TheOtherSide

Sandra Freeman

Published in 2004 by Onlywomen Press Ltd, London, UK.

ISBN 0-906500-81-8

British Library Cataloguing-in-Publication Data.
A Catalogue record for this book is available from the British Library.

Typeset by Chris Fayers
Printed and bound in India by Gopsons Papers Limited.

For Bobby

Acknowledgments

Heartfelt thanks to Christine Bostock for all her patience and hours of deciphering my handwriting, to Jenny Ritchie for the proof reading, and to Faith O'Reilly for support in every way.

Foreword . . .

Only one character in this book, Pablo Picasso, actually lived. Many others are inspired by the artists and writers who moved in Bohemian circles in Paris at the time the novel is set, just before the First World War. Some have some kind of family resemblance to characters in fiction about the same period. But they have all taken on their own life, even Picasso, so there is no attempt to tell anything how it was, or even could have been. Nevertheless, this book would not have been written without the author's knowledge of, and love for, the following: Colette, Radclyffe Hall, D.H. Lawrence, and Gertrude Stein.

Chapter 1
Toby

Charlie had ordered the walnut tree to be cut down immediately after Toby's funeral. The wood was stored separately to be burnt when the pain had dulled. Only a few of the guests who were chatting on the lawn in the warm sunshine knew of its significance. William and Victoria Langham Price had planted the tree when the twins were born, had watched it grow and bear fruit. When Colonel Langham Price was shot in the Boer War Victoria sat in its shade and talked to her husband's ghost about their wayward children, whose names were carved with increasing confidence in the bark. Toby and Charlie, Charlie and Toby, etched deep in a spiral record of their closeness, year by year until Charlie went away. Now Victoria was dead, and Toby. The twins had stood together at their mother's graveside, numbed by the bitter wind from the sea, six months later Charlie had watched as Toby's coffin was lowered into the ground beside his parents. On Midsummer's day his body had been found at the base of the cliffs, not yet washed away into the English Channel. There had been an engagement party on Midsummer's Eve, apparently a frenetic affair with friends and family – mostly on Violet's side, since Toby's friends declined to come and he had only a few cousins. Charlie was still in Paris, at a first night not to be missed. It would seem that Toby drank a lot of champagne and disappeared some time after midnight. Violet was dancing with one of her uncles, she said afterwards she thought Toby had gone into the garden to smoke a cigarette and look at the stars. It was not until two o'clock in the morning that his absence began to cause some concern.

"Couldn't you have left that tree?" Charlie turned from contemplating the workmen expertly slicing off the top branches, to face Violet standing there in her black silk, her face still wet with tears. The desolate fiancée, no more grand September wedding, no future life in Finborough Place, no role as gracious lady of the manor. What was Violet to do now?

"No. There is no more 'Toby and Charlie'. There is just Charlie."

"Are you going to live here? I thought you were settled in Paris."

"My dear, I'm the last Sussex Langham Price. Finborough Place is my responsibility. I know it was going to be yours. You would have suited it. Added glamour. You and Toby were a glamorous couple. You look very good in black, by the way. I'm sorry it didn't work out. You'd waited a long time. Too long. A few lost opportunities on the way. I do hope there's someone waiting in the wings. Otherwise perhaps you could be my housekeeper. It wouldn't be a bad life. I'd make you very comfortable. No marriage, no children, but then I doubt whether Toby would have been able to give you those."

"How dare you talk to me like that! You are unspeakable. I hate you, Charlie! I despise you. Toby was good and kind and gentle. You are so hard, so cruel." Violet's pale face flushed an unpleasant red.

"I survived, Toby didn't. My sensitive brother eventually opted out. You knew this marriage was wrong didn't you?"

"The marriage was what he needed. I would have cherished him. He would have been all right with me. He wanted a normal life, wanted a family. We would have been happy. You were jealous of that. You will never have that kind of peace."

Violet's face was white again. Her eyes were wide. Beneath the anger lay desire, buried deep. Both remembered another summer's day, a ride on the cliff tops, sitting on the springy turf in a fold of the hills. No-one else around. A gentle breeze from the water like blue glass turning milky towards the shore. They were very young. There was real passion between them, the urgency of a first time. As they rode home their bodies trembled. Before parting they dismounted and kissed each other time and time again with a frenzy Charlie had never known since. When Charlie called the following day, Violet was sick. The next time they met she made Charlie promise that what had happened between them would never be mentioned again. They had been mad, she said. It was wrong. They must forget it.

Now Charlie wanted to bite those lips again - the lips of the almost widow, distraught in her loss. Violet felt a melting in her womb, a hardening of her breasts in her very act of denial.

"I'm sorry Violet." Charlie began to move away. "We're going to be neighbours again. We must both review our lives. I know you cared for Toby, you know how much I loved him. We should be friends and help each other."

Violet took the extended hand, before walking away, back to the guests she had invited.

A week before he died Toby had written to Charlie in Paris. The pitiful cry of a doomed man.

"Oh my God, why did I make that promise? I should have stood firm. Mother gripped me so hard- she could scarcely speak but she found such strength at that moment. "Marry Violet, Toby. Marry Violet, have sons." She said it over and over again until she died. I told myself that she was right. That's what I should do. Now it's going to happen, I dread it so much. I have nightmares. George says it won't matter. We'll still be lovers. It happens all the time. It will be even more exciting and I'll be a respectable married man. It won't be like that, Charlie, it won't. Violet won't let it be. She will cling to me, totally possess me. She would be a good wife, a good mother, but I don't desire her. How can I father children? It will be living hell. What can I do, tell me, what can I do?"

Charlie had been busy with preparations for the play. There were lots of complications, as usual. Some rewriting to be done, at the insistence of the leading actress,

with whom Charlie had been having a somewhat meaningless affair. So the letter was put aside until the moment
when Toby set off alone in the dark for the edge of the
world. At one in the morning, after the champagne, the
relief of the success, Charlie sat down to write "Don't do
it. Don't get married. Mother is dead. Live your own life
at last. " Poor Toby. Poor, poor Toby. Incapable of doing
his 'duty' as a son, afraid to admit his love for George,
there was only one way out. Of course it was an accident, they all said, too much to drink, gazing at the sky,
losing his balance. What a tragedy! A rich young man with
a brilliant future, a beautiful fiancée. Heir to a great estate.

Charlie imagined the conversations as the guests wandered in the park. They would be shaking their heads
over the loss of the good twin, wondering how the bad
one would deal with the family property. The bad one
who had left home to live in Paris. Who wrote plays, in
French, performed in London in private clubs. "I believe
they are quite shocking, my dear." Who was reputed to
have a house in Brighton where disgusting acts took
place. "But how do you know, darling?" "Well, Celia
knows someone who has a cousin, who has heard from
a friend . . ." "Really? I'm not surprised." "I'm sure the
estate will go to rack and ruin. Who knows what sort of
carryings on there will be in those elegant rooms." "Don't!
I can't bear to think about it."

Charlie loved Finborough Place. The house in Brighton
was a way of being near. Of keeping in touch. It was
where Toby met George, whenever he could get away
from Mother for long enough. Charlie kept a motor car
there and sometimes the twins would drive back across
the downs in the moonlight, so that Charlie could admire
the clean outline of the Palladian mansion against the
chalk hills. The house, the gardens, would be a heavy
responsibility. There were gardeners of course, estate
workers who lived in the village, a few servants. A housekeeper would need to be found. Violet would have done
that very well. Pity. It would have been thrilling to come
home to find her not only at the dinner table but also
in the bedroom. She was a lovely woman. Surely she

must have lovers. There was a sensuality about her mouth, a fullness in her breasts, a languor in her movements, could drive men wild. Charlie sighed. No, it would be wiser to find a married couple, solid trustworthy retainers. It would take time. Gaby would keep an eye on the house in Paris until important decisions had been made.

People began to move indoors out of the sun, which was unusually hot for England. Charlie strolled over to the rose garden, their mother's pride and joy. Old roses, tea roses, climbers of every shape and colour spread a glorious patchwork between the mellow brick walls. The mingled scents were almost overpowering. Mrs. Langham Price was always in close correspondence with a Derbyshire rose grower, who had produced a large deep red floribunda for her, named "The Colonel" in memory of her husband. Charlie thought it exquisite. This year's weather was ideal for roses – the right amount of sun, just enough rain. The shrub was covered in blooms. "Blood red" went through Charlie's mind. Did Mother want that? To be reminded of her husband shot to pieces in Africa?" There had been no blood around Toby's body, no harsh stain on the whiteness of the chalk. Simply a broken neck.

"A fine sight, eh, Charlie?" A wheezy voice, that of an elderly man, interrupted the morbid reverie. Brigadier Jamieson, one of their father's fellow soldiers, a friend of the family, godfather to the twins, stood leaning on his stick. He was one of the few of their parents' circle that Charlie trusted. Up to a point. There was no need for confidences, for the Brigadier made it clear that he guessed a great deal about his godchildren and understood. At this moment, his shrewd eyes conveyed a sympathy based on an unspoken knowledge of Toby's dilemma. He shook his head. "Your brother was never happy, would never have been happy. You protected him as well as you were able, always. You couldn't have done more. He was so fragile. Your loss is terrible. I think you'll never love anyone as you loved him, but even you couldn't save him." He paused. "You were always the one with the guts. Charlie, you'll never let

11

the world make you do what you don't want to do, will you? Forgive me for speaking bluntly, we don't meet very often and I suppose as your godfather I am the only parent you have left. I'm not well, I'm old, so I need to say what I have to say before it's too late. I've watched Toby over the years, seen his anxious face, beside your defiance. When he fell down you always picked him up, dried his tears. I never saw you cry, ever. When you went to live in Paris, there was no-one to pick him up any more. I don't know what you get up to, I hear stories of course, some may be true, I don't care. You're brave, and strong. I'd go into battle with you any day." His eyes twinkled. "By god you'd look good in a uniform. You have your father's bearing, do you know that? That's by the way. It was the world that did for Toby, all those in there." He gestured with stick to the house. "They won't do for you. Stand firm. Don't retreat like your brother, they'll shoot you in the back." So saying, he turned away and made his way through the herb garden to his wife who had left her tea to look for him.

In the middle of the rose garden stood a sundial. The shadow fell towards half-past five o'clock. There was a trickling out through the French windows down across the terrace. Chauffeurs waking up from a doze or breaking away from the groups where they exchanged gossip. The guests were starting to go home. They would try to find Charlie first. Yet again they would utter platitudes about life and death. It would be better to hide, only come out at dusk. Would they worry? Would they be afraid the last member of the family was also gone forever? No chance of that. Charlie was sure-footed, Charlie had scrambled over the cliffs, ridden, run and jumped over every part of the springy turf. Charlie wouldn't slip, fall . . . jump. No, if Charlie was not to be found it would be through natural perversity, a wilful flouting of every convention. So they would go home to normality.

A gate in the far wall of the rose garden led into a maze. Well-kept rectangles of box hedge seven foot high. In the centre a circular stone bench around a modest nymph whose drapery left nothing exposed but back, arms and one plump leg. Charlie had often tried to imagine the concealed breasts and undoubtedly plump buttocks. This was the place to sit until one could be quite sure of being alone. To begin to grieve, remembering the shared pleasures, trying to wipe out the obsessive image of the slender limp body, glassy eyes turned to the sky.

The last time the twins had met was at their mother's funeral. In spite of the cold, the frost which had lasted all day long under the dark grey clouds, they had sat all afternoon in the maze, talking about the future. Toby had spoken of his promise to marry. He was deeply disturbed. Marriage was a fact he would have to face sooner or later. Violet loved him, she was a good woman, she would inherit her parents' farm, it was a perfect union, they had all known each other for years, played together as children, it would be all right, wouldn't it? He couldn't love her as she wanted, he was fond of her, respected her, surely he could be a good husband, couldn't he? Couldn't he? Charlie had tried to give him the reassurance he needed. Words going round in circles, avoiding the truth, both of them hoping they could create another truth through confident utterance. Toby wanted to give Charlie half the estate, Charlie refused, being quite wealthy enough already. Mrs. Langham Price had made a settlement when she banished her wayward offspring, several hits in the Parisian Boulevard theatres, careful investment, had made sure that the black sheep would never be poor. Toby argued that it wouldn't be fair if the children he and Violet would make would inherit what was Charlie's by right; Charlie said any children of Toby's would be welcome to every last penny. So they comforted themselves with a vision which they ought to have acknowledged impossible. Alone as the birds began their evening songs, reliving these conversations, Charlie wished they had been able to be honest.

Outside the maze the countryside still glowed although the sun had set. Inside the darkness thickened. Charlie could have found the way out eyes closed. Emerging into the soft light, seeing the white house settled in the fields, the new owner felt a curious mixture of melancholy and exhilaration.

"Miss Charlotte"

A young man, a very handsome young man stepped out in front of her. He was one of the villagers who worked on the estate, odd job man, chauffeur, (they had recently bought a very fine car), occasional gardener. His mother Mrs. Branson cooked and his sister cleaned. They were stopping late tonight, waiting for Charlie to give them permission to leave.

"You can go home, Dan. And tell you mother and family they can go too – just leave the lights on in the library. I'd rather be on my own now."

She expected him to go. He looked down, then stared into her face with an unpleasant expression.

"Miss Charlotte, Toby, Mr. Toby, used to give me an allowance. I'm saving up to go to London, you see."

"Oh no!" thought Charlie.

"An allowance? What for?"

"Things. Services." His meaning was plain.

"As you know, Mr. Toby is dead, so there will be no need of 'services'."

He held his ground.

"Yes but there was the matter of privacy."

"Privacy?"

"Things between him and me that other people shouldn't really know about. I never let on, even to Mum and Emily. Mr. Toby understood how much I would need to save up. He was very generous."

So he was, thought Charlie. Generous and vulnerable. To youthful beauty, to blackmail.

"Well my young friend . . ."

Dan's insolent gaze faltered a little at her tone.

"I am not generous. Not to blackmailers. There will be no more 'allowances'. It's common knowledge that I'm not interested in the services of young men. I have every reason to believe your mother is a good, honest woman who will give you the beating you deserve if I tell her what you've been up to. Is that clear?"

He hesitated, not quite convinced that he'd lost.

"Is that clear?"

It was.

"Off you go. Sorry, old chap. All good things come to an end. No hard feelings." She held out her hand, smiling.

As if mesmerised Dan shook it, before moving away, quite bemused. There were lights in several rooms. Charlie and her birthright stared at each other.

"I'm passionate about you, old dear," said Charlie, "but what on earth am I going to do with you?"

Chapter 2
Gaby

The next morning before the rising sun lit up the bedroom with a sudden brilliance, the dawn chorus made it impossible to sleep. Charlie had lain awake watching the increasing brightness of the stars in the moonless night until a luminous blue flooded the sky preceding the break of day. A magical moment Gaby always said, even in Paris, the moment when Charlie's eyes finally closed. There were not enough birds in the garden in Passy to interfere with her natural rhythm. Here the lime tree particularly close to the house seemed to have a feathered claw on every branch. She shut the window grumpily, making a mental note to trim back the ivy already pushing its way over the sill, climbed back into bed, decided against an attempt at oblivion and looked around at the room she had almost forgotten.

It had been kept for her, in spite of the fact that she was not expected to stay here any more. There were so many rooms, enough for any number of guests without using this one. The furnishing was simple – a large wardrobe (Charlie had always loved clothes), a bookcase with a selection from the library (books which she was sure neither of her parents had read), a desk at which she had written short plays and stories, paintings she had chosen over the years, mainly horses, and a toy theatre. Would she prefer another room now, she wondered. Her parents' room had been so much bigger, lighter, facing the lake. Could she sleep in her parents' bed? Perhaps with a lover. The thought pleased her, taking a lover into her parents' bed. Would that have been the scene of failed attempts at love making between Toby and Violet? Could she take Violet in her father's bed? She let her mind dwell pleasantly on this for a while, before dismissing the idea. Not Violet, another woman, a beautiful stranger. Charlie's lovemaking had become rather mechanical of late. She and Gaby had talked about it.

Gaby! She had almost forgotten that she was to meet Gaby today in Brighton, in the cottage in Vine Place. Though they had been friends for years Gaby had never been to Brighton, nor even to London. England had nothing to attract a Parisian, or so she thought, London was a fearful place, its grimy foggy streets concealing thieves and murderers. And Brighton, what was Brighton beside Le Touquet? She had unselfishly agreed to make the trip to support Charlie at this difficult time. She had just finished her latest novel, so the moment was propitious. She needed a break, some distance on a work which had cost her much effort. She also had a new lover whilst not quite finished with her partner of several years. It was a welcome relief to escape from the tense atmosphere. Charlie had made the journey as easy as possible for her by arranging for a young actor she knew to meet Gaby in Newhaven and take her to Vine Place for the night. She had given him enough money to pay for an oyster supper at Wheeler's. She knew Gaby would appreciate her escort, who was handsome, witty and considerate. He would regale her with theatrical gossip, they would exchange anecdotes, for Gaby had toured as a music hall performer for several years.

She was tempted to drive to Brighton straight away, surprise Gaby in bed with a cup of hot chocolate, but it was far too early. Instead she wandered down to the kitchen to make coffee before Mrs. Branson arrived. Although everything was neatly arranged it took Charlie some time to find what she needed. There was an order not immediately apparent. Half an hour later she took a tray outside to sit on the walnut tree stump.

"I should make this into some kind of rustic table," she thought. "Make sure it's quite dead and turn it into something different." After lying awake remembering her childhood, she was ready to turn her back on the past. If this was to be her house she would make it into what she wanted. Take away the portraits of her grandparents and great-grandparents from the large reception room; hang them in a quiet corner where they wouldn't frown with disapproval at her bohemian friends. She would ask Gaby to give her some ideas about redecoration. She couldn't live with the furniture - her mother's taste had never been formed, she had been happy to live with the Victorian clutter inherited from her husbands' parents. Violet would certainly have swept all that away, spending a great deal of money on the latest fashions. Charlie would do the same, but her choice would doubtless be shocking to the Sussex yeomanry. She and Gaby together had furnished the villa in Passy, perhaps they would ship all she needed from Paris. After all, Charlie had become so much more French than English.

When she went back to the kitchen Mrs. Branson was already busy with some mysterious preparations. Charlie was very fond of her. She was honest and reliable, as outspoken sometimes as Charlie herself. She had worked for the family ever since she had come to the village to marry Ted Branson. Her children had helped around the place as soon as they were able. Apart from Emily and Dan there had been a baby born at the same time as the twins. He had died after a few days. Mrs. Langham Price had never discussed intimate matters, but Charlie had a suspicion that given Mrs. Branson's excess of milk and the other young mother's delicate condition the two had shared the feeding of the twins, one each. Charlie was sure she must have been the one suckled at Mrs. Branson's full breast. For this reason she felt that however shocking her behaviour she would always be defended by the cook against criticism from the other villagers.

"Mrs. Branson, I won't be home for lunch, but I'll be bringing a friend back for dinner. Maybe one or two. Yes, there'll probably be three besides me. Will that be all right? Would you ask Emily to make up three beds? We'll have to have a talk about salaries. I'm not sure what the arrangement was. I don't know much at all about how the household is run, so you'll have to teach me. I expect you'd already begun plans with Violet."

18

Violet had doubtless taken charge as soon as Toby had asked her to marry him.

"Will you be living here then, Miss Charlotte?" It was difficult to know what kind of an answer Mrs. Branson hoped for.

"Much of the time, I expect. I'm not sure yet. I'll be staying for a while. It's very odd to be called 'Miss Charlotte' you know. All my friends call me Charlie, perhaps you could do the same. Charlotte doesn't suit me at all."

Mrs Branson considered this. There was just a hint of amusement in her brown eyes. "Miss Charlie . . ." There was a long pause. "Or . . . Master Charlie?" And the two of them burst out laughing.

By the time Charlie had put her car in the garage and walked through the streets to Vine Place it was late enough to take the chocolate up to Gaby. There was a resemblance between the two houses, the French and English. Both were hidden away, pretending to be cottages in the heart of a town. Even before she opened her gate she smelled the honeysuckle which grew around it. There was a small courtyard garden with narrow borders planted with herbs. Pots of lavender stood in the corners. There were a few shrubs which flowered in the spring and bore bright red berries in the winter. There was no gardener here, so the plants looked after themselves. It was a delightful place, throughout the seasons, particularly so in early summer. As Charlie approached the front door, it opened. Gaby stepped out, fully dressed, holding a cup of very weak tea.

"Bonjour, Charlie, ça va?"

(Gaby and Charlie always spoke French together, but for the sake of the English speaking readers, the author will translate their conversations.)

"Gaby! Dressed at this hour and drinking tea! Tea for goodness sake!"

"I found it. As I am in England, I thought that's what I should have. But I don't think I got it right. I poured hot water into my cup – by the way that's a charming kettle you have, I've never seen a real one like that before, only in pictures – I poured hot water into my cup and sprinkled a few leaves on top. Taste it. Is it all right?"

Charlie tasted.

"It's disgusting. I'll show you later how to make tea. Why aren't you still in bed? Don't tell me your escort didn't show you the town last night? You should be exhausted."

"Oh he was so sweet. I could have eaten him all up. Yes, after supper he took me to a party, where we met lots of friends of yours. We drank more champagne, we danced, we came back here very late, he kissed my hand, bid me goodnight, which saved me the trouble of explaining that, although I found him very attractive, I am the faithful type and mindful of my lover back home. Mind you, my dear, there was a ravishing young woman at the party, said you and she had an affair a few years ago. Red hair, green eyes, Irish. Now if she hadn't been with a very formidable person built like a wardrobe, I would have been strongly tempted to exercise all my powers of seduction. How could you let her get away?"

Charlie smiled. "Her beauty is all on the surface."

"Who cares? After all that I was afraid I'd be too excited to sleep, but no, as soon as I climbed into that large bed of yours, it was instant oblivion. Then I was awoken by a cat throwing itself at my bedroom window. You know I can never resist a cat. Anyway, he was so insistent, so dominating. I'm sure he's a he, he's so big, so handsome – I suppose he's yours because I found the sort of things in the cupboard that cats might like."

"Actually, there were things I though *you* might like if you were hungry during the night." Gaby's appetite for food and wine was notorious. "He's not mine. He behaves like all cats, he moves in when I'm here to see what he can find. You see, I can't resist him either. His name is Sapphire.

The animal in question strolled out to greet Charlie. He was a magnificent Siamese, in peak condition. His miaow was deep and sonorous.

"He talks a lot," said Gaby. "I heard what he had to say about life here in Brighton, then I told him about my

cats in Paris. Luckily, I speak his language." And she proceeded to give an imitation of Siamese cat which would
have fooled anyone listening. She ended with a few sharp
cries, which must have meant "Go home now", since
Sapphire immediately disappeared over the garden wall.

They went inside. The sun was high enough above the
roofs of the neighbouring terrace to shine in through the
living room window. Gaby sank back into the feathered
cushions of a large sofa. "This is very English," she said,
looking around. Charlie refrained from saying "How
would you know, you've never been to England before."
Looking around she supposed it was, in an indefinable
way, very English. She spoke almost perfect French, she
wrote mostly in French, had lived in France for many
years, liked the life, the attitudes, had French ideas for
goodness sake, yet underneath it all was an Englishness
she took for granted, which she would have to rediscover
and cultivate if she were to become a country squire.

"I can understand you more since I've been here, my
little Charlie," Gaby stroked her cheek. "Already in
London, but especially in Brighton. I'm beginning to put
you into place. The pieces are fitting together. The last
one will be the most important. It will be very strange."

Gaby herself was from a country background, a not
too well-off middle class family who lived in a ramshackle
house held together by wisteria and Virginia creeper.
They had what was considered to be a large garden, in
which the four children could tire themselves. Charlie
was sure she had an image of this in her mind, so that
she would be overwhelmed by the vast parkland, the
elegant mansion. What would she make of it? How would
this last piece fit into her jigsaw of Charlie's persona?

"We're going to spend the day idling on the promenade. I'm taking you back to Finborough Place for dinner. I'm going to invite Toby's lover George too, and his
friend Cedric. Toby never took George home. He and
Cedric can stay, then tomorrow we'll go to the cemetery.
Maybe to the cliffs."

George and Cedric said they couldn't accept. Gaby and
Charlie took a tramway along the seafront. Between the

piers. They listened to the brass band on Hove lawns where holiday crowds had already gathered. They talked, took tea with an old acquaintance in Adelaide Crescent, talked more, walked back to pick up Charlie's motor car. Gaby was very impressed, since motor cars of any kind were still rare. She was nervous in the busy streets, only relaxing when they headed out on to the coast road. She jumped every time the horn was sounded.

"Please don't run over the rabbits," she pleaded.

The pink cottages, the squat church tower with its small spire in Finborough village drew forth exclamations of joy, but the first sight of the house as they turned into the long drive reduced even the exuberant Frenchwoman to silence. Charlie stopped the engine, to give them chance to admire the classical lines in silence. At length Gaby turned to look at her companion with deep seriousness.

"Ah! Now I am really going to see you as a stranger. Oh my god, I am going to have dinner at the chateau. With an aristocrat. I will have to be on my very best behaviour." She spoke with an exaggerated country accent.

Charlie knew this was playful. Gaby's present, soon-to-be-ex, lover, was a duchess. Her soon-to-be partner had a castle in the South. She climbed down and cranked the engine again.

"This is not aristocratic, though. It is far too noisy, too modern. Oops . . ." She nearly lost her hat as they came to a halt.

Mrs. Branson took the news that there would only be two for dinner with her usual equanimity. Familiar as ever, Gaby asked her what they were to eat, then followed her into the kitchen to exchange recipes. She discovered that Mrs. Branson was a very excellent cook indeed, who knew of at least half a dozen Sussex recipes for wild rabbit. "And her apple tart – she showed me how she puts the pastry all round the apples, with cloves and cinnamon. She has true talent. I thought the British knew nothing about food. I was so wrong. About so many things."

Yes you were, thought Charlie, and right about so many others.

"Well, perhaps you can teach her something about wines," she said aloud.

"Aren't we going to drink ale?" Another misconception.

"No we are not. Toby kept a good cellar. Now, what would go well with coney pie?"

It was obvious that Mrs. Branson hoped Gaby would stay for a long time, if not for ever. She blushed becomingly when Gaby invited her and Dan and Emily to join them in the dining room. "The table is far too big for two. You don't mind, Charlie, do you? We can be informal, can't we?"

Such an extent of informality was inconceivable to the cook, who beat a hasty retreat to the servants' quarters.

"You're wicked, Gaby. You knew she would refuse."

Gaby gave a very Gallic shrug.

"Why not? She seems almost part of your family."

"Hmm. I've put her straight about you anyhow. I've told her you are divorced, but may marry again soon. You definitely need a separate room."

"Really?" There was a tinge of disappointment in her tone. "With you it wouldn't be infidelity."

"Oh yes it would. We never have been, and we never should be, lovers. I value your friendship too much to put it at risk."

It was true they never had slept together, although they nearly did on more than one occasion.

Gaby was about to argue that there would be no risk, it would be a delicious moment, nothing more, but she changed the subject instead.

"Are you leaving your house in Passy empty for long?"

"I suppose so. I must stay here for at least a few months. The play's going smoothly now and anyway I have to talk to London managements. Does it matter? Maybe I should get Bernadette to live in if she will." Charlie's housekeeper went home every evening, in spite of the fact that there was room enough for her to stay and she had no family.

"You could let it."

"Let it! There's absolutely no need to do that."

"Lend it then."

"To whom?"

She suspected some clandestine affair.

"An artist. An Englishwoman. She's very good I believe. She's been living in Germany and has quite a reputation. Elisabeth von Kornfeld knows her. She met her when she was back in Frankfurt. Apparently she's tired of Germany now, wants to come to Paris, which she scorned before. Elisabeth has set up an exhibition for her in a month's time. She may only be a bird of passage. She will need somewhere to stay where she can work."

"Why should I lend my house to a stranger?" was Charlie's immediate thought. "An artist might make an awful mess."

"She carves and paints. You have a lot of space in your summer house."

"Yes, I have. It's my space. I don't want anyone else interfering with it."

She could tell by the quality of Gaby's silence that this was considered to be a very selfish attitude.

"I don't know anything about the woman except what you've just told me and that's not much."

"She is quite wealthy."

"I've met some very nasty wealthy people."

"If you could come over the water for a few days, you could see her at her private view, make up your mind. Meanwhile she will stay with Elisabeth."

As far as Charlie was concerned her mind was already made up. She did not want a tenant.

"You're right. She's probably horrible and ugly with big muscles. Not your type at all." This was said with Gaby's famous impish grin. "Do you think Toby kept good liqueur?"

Chapter 3
Anna

Countess Elisabeth von Kornfeld lived in an eighteenth century apartment on the Ile St Louis. She was at home to German, Russian and English émigrés and a few carefully selected French natives. A widow in her later years, she had travelled widely, accruing an immense knowledge of European culture. She was unusual in her appreciation of the contemporary, even avant-garde. She bought generously, despatching each new piece to her residence in Brittany, where she had one of the finest collections to be found in France. Her walls in Paris were covered with canvasses of the 1700s, including a Watteau and two Fragonards. She was an excellent pianist, the patron of many young musicians. She adored Charlie, believing her to be head and shoulders above all other living dramatists writing in French. As she spoke seven languages she had translated several of Charlie's texts for the Northern European stage.

She had been very excited by the work of the young English painter when she discovered her in Germany. Here was an unusual vigour combined with tight control. Her sculptures were grotesque, frightening. The painting too had an energy, both in form and colour, that seemed to reflect some unresolved disturbance in the woman herself. Anna would say little about her life. Simply that she had gone to Germany with a friend because England seemed a tired place. She lived alone. She had attracted much attention amongst artistic circles; mystery is always intriguing, especially in someone so beautiful.

"Beautiful and dangerous," thought Elisabeth as she watched Anna making sketches from the long windows of the salon. "She could break hearts. I expect she left England on account of some unfortunate love affair. I'd like to know. Perhaps when she trusts me more, I'll discover the truth. At least she seems tough enough to take on Paris, without being lost in somebody's bed. They'll try, of course. Ask her to model first, make love to her, hope she'll turn into muse and housekeeper." Elisabeth had seen this happen more than once. "I have the feeling that she would always be the victor in the battle of the sexes."

Anna turned away from the window, closed her sketch book.

"I think I'll go for a walk," she said.

"Of course, but do wear a hat. The sun is fiercer than you think. I have friends coming round at five, maybe you would like to meet them." (They'd love to meet you, she thought.)

Anna disappeared into her room and emerged holding a hat of simple white straw. She was dressed in emerald green with white shoes.

"If you don't mind, I'd rather not be precise about the time. I might walk for a long way, I might sit in a café and sketch." She carried a very small sketch book and pencil in a white leather purse.

"As you wish, my dear." Elisabeth was wise enough not to insist.

Out in the narrow street Anna drew a deep breath. The sooner she could find lodgings of her own the better. Staying in another person's house was stifling, in spite of Elisabeth's kindness. There had been a suggestion that an English playwright might have a house to let near the Bois de Boulogne. Anna hoped that she could move there soon. She stood on the small bridge linking the two islands, looking down at the Seine. She had always considered Paris to be a frivolous city, too superficial for her taste. Yet it was a magnet for creative talent. She must come here, test herself. She was still young, twenty-seven years old, with a strong drive to make an international name for herself. There were Americans here, who had money to buy, to ship works of art back to New York.

She had a vision of exhibitions in London, Paris, Berlin, her work sold out to collectors. She began to walk towards the Ile de la Cité, making for the Palais de Justice and the wonderful stained glass window within the Sainte Chapelle. Her rational self repeated that she was not a great painter, simply a good one, that fame and fortune were but a dream. She was already comfortably off, rich enough to afford to stay wherever she chose for as long as she wished. She had no idea how long that would be, really she had no positive plans.

Before she left Germany, she received a proposal of marriage. A baron from an industrial family, three years younger than she, a well set-up young man, who had fallen in love with her at a private view. She had looked particularly striking on that occasion, her dress of cream satin and lace clinging softly to her slender form. Men flocked around her vying for her attention. The young baron was so smitten that he was unable to say a word; Three days later he had sent his card with an invitation to dinner. She had accepted without knowing anything about him except his name. She was bored, needing to change her ideas, so a young man outside the usual circle could be interesting. Her first impression when he came to call for her was of a tender plant. He was extremely good-looking in a delicate way, his blond moustache almost a fine down. She was immediately protective, addressing him with unaccustomed gentleness. He brought out in her a kindness which was almost maternal. His kisses had a child-like sweetness, so much so that Anna supposed he thought of her as an adored elder sister. He never asked her to sleep with him so his proposal was a shock. She had refused other suitors with no compunction, but this one stood trembling with so much hope that she asked for time to think. It was only when she saw the tears in his eyes that she realised how much she had misled him. Two days later she sent him a note, begging his forgiveness for any misunderstanding. She hoped they could continue to be friends; whilst knowing this was impossible.

What would life have been like as a German baroness?

Suffocating, she was sure. Dreadful social expectations which she could not bear. She had to be free. He was too soft to arouse desire, though she would have learned to love him, already did in a way. Generally speaking she was cold, only being aroused by provocation, a challenge to a battle of wills she must win. Was her whole life to be a battleground, fighting to gain recognition as an artist, as an independent woman, who refused to be dominated by her lovers? Since turning her back on this last proposal she had begun to experience a slight sense of panic. She didn't want it to be like this, she longed for the kind of attachment other women seemed to find so simple. She didn't understand what was normally meant by 'falling in love'. Had she ever fallen in love? Two years ago she had a lover, a man whose demon force matched hers. Each had tried to possess the other. His physical strength, his masculine resolve, were finally beaten by the steel of her resistance. He had shot himself. Anna's initial, terrifying indifference had been replaced by guilt. When she first looked at the bloody corpse she felt nothing; now the destroyed face haunted her. Yet it wasn't her fault. He had forced her that last time against her will. He had died because his fierce, hard will had been opposed. He was a spoilt rich boy who would always have his own way. It wasn't her fault, she told herself time and time again. He was a heartless brute, who had stalked her like a predator. He hadn't loved her. Had she loved him? Had she been in love with him? Since then she had been dead too, her emotions numbed.

She had reached the chapel. At her first visit she was so entranced by the painted walls downstairs that she almost left without seeing the glory upstairs. An elderly Frenchman who had been watching her since she came in, stopped her. "Mais vous ne sortez pas encore, mademoiselle! Montez, je vous prie, montez!" Now she came whenever she could, it was so near Elisabeth's apartment.

There were tall windows on every side so that brightness shone at all times through the rich patterns of deep blue and red. Anna didn't care for the stories that were told: the passion, the suffering, the transcendental victory. She was moved to the depths of her soul by a light and colour she had never seen before. She could live and die in this place in a state of ecstasy. This was surely heaven; here, within a great work of art, surrounded by total perfection. She never told Elisabeth she came here, she pretended instead she looked at the shops along the Rue Saint Honoré.

Two hours had passed when she returned to the Ile St Louis. As she climbed the stairs to the salon she could already hear the sound of voices. She found the whole social circumstance of salon entertainment tedious but she knew it had to be endured. Every so often she would experience acute discomfort, a feeling of being totally out of place. Yet she had no place. She had cut herself off from London, where she had many acquaintances, if not friends, from her family in the Derbyshire countryside where she had lived all her young life. She had not even told her elder sister, in whom she had largely confided, where she was living in Paris. It was strange that Elisabeth's hospitality made her feel a little like a kept woman.

"Anna, my dear, come and meet Mabel Block and Belle W. Mayer. They've heard all about you," Elisabeth and her guests rose from their chairs.

What had they heard? Anna asked herself. How she hated those words.

"How do you do, Miss Waltham," Mabel Block's voice was mellow, sonorous, the American accent hardly noticeable.

"How do you do, Miss Waltham." Belle W. Mayer's was slightly more marked, her words a little more clipped.

"How do you do, so pleased to meet you." A vigorous shaking of hands, Anglo-Saxon, not continental greeting.

They were a couple Anna immediately wanted to paint. She rarely did portraits and never to commission. However, the two women before her were such a contrast that they inspired her. Mabel was broad, solid, her hair drawn tightly back from a high brow. Her face was egg shaped, the features most harmoniously placed. The eyes were long, dark, large, the mouth humorous. She was wearing a white pin-tucked shirt, a long brown skirt, brown stockings and sandals. Her companion was about the same height but slight, so she seemed altogether smaller. The intensity of her gaze was shielded by her heavy lids. Her cheekbones, her long nose in a long pale oval were defined with startling clarity. Her sensual lips contrasted with her pallor. She was clothed in a long-sleeved dress which fitted closely to the waist then followed the contours of her hips and thighs. It was make of a batik material, riotously patterned with purple, green and red flowers. Anna found herself the subject of their intense scrutiny.

"Elisabeth has told us so much about your work, we are looking forward to your exhibition." There was a slightly caressing note in the deeper voice. "We know very few women painters."

"I am a painter and a sculptor. The fact that I am a woman is not important."

"Not to you, Miss Waltham, not to you. But to others. I'm afraid that if you stand beside your work they might notice you before they see the picture." This time she was definitely teasing.

Who did she mean by 'they? The critics, other artists, men, even Mabel herself, whose appreciative gaze was taking in every detail? Was she flirting? Anna sensed a challenge, to which, who knows, it might be fun to respond.

"Then perhaps I should not appear until the very end of the private view."

"That would indeed be a shame. After all, the excitement caused by your presence might stimulate sales." This was clear provocation.

"Mabel, I think we must leave now. We are already late for you appointment with Pablo." Mabel's companion had taken a step closer to her and spoke with a proprietary air. Mabel put an affectionate arm around her shoulders.

"Of course, my dear, you're right. Belle is always right, Miss Waltham. She is my timekeeper, my housekeeper, my secretary, my very, very dear . . . friend." There was unmistakable meaning in the pause. "A Bientôt, then."

This time instead of shaking Anna's hand, she kissed it. "You will come to our at home on Saturday, I hope."

"Goodbye, Miss Waltham. Sorry to leave so soon. I do have to keep Mabel in order."

Was this a warning? The door had scarcely closed before Elisabeth hugged her protégée.

"I'm so glad you came home in time at least to see them. You will come on Saturday, won't you? Mabel is a wonderful patron to so many artists. She and her brother have a great collection. And she commissioned a portrait from Picasso which I don't like at all. *She* does though. She had to sit ninety times on a broken down armchair in his freezing studio. He couldn't get her face right so in the end he painted it from memory, as a sort of mask."

"What about Belle?"

"Belle has her own means. She cares more about writing than art. She copies out everything Mabel writes because she believes she's a genius."

"Is she?"

The generous minded Elisabeth struggled to be tactful. "I think she must be ahead of her time. She is a poet. Poetry is often difficult to understand. I am not English, so I can't really appreciate her style. It isn't like any other writer I know, so perhaps, yes, perhaps she is a genius."

"Do they live together, Mabel and Belle?"

"They live with Mabel's brother. It is all rather tense since Belle moved in."

Anna supposed it would be.

"Belle takes care of them both, she is a very good cook. There is jealousy. Mabel and Belle are like a marriage."

Anna found the idea of a marriage between two women strange. Marriage was a state she had never desired. Between a man and woman it was expected in the end, even amongst the bohemian circles she moved in. Between women there was no need to talk in those terms. What did it mean? Was Mabel the 'husband' and Belle 'the wife'? One produced great books whilst the other cooked, swept and cleaned? Or was it simply a pledge, until death do them part? Then would they expect lifelong fidelity? The gleam in Mabel's eye belied that, though Belle's warning suggested it was her expectation. She decided that she would like to see them again in their home, surrounded by their friends.

Mabel's Saturday evenings were famous. It was a French tradition for artists of all kinds to meet in the house of a wealthy woman. Intellectuals mingled with socialites, with poets, painters, musicians, making a rich cultural seedbed. The Block residence was on the left bank of the Seine, near the Latin Quarter, through the Luxembourg gardens. It was within easy walking distance of the Ile Saint Louis, so Elisabeth made her way there every week when she was in Paris. On this particular evening it was very hot, so she and Anna put on their lightest dresses and strolled languidly along the quays. Whole families were out in the gardens, the big pond colourful with toy boats. Children of all ages were gathered around the Punch and Judy show. The two women stopped to watch, Anna taking the opportunity to make quick sketches of the intent young faces. So reluctant were they to go indoors that by the time they reached their destination the big studio was full of an animated crowd drinking red wine.

"Elisabeth! My dear! Thank goodness you're here. There are too many men. And you have brought a friend." This was said with a heavy French accent. The speaker was clearly very drunk. She held firmly on to Elisabeth's arm to stop herself falling over. "They're all ignoring me, as usual. My name is Marie" She managed to kiss Anna on both cheeks without letting go of her support. "Who are you?"

"This is Anna Waltham. Anna, this is Marie Laurence, also a painter."

"Not yet. I'm learning. I'm learning fast. One day I will be as famous as Pablo, or Henri, as any of them. You are very kind to describe me in that way." She gave Elisabeth a kiss, then turned to Anna. "Mostly I am introduced as Guillaume's mistress. I don't mind too much, I'm proud of him. Would you like some wine?"

Anna looked around. Were these people any different

from the crowd she had known in London? The café set her lover Robin had despised? The atmosphere was more charged; she had a sense that here was a source of creative energy, refreshing, revitalising. So often she had returned to her London flat quite drained and unable to work the next day. It might just be that her British friends drank to forget that their talent was mediocre whilst here was perhaps the unquenchable force of real genius.

"Mademoiselle, I don't believe we have met?"

The speaker was a small compact man, who emanated extraordinary power. His diabolical black eyes made Anna afraid. He saw everything – her body, her soul and beyond.

"I am Pablo Picasso. You are . . . ?"

"Anna Waltham"

"Who are you with, Mademoiselle?"

"What do you mean?"

"Who is your lover? Where is he? I would like to congratulate him on his taste."

Though this was intended as a compliment, Anna flushed with anger.

"You are extremely impertinent, Monsieur. I am here alone, I shall stay alone." (She knew Elisabeth did not count in this kind of conversation.)

Picasso smiled. He clearly liked this response.

"I beg your pardon. You are a friend of Mabel and Belle, then." He shrugged. "I didn't think . . . you don't look like them.

His assumptions were quite insufferable.

"I repeat, I am alone. I have only just met Mabel and Belle."

"Why are you here then? No-one is invited without a reason."

Anna was provoked into an honest response which she was sure she would regret.

"I am a painter and sculptor. I am going to have an exhibition."

"Ah!" was all Picasso said.

"Pablo, I was going to introduce you two, but I see there's no need. Isn't Miss Waltham just beautiful?

33

Wouldn't you like to do her portrait?"

Picasso laughed heartily.

"Of course! But my prices have gone up since I painted you, Mabel. She would have to be rich to afford me, are you rich, Miss Waltham?"

Did she have to suffer this? Was it a necessary rite of passage?

"I have painted my own portrait several times, Monsieur Picasso, thank you. I would be pleased to paint you, but I hear that you would rather earn money than spend it and my prices are high too."

Both these last statements were lies, however the retort had the desired effect.

"Ooh là là! I wish you luck then. I look forward to seeing your show. Water colours I presume?"

"I will make sure you have an invitation."

"Thank you."

He moved away.

Anna was irritated. She had just offended someone whose work she admired, who had, no doubt, a strong influence over public opinion.

"Bravo, Miss Waltham. May I call you Anna? It's not often women stand up to Pablo in that way. I adore him, but I seldom approve of him."

Was Mabel teasing her again?

"I was very rude, I'm sorry."

"Not at all. Just because one is a genius, it doesn't mean all women will fall at one's feet. Most do, it takes a certain kind to refuse."

What kind, wondered Anna. What kind of a woman am I? What kind does Mabel think I am?

"I'd like you to meet Pauline. She's a poet. A compatriot of mine. Come."

Across the room Belle watched them anxiously, but she was too busy handing around canapés to intervene.

Pauline was a frail, insubstantial thing. Her muslin gown, her long blond hair loosely knotted at the nape of her fragile neck, tendrils escaping over her shoulders, gave her a mediaeval look. She seemed more spirit than flesh. An embrace from Mabel could have crushed her.

"Mabel, I have to leave now. *She* is being unbearable. She is so demanding."

As she spoke Anna caught the faint smell of eau de cologne.

"I understand. This is Miss Waltham. Perhaps you will come to her exhibition then you can talk."

"Oh yes. Perhaps, it depends. I can't make promises. I must do whatever she wants you know. Goodbye."

She drifted out, trailing chiffon. A tortoiseshell comb fell from her hair. Anna picked it up.

"Keep it. Some day she might be famous. When she's dead, which won't be long. We're honoured she came at all tonight. Usually she keeps to the company of women, mainly French. I've heard she gives great suppers but never eats."

"What did she mean when she said she can't make promises?"

"She claims to have a dominating lover, a kind of female satyr. She has described to me in great detail what they do together. Unimaginable. Yet her poetry is so vague."

Belle had distributed all the canapés and was once more at Mabel's side.

"I do wish that woman would have a square meal. I can hardly bear the sight of her. For goodness sake, you don't have to be so affected just because you write poetry. Look at Mabel. She really likes her food, don't you, fattuski?"

"Especially cooked by you, baby queen."

They exchanged an intimate, loving smile.

"You must eat with us properly one night. I always supervise the meal, choose the recipes. In the menu there should be a climax and a culmination. One will suffice."

Mabel kissed the tips of Belle's fingers. Anna felt a great tenderness for these extraordinary women. Their love was so open. If it delighted Belle to devote herself to Mabel's every need, if it was her mission to make the world realise Mabel's talent, so be it. Their complementarity made for perfect harmony.

It was now quite dark. Quarrels were beginning. Marie

was lying unconscious on a sofa whilst her lover almost came to blows arguing over the meaning of 'reality'. Picasso was locked in a tight embrace with a handsome girl Anna took to be his mistress. A wild young man was thumping out a frenzied piece on the piano. Anna was suddenly overwhelmed. So was Elisabeth. She made her way over to the dazed Englishwoman. "I think we should go," she whispered. "Before anyone starts taking their clothes off."

It was cool in the streets. Children were still playing in the gardens in the géntle glow of the lamps. Students sat at the cafes along the Boulevard Saint Michel, laughing, gesturing, talking, talking, talking. "How the French love to talk," thought Anna. "How well they do it. It is such an elegant language." She resolved to learn it better.

They reached the point of the quay where they should cross the little bridge to the island. There was a small, uncrowded café on the corner of a narrow alleyway.

"Shall we sit here for a moment, have a drink and look at the river before we go to bed?" Elisabeth suggested. "The rest of Paris is just waking up."

They ordered glasses of white wine. Pleasure boats sailed past, lit by candles. The moon was almost full. The towers of Notre Dame were big against the bright sky

"I hope you enjoyed the evening," said Elisabeth.

Oh yes, Anna had enjoyed the evening.

"At least you have met a few people. That is important."

Anna reflected how lucky she was to have Elisabeth as her patron, to introduce her to the city. A brightly coloured barge chugged by. A woman, man, child and dog all sitting up on deck.

"I might like Paris after all," she thought.

Chapter 4
Private View

Gaby fell in love with Sussex. She was entranced by the village, the thatched cottages, the flint church and pub, especially the pub, where her Gallic charm won all hearts. The little English she had was spoken with an accent which represented French laxity of morals, so the farmers were spellbound as she waved her delicate hands and flirted with her sea-green eyes. She spent the morning wandering in the garden and in the afternoon Charlie generally took her for a drive, visiting castles or manor houses. She became a local talking point; speculation was rife as to whether she would be the future lady of Finborough Place, especially as the two women went shopping for new curtains and wallpaper. One evening Violet came to call. She was slightly thinner, more drawn than when Charlie had last seen her at the funeral. She was dressed in black, whereas Charlie made a point of wearing her brightest colours; which it must be said were still fairly muted, apart from a bright green cravat.

"She's come to see what all the talk is about," thought Charlie.

"So this is the grieving fiancée," thought Gaby.

"It's true she's very alluring," thought Violet. "So that's Charlie's type now."

Charlie felt sorry for her. She had gambled on making a go of marriage with Toby when she might have had a less glamorous match. Having lost, her future was uncertain. "Is she hoping to try her luck with me?" Charlie wondered. "Is she sizing up what she thinks is the competition?"

If Violet had entertained any hopes whatsoever in that direction, the sight of the sophisticated Frenchwoman demolished them. With her Charlie was another person, whom Violet didn't recognise. She felt excluded by the rapport between the two, a silent language based on experience beyond Violet's understanding. Gaby talked in halting English out of politeness, but every so often Charlie would explain something to her in rapid French. Then Violet lost sight of the tomboy she had so much admired when they played together as children. She saw instead the international dramatist, at home in London and Paris, the debonair dandy who might have her pick of attractive women. Confused, unconfident, she went home to her parents' farm, shut herself in her bedroom and cried.

All good things must come to an end, it is said. One Monday morning Gaby announced that she had to return to Paris.

"Won't you come with me to this Englishwoman's exhibition?" she asked.

She had not spoken of this again after first mentioning the subject. Charlie had quite forgotten the business of letting the house in Passy.

"When will you go?"

"The day after tomorrow, or that day after that. Before the end of the week. The private view is on Friday."

It was a sensible idea to have someone living in if Charlie was to be away for some time, she accepted that. It was just that that house was most personal to her. It was where she worked. The cottage in Vine Place had been shared with friends, with Toby; it was associated with pleasure. Could she let another person use her workspace? Would Finborough Place be where she wrote now? It was too soon to imagine that. She might turn her old bedroom into a study, not yet, though. Writing was out of the question for the moment anyway.

"If we leave on Thursday I'll go with you. I can't organise things any earlier. I won't stay long. I'll see how the play's going, pop into a performance."

"Fine."

"I'll get Dan to drive us to Newhaven."

After an initial period of sulking Dan had become

Charlie's right-hand man. She paid him a good wage, which more than compensated for the sums he had extracted from Toby He was also besotted with Gaby, who was equally drawn to young men and women.

"I would like to have your Dan as a pet," she sighed more than once.

"He's not ready for the big city yet, my dear. I need him here."

Gaby decided in that case, if she had stayed much longer, she would certainly have taught the boy all about the delights of sleeping with an older woman.

It was raining and windy the day they caught the ferry. They were already very wet when they arrived at Newhaven, although the journey in the car was short. Gaby remembered that seasickness was one of the reasons she had stayed away from the British Isles. Charlie was used to rough seas, having been out with the fishermen until they realised she wasn't a boy. She stood on deck, in spite of the weather, looking back at the white cliffs. The image of a body on the rocks came back to her. Gaby's presence had helped to keep the bad dreams at bay; now her tears began to drip on to the handrail. Any observer might have thought they were raindrops.

Often, when she arrived in Dieppe, Charlie would have a meal in one of the many restaurants beside the harbour. If she was lucky the Dover sole, which she always preferred, was from the morning's catch. This time she was too melancholy to feel hungry and Gaby swore she wouldn't be able to eat for days. Several times during the crossing she had moaned that she was going to die. Since they had to wait several hours for a train to Paris they managed to stagger (Charlie holding Gaby up) to the café in the main street beloved of both Proust and Oscar Wilde, where they sipped a large brandy.

"I think I will live," announced Gaby, not having spoken for an exceptional length of time. "In fact, after this cognac, I might even fancy a plate of mussels." She rolled the liquid around the glass. "It's very good, this cognac."

"Nothing but the best for you, my dear. Who'd give second-rate stuff to a connoisseur?"

Gaby's eyes were beginning to regain their normal intelligence. She looked seriously at her friend.

"Well Charlie? Have you left too much of yourself over the channel? Are we going to lose you?"

Charlie didn't know.

"I'm sorry. Dieppe is too close to England. I'll ask you again when you've been back in Passy for a few nights. When you see how your friends have missed you. When you listen to your French words spoken by good actors to your audience, the audience who never misses one of your plays. Then I'll ask you where you think you belong."

It wasn't just a question of belonging, thought Charlie. It was about responsibility as well. Gaby would never understand that. She had not imagined she would be responsible for Finborough Place. She had never become quite as irresponsible as she had hoped when she first left England. Her plan, such as it was, had been to rent a room with few possessions, to spend time during the day thinking of nothing but the words on the page. At night she would look for sex. Her remarkable good looks made finding sex easy. This brought with it an introduction to the wealthy and influential. The little garret, a bohemian fantasy, was no longer appropriate. She had money, she might as well use it. So she acquired possessions as she acquired lovers. Success in the theatre meant an end to pondering at length over style and meaning. There were deadlines, rewritings, demands from producers, directors and actors. This was not the freedom she expected. Too much order. Yet she had made this. She had a profession, she owned property. In these first heady days she sought out only the women with whom she could not fall in love. Exciting women who thrilled her. They were no more interested than she was in emotional attachments. Recently she had begun to feel uneasy, overwhelmed by all she had created. It might be good to share it with someone. What did that mean, though, sharing? Even the suggestion that a stranger could use her home, live amongst her things, was distasteful. She and Toby had managed to maintain a separateness whilst being there for the others' needs. How she would miss him! Gaby had helped her so much but friendship could only go so far.

"I have to finish it with the Duchess. I have missed Giles very much. I want to be with him. It's not fair to her. I must be brave, tell her it's over."

Charlie had almost forgotten Gaby's dilemma.

"Giles would like to marry me."

Gaby married! There would be an end to their evenings together.

"Thank you for making me get away from it all, Charlie, giving me chance to see clearly."

Make her get away? Is that what she did?

"He has asked me to go with him to his family house in Provence in the autumn." She paused. "It will be a new life, Charlie. I would like a child."

Charlie was silent. Gaby as wife, Gaby as mother, would mean a new life for Charlie too. Another loss.

"It is the right moment."

Charlie gave no answer.

"I am going to order moules marinières. Would you like some? With some cold white wine?"

Why not, thought Charlie, why not?

"I have to say, although your excellent Mrs Branson did her best, I missed French cooking. Puddings are bad for the digestion, I think. Boiled beef fat pastry is an odd invention."

"What I would like now," thought Charlie, "is a plate of steaming steak and kidney with a suet crust as light as a feather."

"Come to Provence. I'll teach you how to make the most of vegetables. The aubergines are especially good!" Quite restored she chattered on, picking the moules delicately from their shells, dipping bread into the white wine sauce. Suddenly Charlie felt lonely.

The day of the private view Anna was in a bad mood. Hanging the paintings, arranging the sculptures the day before had been a long, irritating process, shifting them all around for the best effect. Elisabeth had given unwanted advice without understanding Anna's intent. The gallery was large and well lit, situated centrally in the Rue des Arts. A hundred invitations had been sent out to the cream of Parisian society.

"You're sure to sell," Elisabeth promised. "I can think of at least ten likely buyers."

Anna found this hard to believe. These were not pretty pictures; they were demanding, almost aggressive.

"They are new, therefore, exciting," Elisabeth explained. "I have aroused much curiosity. I have also presented you as a good investment. I hope you don't mind."

Why should she mind? There were those who bought paintings because they fell in love with them, must possess them, and those who bought because at some future date they could sell for several times as much. When she first started to show she only wanted to sell to those in love, who would cherish what she had made, until she realised that there was some value in being considered a good enough placement for capital funds.

"No, I don't mind. I hope you're right."

"What are you going to wear?"

Not only did this woman presume to know how the works should be displayed, she wanted to practice her window dressing skills on the artist herself! This is too much, thought Anna.

"I haven't decided."

"Could we have a look through your wardrobe?"

Anna refrained from saying most certainly not. She owed Elisabeth a lot and, after all, it was only kindness. She laid out dresses, hats, stocking and shoes carefully on the bed.

"Try that one."

They spent two hours trying various combinations. It was not enough to see the clothes themselves, she must wear them. There were three dresses Elisabeth liked very much, it was then a question of deciding on the stockings. In the end a pale pink beaded chiffon was chosen with stockings of almost the same colour and white shoes with little pearl buttons.

"Exquisite," Elisabeth pronounced. Her own wardrobe

offered a limited range of subtle colours, nothing vibrant, nothing shocking.

Pale pink was Anna's least favourite colour. She had bought this dress because of its meticulous workmanship, from a seamstress friend who needed money to feed her children. She had worn it out to dinner the evening her young baron had made his marriage proposal, so it had rather unpleasant associations.

"I'm not sure this is what I want," she said.

"Believe me, you look ravishing. It is important."

When Elisabeth had gone next door to consider her own costume, Anna took a hard look at herself in the long mirror.

"A china doll."

Elisabeth's final choice for herself was primrose yellow broderie anglaise. A topaz necklace was her only piece of jewellery. She offered to lend Anna her pink pearls.

"No thank you. Please go ahead of me. I need time to prepare myself quietly."

"I understand. You must be feeling very nervous." She took Anna's hand. "Everything will be fine. Don't forget your gloves. White of course."

"Thank you. No, I won't forget the gloves."

"Do you want me to come back for you? Or send someone? Surely you don't want to arrive alone?"

That's just what she did want. To arrive alone, to be left alone.

"I shall be perfectly all right, honestly." She squeezed her hostess' arm. "Thank you for everything. See you soon."

Elisabeth frowned. This was not quite in order. She had planned it all so carefully, she was afraid of the unexpected.

"Elisabeth, I insist. I must have time on my own."

Elisabeth recognized what she called 'the artistic temperament'. Opposition to this wilfulness would be unwise.

"Don't be too long dear, will you? I wouldn't like people to leave before meeting you."

Anna said nothing. Her look was enough to send Elisabeth finally out of the door. Anna began to take off the pink dress.

A hundred invitations brought out more than a hundred guests. Elisabeth had the foresight to prepare everything beforehand down to the last detail. Price lists were on small tables placed strategically around the room, there was a large desk with catalogues for sale and a huge bunch of lilies for decoration. The first comers, who arrived exactly on time, had an opportunity to study the works. Soon a lively throng made viewing almost impossible. Mabel and Belle were amongst the early arrivals.

"Well, I must say, I'm surprised," was Mabel's first comment. "The girl's got power. My goodness, who'd have thought it!" And she immediately reserved three of the larger canvases. Belle liked a couple of the sculptures, so they bought those too.

Pablo was not far behind them, with Fernande. She too wanted a sculpture but Pablo was certainly not in the business of buying.

"What do you think then, Maître?" asked Mabel.

"Interesting," he replied, then, seeing her raised eyebrows, "not bad. She has a certain something."

Elisabeth began to feel distinctly edgy. She made a discreet sign to two young men that they should start to serve champagne. A little drink enlivened conversation, animated conversation about the pictures encouraged sales. Not too much, though, it was a very delicate balance. Marie and Guillaume had just appeared – she must make sure that Marie had no more than two glasses at this stage. Now the room was filling rapidly. Where was Anna?

"My dear, what an extraordinary show!" This was Gaby, accompanied by a grumpy looking Charlie. "So dynamic, almost frightening."

"Gaby, how nice to see you! And Charlie too. I was so sorry to hear of your loss, Charlie."

"Thank you, I received your card." One of many from friends and acquaintances.

Charlie neither liked nor disliked Elisabeth, she didn't find her very interesting. In the end, thought Charlie,

Elisabeth had few ideas of her own. She was generous almost to a fault, almost smothering her protégés, but she used her wealth to buy reflected glory, only encouraging those she judged to have the capacity to become famous.

Charlie felt as uncomfortable at private views as at first nights.

"But where is the artist? I can't see anyone I don't know here." Few Parisian socialites and bohemians were unknown to Gaby.

There was sudden hush. Here at last, was the artist, pausing on the threshold before making an entrance.

Oh, but she was an exotic bloom. Green slippers glittering with silver embroidery, a skirt of mysterious fabric which shimmered sea-green and turquoise, a blood red silk blouse, a turquoise necklace and on her head a turban the same colours as her skirt. Her arms were bare to the elbow, she had no gloves, instead jewelled bracelets tinkled around her wrists.

"Bravo," shouted Gaby, and everyone applauded.

Elisabeth recovered from her shock sufficiently to take the apparition by the hand.

"Dear friends," she said, "allow me to present Miss Anna Waltham."

Another round of applause as Anna was firmly led in towards prospective customers.

"What a woman!" thought Mabel.

"I'm not sure about the red" thought Belle.

"Now here's a force to be reckoned with," thought Gaby.

"Yes, I would like to paint her," thought Picasso, and several others.

"Oh really! She looks so vulgar," thought Elisabeth.

As for Charlie, she considered it all the height of affectation. Was the woman a painter or an actress? She herself was plainly dressed in a severe but expensive white linen suit. Her shirt too was white, of an impeccable cut. She was unaware that in this crowd the combination of whiteness with her sunburnt skin, her pale blue eyes, her thickly curling blond hair which was cut short, she

too stood out. In other circumstances she might have
worn trousers, but not here. Gaby's partner the duchess
held soirées for women only, when half the guests wore
complete male attire. The duchess herself never dressed
as a woman. One day Charlie might dare to throw away
her skirts; not yet.

Elisabeth was in close conversation with Gaby. Anna
was surrounded. Charlie picked up a sculpture in wood.
Its smooth rounded contours felt good in her hand, perhaps she would buy it. She wasn't sure what it was,
some kind of bird shape, she supposed, but the colour
and the polish of the wood pleased her. There were
larger pieces in marble which she found fascinating. The
paintings she would come back to examine some other
day, perhaps.

"Elisabeth says would you join her and a few friends
for supper. Then you can meet Miss Waltham properly
and see what you think." Gaby in her turn was rolling
the bird shape in her palms.

"What I think?" Charlie had almost forgotten that this
bright creature was her possible tenant. So far what she
thought was that there was an unpleasant harshness about
her brilliance.

"I'm not sure about letting."

"You keep saying that. Do at least give her a chance.
You don't want her to be stuck with Elisabeth for too
long, do you?"

Charlie wouldn't wish that on anyone.

"I'm not feeling sociable. I'd been counting on an early
night."

"Oh come on. You must shake off these country habits.
You never knew the meaning of early night."

It was true. If she went home she would in all likeli-
hood sit alone with her dark thoughts. It would be better to wear herself out with food, drink and the noise
of a café.

The party didn't break up until very late indeed.
Elisabeth's attempts to arrange the seating were thwarted.
Mabel placed Anna firmly between her and Belle and
Charlie was trapped by two men who went to all her

plays several times over, who were dying to meet her.
As they all began to leave, Anna herself caught up with
Charlie just outside.

"I've been told you have a house you might be willing to let." Her voice was light, pleasant, underlined with
an odd accent.

"I don't know." Charlie almost meant, "I don't think
so."

"Could I possibly come to see it?"

Under the lamp her eyes were a deep almost purple
blue.

"I don't know."

"I desperately need to find somewhere of my own to
work."

"Come round tomorrow for lunch. Twelve o'clock. It
will be a light meal."

"Thank you." As she held out her hand the bracelets
sounded almost tuneful.

On impulse Charlie raised the hand to her lips and
kissed the tips of the pale fingers. She looked up quickly
to see the response.

Was it amusement, mockery, or sympathy?

"Until tomorrow. Goodnight."

"Goodnight."

Charlie's villa was a long way from the café. Should
she take a cab? She chose to walk along the quays before
crossing the river. Had she been wearing her trousers,
she would have been propositioned along the way. As
it was, one or two hopefuls tried to catch her eye. She
hesitated as she passed the door of an actress who had
a small part in her last play. It had been clear the girl
has wanted to get to know her a lot better. Should she
knock? She walked on. She wasn't in the mood.

Chapter 5
Passy

La Villa Marguerite was much bigger than it looked. Named after a famous courtesan whose last lover had it built specially for her, it had square rooms of a comfortable size, ceilings of a sensible height and a particularly tasteful drawing room, where 'Marguerite' used to entertain. At the end of the garden the summer house was a quiet retreat next to a disused stable block. It was a place for all seasons since there was a wood-burning stove in the corner of the main area. Charlie only used it in the warmer months when she could open the long windows. All her books, her manuscripts and her writing materials were in the main building in a small library where she worked throughout most of the year. As she opened the shutters the sparsely furnished room filled with light. Of course, it would make an excellent studio. Both Gaby and Elisabeth had given her to understand that she almost had a duty to allow it to be used in this way. She might not come back here until winter if then, wouldn't it be a terrible waste for everything to be empty, unused? She never dreamed she would become so possessive, it had crept up on her through the years. This was her house, where she was, reflecting who she was. But that was as long as she was denied Finborough Place. As she was rejected, she turned her back on who she had been and made herself someone else, the someone else who lived here. Having been forced to revisit her old self in her old home (real home?) shouldn't she begin to let go of this one? She had argued with herself during the night, pacing from room to room. But she must have a base in Paris, she must! The idea of it being taken

over made her very insecure. It wasn't fair to ask her to
give up this refuge when she had just lost Toby. Nobody
understood how shaken up she was. Her friends only
saw a very rich woman with three homes, they didn't
know how she needed to cling on to each. When the
doorbell rang at twelve o'clock she had decided she
would most definitely not let or lend the Villa Marguerite.

Today Anna was wearing a very dark blue linen dress,
pale blue stockings. When she took off her white straw
hat, Charlie saw that her hair was a deep, rich brown.

"I'll give her lunch before I disappoint her," she
thought. "I suppose she might have some interesting
things to say. There's something irritating about her,
though. Too self-contained. Rather cool. Probably not
very emotional at all."

She had not been able to get near enough to the paintings to experience their disturbance.

"Do come through," she said. "I've asked for lunch to
be served in the garden."

Was there a slight reaction to the word 'served'?

"So how do you like Paris?" asked Charlie.

"I think I like it well enough."

Not a very encouraging response. Well enough for
what?

"You intend to stay?"

"Certainly not for ever. I don't know for how long."

"Where are you from?"

Anna didn't know what she meant.

"You were living in Germany, but you're English.
Where is your home in England?"

"I don't have a home in England. I don't have a home.
I move around."

Again Charlie was intrigued by the accent.

"Where are *you* from, Miss Langham Price?" She pronounced the name as though she were underlining it.

"Sussex."

"Ah!"

"I have to spend some time there sorting out the family estate."

"Ah!"

She was beginning to make Charlie cross.

"Do you know Sussex, Miss Waltham?"

"A bit. Some of the friends I studied with in London lived there."

"Did you visit them?"

"Sometimes, Miss Langham Price."

This was painful, insolent.

"Look, Anna, please call me Charlie. This formality is ridiculous. I never want to be called 'Miss Langham Price' nor 'Charlotte'. Why are you being so distant?"

Anna blushed.

"Last night at supper you were speaking French. You looked like good fun. Today, when you spoke to me in English, I didn't recognise you. You sounded . . . I don't know."

What she could have said was, "You sounded like the wealthy county types I can't bear."

"I didn't sound like Miss Langham Price, for god's sake! Oh please, please tell me I didn't sound like that!"

Her expression was so horrified that Anna started to laugh.

"That's better. Now you're human. Much less frightening."

"I frightened you! But you frightened me!"

For the first time they studied each other closely. What Anna saw was an athletic form, long legs, small breasts, muscular short neck, fine wrists, muscular forearms, the upper arms hidden by the sleeves of a pale blue kimono, exactly the same shade as the eyes. A noble head with delicate features. Thick blond hair like a curly halo. A proud set to the chin, a mouth neither too large nor too small.

"Has anyone ever drawn her?" she wondered. Then she caught sight of a pastel hanging in a rather dark corner. "Oh no, that's far too sweet, too pretty. It doesn't do her justice. She probably doesn't like it either, that's why it's almost hidden.

What Charlie saw was an extremely beautiful woman. The plain dress fitted to perfection over hips and thighs. Nothing angular, smooth roundness from head to toe.

And a face that Helen of Troy might have envied.

She did not desire her. The invisible barriers she sensed were too strong. "She does not want to be touched. Woe betide anyone who comes too near."

The temperature in the little garden was most pleasant, a relief from the great heat which had kept the Parisians in an almost comatose state between the hours of twelve and six. They ate quails followed by goats' cheese and fresh figs from a tree by the fountain.

"How lucky you are to have such a pretty quiet place to work. It must be very rare here."

"I am lucky to have friends who know where to look."

"You've lived in Paris for a long time?"

"Some years."

"Why Paris? Why not London? Why write in French?"

"Personal reasons."

"I'm sorry"

"I could ask you the same questions. Why Germany? Why not London? Why do you have no home?"

Anna looked down, brushing crumbs off the table, smoothing her napkin.

"I've said I'm sorry. Thank you for lunch. You have been most kind, but it's obvious you don't like me, so there's no point in talking about the house." She stood up.

It's not that I don't like her, thought Charlie. How could I dislike her? I don't know her and am never likely to.

"Please sit down again. We seem to have got off on the wrong footing. I'll show you round when we're ready. Do you smoke? I smoke small cigars, myself, but I do have cigarettes."

Anna didn't smoke, but she liked to watch the way Charlie held the cigar in her slim fingers. As she raised it to her lips the kimono sleeve fell back, revealing strong biceps. That's the way Anna might like to draw her, right hand holding a cigar away from her face, left arm bent across the body to support the right elbow. They talked about flowers whilst they were outside, about light and space when they went into the summerhouse. It was plain that Anna felt quite at home with it all, judging the amount of wall space, appreciating the simplicity of the furnishing. She was careful to compliment Charlie on her writer's retreat without making any assumptions, however, that it could be an artist's studio.

It suits her, dammit, thought Charlie, she looks good in here.

The rest of the house evoked less interest. The appreciative remarks were less spontaneous, although they spent a long time discussing the paintings and drawings acquired over the years. Anna's private assessment of the collection was that it was rather safe even though she congratulated Charlie on having so many fine works.

"I'm not as daring as Mabel," said Charlie. "Her studio overwhelms me."

Mabel's 'studio' was more like a gallery filled from floor to ceiling with pictures by all the interesting artists of the day. Some would have to be taken down to make space for Anna's. "I didn't get a chance to look at yours properly. I'll go back when there are fewer people." This was a fortunate truth, saving Charlie from any polite lies, since she hadn't cared much for what she glimpsed through the crowd.

"I'm sure my painting isn't to your taste. But you might like the carving. Thank you for showing me around. I have an appointment in half an hour with a client, so I'll say goodbye."

"So she's leaving it to me to say something about renting the house," thought Charlie. "Doesn't she want it after all?" Perversely, she was annoyed by this apparent indifference.

"Do you want to stay here whilst I'm away?" A straightforward question. Anna seemed disconcerted.

"I would very much-like to." She paused. "It would be a great privilege. What would the rent be?"

"No more than you could easily afford. I'll be going back to England at the end of next week. Could you move in then?"

"Oh yes. But I would like to know how much . . ."

"Don't worry about that. We'll discuss it later."

She would ask for a small sum, a nominal amount. Money didn't matter.

That evening as she was preparing for a supper party at Pauline's, she wondered why she had changed her mind. Gaby would be pleased. Did she need Gaby's approval? Charlie's wealth, her looks, her success, meant she would never be short of admirers, she had a veritable fan club, but there was a faction which spread gossip about her, a clutch of ex-lovers whose rejection had inspired a malicious desire for revenge. The 'doomed women' as a male poet had called them, protected each other against 'normal' society; amongst themselves they could be vicious. Gaby had never wavered in her support of Charlie, even though she often disapproved of her cavalier attitude. After all, there were times when Gaby's actions gave rise to intense suspicion, when Charlie stood by her against group hostility. So, was it really to please Gaby that she was going to hand over her keys? She secured her cravat with a jewelled pin, examined her image critically. A handsome young man looked back at her, a dandy careful of every detail. Expensive simplicity. The jacket and trousers hung more loosely than before, her appetite had been poor during the last few weeks. She frowned, she usually desired a perfect fit. Never mind, she still looked good enough to turn heads, men and women alike.

Pauline's apartment was a few streets away, towards the Seine. It was a world of oriental fantasy. The bourgeois salon had been turned into an enormous tent, draperies of all colours over the ceiling and walls. Persian rugs were spread in profusion, there were cushions and low couches, ornate lamps, vases and coffee pots in burnished metal. You could have been in a harem, since women in embroidered bodices and flowing trousers were stretched out languidly, sipping from tiny goblets, or, in a few cases, sucking on a long tube attached to a bulbous pot. There were a few figures dressed in a similar way to Charlie standing by the wall and smoking cigarettes. Most of them Charlie recognised. During the day they might be seen exercising their horses in the Bois de Boulogne, with or without their husbands. They would not dare to walk through the streets in male attire, as Charlie did, their present personas were strictly for darkened rooms.

"Charlie! How good to see you! So sorry to hear about your loss." The Marquise de Sotteville swaggered over, smiling dangerously. Her present lover was a dancer previously with Charlie herself for a month or two until she tired of her. This dancer was now full-length on the floor, lost in her opium dreams.

"I hear we might not have the pleasure of your company for a while?" The pleasure of talking about my affairs, thought Charlie grimly.

"Adrienne was here last week. She looked dreadful, poor thing."

The implication was, "look what you did to this woman. She was destroyed when you cast her aside!"

"I'd heard she was making a set for a Russian princess."

"Lies, all lies. She was sobbing on my shoulder most of the evening. Her heart is broken."

"Again" thought Charlie. It was amazing how many times her heart had been broken. Fortunately it could be patched up again by the glue of a rich new lover.

"Do give her my regards. Excuse me, I have to say hello to Pauline."

Pauline was sliding across the floor, holding a steaming cup.

"Have a sip." She proffered the cup.

Charlie smelled it. It was disgusting. And dark green. She pretended to taste.

"Isn't it delicious?" Pauline's breath had the usual fragrance of eau de cologne. She wafted back to the kitchen, where she never cooked, scarcely ever ate.

"If Gaby doesn't come, I'll go home," thought Charlie. There was no one else here of any interest. Pauline emerged again, clapped her hands.

"Listen everyone." Her American accent was still strong. Most French people found it attractive. "The entertainment is about to begin. Allow me to present the famous Turkish belly-dancer, Fatima."

Gaby had told Charlie this was to happen, but Gaby wasn't here and Charlie had forgotten all about it. Could she leave before the show began?

She couldn't. Even as Pauline finished speaking, Fatima rose from her velvet cushions. She was entrancing. Charlie didn't know what she had expected of a belly dancer, certainly not this. Her young fluid body had an extraordinary boneless grace. The skilled movements must have been learnt in childhood, so accomplished were they. The whole company, apart from the unconscious, were spellbound.

"Who's the lucky devil will take her home tonight," the Marquise whispered in Charlie's ear. Charlie moved away from her angrily. The eroticism of the dance transcended lewdness. The purity of sexual expression, the essential femininity, was almost a religious mystery. The expansion and contraction of the muscles, rippling across her stomach and belly was the very breath of life.

When the dance ended there was a moment of respectful silence before the applause.

"Bravo, oh bravo!"

Gaby and the Duchess had managed to be present most of the performance, slipping in unnoticed just after the beginning.

"Come on Gaby – it's your turn now," a drunken voice called out from a corner.

Gaby's dancing was a bit of a joke. She had taken lessons from a leading mime artist who thought she was cute enough, if not professional enough, to work with him on tour.

"Yes, come on Gaby. You and the Duchess do the Egyptian thing."

This was a sketch which had created a scandal when the Duchess had trodden the boards as an Egyptologist unwrapping a mummy to discover Gaby as a very scantily clad Princess. The two seized each other in a passionate embrace lasting several minutes. Gaby's ex-husband had been most excited by the spectacle.

"We're not dressed for it." Although Gaby's costume this evening made her look like a character from the Arabian Nights, the Egyptian sketch would have demanded yards of bandage to be slowly unwrapped by the archaeologist.

"Just the end bit will do," suggested the Marquise. "Or wouldn't it be appropriate?"

"No it would not." The Duchess' voice was tense. She walked stiffly over to exchange words with her hostess.

"Gaby, you've told her!" Charlie tried not to make this sound like an accusation. It had to happen. Gaby seemed genuinely distressed.

"Charlie, will you talk to her?"

"What can I say?"

"Tell her I love her, that I'll always love her."

Oh yes, thought Charlie, she's going to believe that, when you abandon her for a man.

"Haven't you told her yourself?"

"Of course I have. I never want to hurt her, truly I don't. She's so fragile. But I must do this. Charlie, she respects you. She thinks you understand her."

"I do."

"I can't bear her to be so sad. She mustn't be jealous of Giles. It's not the same as with her."

There you have it, thought Charlie. It's not the same. That's the Duchess' tragedy.

"All right. I'll talk to her . . . man to man."

Gaby kissed her on the cheek. "Thank you."

Man to man. It wasn't entirely ironic. Gaby had an all-embracing sexuality which included plants and animals as well as men and women. However hard she tried, she would never understand the single-mindedness of the Duchess, who was taking the initiative and coming towards Charlie.

"Can we go on to the balcony? The face was as tense as her voice.

The air was refreshing after the closeness of the room. The Duchess offered Charlie a cigar which she lit for her with trembling hand.

"It had to happen one day. I've been incredibly lucky to keep her for six years."

She paused, trying hard to keep her voice steady.

"Of course it couldn't last. She's beautiful, she's talented, she's becoming famous, for God's sake! She's . . . she's . . ."

She stopped, swallowed hard, shook her head, leaving Charlie to guess the end of the sentence.

"But after six years," the Duchess continued, in a steadier voice, "one had a sense of security." Pause. "She's been faithful until now, hasn't she?"

Probably, thought Charlie, How would I know?

"Yes, I'm sure she has."

"She always said after her husband I was so tender. So careful of her pleasure. She has a way of describing things makes me feel so humble."

Indeed, thought Charlie, she has a gift for words. Beware. The deepest emotions defy words.

"I thought I was truly blessed to have her by my side. When you compare her with these others," she gestured back into the room, "she is a jewel beyond worth. I can never, never, never, stop loving her." Her voice shook again, she took a long drag on her cigar.

"She says she'll always love me. What does that mean?"

I don't know, thought Charlie.

"It means nothing!" For the first time there was anger. "Nothing! She is everything to me, everything. I can't live without her. She thinks she can go off with this man, sleep with this man, marry this man and keep me waiting like some forgotten mistress. I can't do it! She said what we have is deeper than sex, it will outlive desire. That's just a way of saying she doesn't want me any more, isn't it?"

Do I have to answer, thought Charlie. Fortunately, the Duchess continued.

"She wants a child. That's my curse isn't it? I can't give the woman I love a child. I thought I was in heaven, it isn't, it's hell. I should kill myself. Put an end to it."

She threw her cigar butt into the street. It was a long way down. She fixed Charlie with her anguished black eyes.

"You understand, don't you Charlie?"

"Yes, I do."

"I'm going. I'll slip out when Gaby's not looking. Take her home will you? She wanted us to have a last night together. I can't. Goodnight."

They shook hands.

Gaby wept all the way home in the cab. Comforting her, Charlie thought, I'm so glad I'm your friend and not your lover.

Eating breakfast in the garden the next day, Charlie pondered on the question of inheritance. Finborough Place had come down to her through several generations. She was the last of the line. She was still young, she intended to live a long life, so what would happen to the estate after her death need not trouble her now. It was only Gaby's longing to become a mother that made her think about her own lack of maternal instinct and its consequences. What was maternal instinct anyway? Did it exist in the rest of the animal kingdom, or was reproduction simply the response of the male to the female cycle? A ewe didn't go looking for a ram because she wanted to have lambs, did she? Didn't the female submit passively to the male drive? For the first time it occurred to her that as a rich heiress she might have suitors, who might assume she would want at least to continue a blood line if not the family name. Surely it was commonly known she was not in the marriage market? Who would want her as a wife? A wife! She smiled broadly. A wife! She and her mother, she and Mrs. Branson, she and Violet were a different species. She had met wives who resembled her though, amongst the hunting fraternity. Determined, capable women whose husbands gave them their head. The husbands were the problem; Charlie didn't want a husband, she wanted to be one.

Today she would start to make the house ready for Anna. There were papers to be tidied, decisions to be made about what she should take to England. She didn't envisage doing much writing in the near future. She'd finished the English version of the current play, any alterations would be made after discussion with the producers and director. The library at Finborough Place was enough to keep her in reading matter for the rest of her life so she had no need to take books from here. She had clothes in Brighton. Anna clearly had very few possessions, so she supposed it would suit her to come into a house where everything would be to hand. She felt surprisingly optimistic about her impending departure. She was tired of the kind of masquerade she had attended the previous night, of the incestuous nature of the tight-knit circles. Like Gaby, she should move on.

Chapter 6
New Directions

The first few days after Anna moved in, Elisabeth insisted on 'helping her settle down'. This meant hardly leaving her alone 'in case she was too lonely'.

"Just until you find your feet and people get used to the idea of you being here. Perhaps you should have a party, I'll help you with the guest list."

"You're very kind. I'm not too keen on parties."

"A few dinners from time to time, then."

"Elisabeth, I'm here to work."

"Darling, you can't work all the time."

"I don't want to tie myself down to entertaining. I want to be able to visit the parks, make sketches whenever the mood takes me."

"You need someone to show you around."

"I can find my own way."

"But there are some delightful hidden corners."

"I'll start with the Bois de Boulogne."

"You shouldn't be walking on you own in the Bois de Boulogne, my dear."

Anna wondered if she would have to be really rude. Or at least quite blunt. Elisabeth meant well.

"I am so grateful for all you have done for me. I can never thank you enough. But I can only start to work again if I have no distractions. I won't be lonely. I'm never lonely."

"There is an Austrian Count who was at your private view who asked me to introduce you. He seems discreet, considerate, I'm sure he would make a most agreeable supper companion. He is here on business only, so he knows very few people. You may wander in the parks on you own, though I don't advise it, but you certainly need an escort in a restaurant."

If she didn't know her better, Anna might have thought Elisabeth was running some kind of introduction agency.

"I know this man's family. They are all solid, respectable people."

Oh dear, thought Anna.

"Should I tell him he may call on you one evening?"

"No thank you. Elisabeth, I am very tired. I feél a migraine coming on. I must lie down in the dark."

"I'll leave you then."

"Please do."

Why is she so difficult? Elisabeth asked herself as she quietly closed the front door.

Anna, who never had migraines, nor even headaches, went into the studio to lay out her paints. Most of her sculptures had been bought and most of the pictures, even the large ones. She intended to do smaller works here; several stretched and prepared canvases were leaning against the wall. She placed one on the easel, facing the garden. She focussed her attention on a patch of red and yellow lilies. Flowers had not inspired her in Frankfurt. In Derbyshire she had always been amazed by their bright profusion. In Paris she would work from nature without imitation. The light in the studio was constant, in the garden it changed rapidly. What she sought to convey was the flagrant sexuality of the lilies, their brilliant, vulgar display. The air was heavy with the decadent sweetness of their perfume.

She worked until the space outside was entirely in shadow. She was quite pleased with the beginning she had made. She was uncertain of the direction her work would take. During the last months spent in Frankfurt she had done very little, finding nothing much to inspire her. Some days she had felt so tired that she wondered if she was ill, although she told herself exhaustion was simply a natural consequence of sleepless nights. She had begun to have nightmares, a recurrent vision of a stony face with staring, accusing eyes, a terrifying blankness in which she read her own guilt. She stayed awake as long as she could, frustrated by her inability to use these silent hours productively. At Elisabeth's she slept better, lulled by the gentle flowing river. The nightmares came less often, interspersed with more pleasant, although complicated, dreams.

Having tided away her brushes she crossed over into the main house. She wasn't yet hungry. There was food in the larder – cold meat, bread, cheese, fruit, in case she needed it. What should she do with the rest of the evening to make sure she was tired enough to fall into the dreamless sleep she desired? It was her first night alone in this city, a circumstance she had insisted upon, whilst somewhat dreading. She scoured the bookshelves of the small library without enthusiasm. She noticed a neat stack of papers on a table in the corner. They were drawings, designs for a poster. The finished product, advertising Charlie's latest play, was at the bottom of the pile. Of course! That's what she could do, go to see Charlie's play. She had half an hour before it started. She went into the street and hailed a cab.

She was lucky to have a seat. It was a full house, but as she turned away disappointed a young couple arrived who had a spare seat in their box. They turned out to be avid fans of Charlie's, making a point of seeing each play several times.

"There's always something you missed the time before," was the husband's view. "He is a very clever writer."

He? Did the audiences believe the playwright was a man? Charlie Price (the Langham was dropped as being far too cumbersome) ought to be a man, it was certainly not a woman's name. Anna's French was not good enough to understand half the dialogue, since there were expressions she had never heard before. It must be rather risqué, she thought, listening to the ribald laughter. No wonder they had thought it was written by a man. Would she let them into the secret? That would clearly be wrong. She wondered how many people knew. Did it matter anyway?

Did it matter? This question bothered her as she ate her supper in the cosy little dining room next to the kitchen. This room, this house, had a neutral look. Elisabeth's apartment was obviously lived in by a woman. Certain colours, frills, bows, pretty ornaments would all be called 'feminine'. There were no frills here, the colours were muted, yet the label 'masculine' did not come to mind. 'Comfortable', yes, 'opulent' even in the main reception room, everywhere 'tasteful'. Actually, thought Anna, if I had told the young man the play was written by a woman, I would have not been quite truthful. Charlie didn't behave like a woman. To judge by her writing she saw the world as a man might see it. Anna could feel Charlie's peculiar presence all around, protective rather than dominating. She took her glass of wine through to the sitting room, where she settled down to study the pictures on the wall. The collection was indeed extensive, conservatively eclectic.

She was lost in contemplation of a delicate drawing of a young man (or was it?) when there was an insistent knocking at the door. She must have left the outer gate open, not being used to locking up. It was very late. Should she answer? She had better know who it was, it may be a neighbour in trouble. The knocking came again, louder. Surely this was some emergency. She hurried to open the door.

On the step was a distraught young woman. She looked vaguely familiar.

"Where is Charlie?" she demanded.

The combination of throaty voice, chestnut curls and heart shaped face triggered a memory.

"You were in the play!"

"Where is Charlie?" Much more aggressive this time as she pushed her way in.

"I'm afraid Charlie has gone"

"No she's here. She was at Pauline's. I must see her."

"She may have been at Pauline's but she's not here now. She's gone to England."

"I don't believe you. Who are you? What are you doing here?" Aggression was turning to menace.

"Would you like to come in an sit down? I'm Anna Waltham, I am Charlie's tenant."

"Tenant! Charlie doesn't have a 'tenant'. What kind of word is that?"

"Please do come in." Anna felt ridiculously British. The woman was already in. Polite formalities were no use against raw emotion. "By the way, who are you?" she asked weakly.

The intruder was already in Charlie's bedroom, opening the wardrobe and cupboards. Anna found a theatre programme, hastily scanned the cast list, found what she wanted.

"Mademoiselle Lenoir," she called in a firmer voice. "Mademoiselle Lenoir! Adrienne. You will find nothing in there to help. Charlie has gone back to England. I am not her mistress," this was said looking directly into the other's eyes as she stormed out of the bedroom, "if that's what you think. I hardly know her. This is a business arrangement. Now come and sit down or go home."

Adrienne chose to sit down and start weeping. Anna had an impulse to make her some hot sweet tea. Instead she said, "Would you like a glass of brandy?"

No response. The weeping continued. Was it genuine? There has been a scene on stage where she had cried in exactly the same way. Anna found the brandy and the glasses, poured a good measure for each and pushed one towards Adrienne. She waited.

The sobbing subsided into long shuddering breaths. Adrienne picked up her glass.

"Thank you," she whispered. A hundred spectators would have mopped their own eyes. There was an appropriate pause before she added, "forgive me".

She was extremely pretty in a petite Parisian way. She had the longest eyelashes Anna had ever seen, expressive eyes the same colour as her hair. Her waist looked all of eighteen inches, easily spanned by a man's hands. Charlie's hands were small, Anna remembered.

"You are kind. And beautiful."

Two compliments! Anna felt bound to offer one in return.

"I did so enjoy your performance."

"You saw it? When?"

"Tonight."

"Oh, tonight I was awful. You should have been there

the first night. I glittered, I glittered for Charlie. Tonight was rubbish."

"Well, I thought you were fine."

Anna realised she had no idea how to talk to actresses. Observing Adrienne had finished her brandy she poured her another.

"I'm glad you're not Charlie's mistress, for your sake! She has no heart. No heart at all!"

She looked at Anna as if for corroboration, which, naturally, Anna was unable to give. However, she was encouraged by a sympathetic silence, so she continued.

"They warned me. They all told me she would hurt me. If I had no heart either it would have been all right. We would have made wonderful love for a while then said bye bye when we were tired of each other. She tires easily, Charlie. I am the faithful type. Well, I have had many lovers it's true, but to Charlie I would have been the faithful type."

Anna was slightly confused by the distinction. Didn't a 'type' always behave the same way?

"They said 'Be careful, be careful, be careful!' I am not the careful type."

The image of herself Adrienne was presenting became even more confusing.

"I am the impetuous type. Shall I tell you about me and Charlie?"

Why not, thought Anna. It was one way of passing the darkest hours of the night.

"We met at the first rehearsals. Until I got this part, I thought Charlie Price was a man. What a shock when she walked in! For me it was a coup de foudre. Absolutely love at first sight. I was so excited when she looked at me and when she said 'How do you do, Mademoiselle Lenoir,' I couldn't open my mouth. I was lost! You know how it is?"

"Yes," said Anna, thinking, no, not really.

"There was an irresistible attraction between us. She could have taken me to bed then and there. I went home on fire. She stayed away from rehearsals for a few days, to let us get on with it, then she appeared again and took me to supper at Maxim's. The next night we went dancing. For a week she courted me without even kissing me on the lips. Every time her fingers brushed my skin I nearly died with longing. Then she brought me back here and we had pâté de foie gras and a great deal of white wine before she led me into the bedroom. 'I will undress you,' she said. Slowly, so slowly she took off every bit of clothing, kissing each part of me she exposed. At last, when I stood quite naked and trembling, nearly fainting, she took me in her arms."

Her face was aflame with the memory, her eyes glittering. Anna was transfixed.

"I had never known such pleasure. The next morning she gave me an amber brooch in a gold setting. Every night was equal bliss, every morning was a present. 'She must love me a lot,' I thought. I loved her to distraction. I told her so a hundred times as she brought me to a climax. I moaned, I shouted it: 'I love you, I love you, I love you!'"

She knocked back the rest of the brandy.

"I'm not sure you should be talking like this." Anna was conscious of how cool this must have sounded, but it was as if she was betraying some sort of trust by listening to such a frank account. Adrienne was not to be stopped.

"She possessed me! I would have become her slave. I was so proud to be on her arm on the boulevards. I was in paradise. Now I am in hell."

Anna couldn't help thinking this sounded like a curtain line from a cheap melodrama. She wasn't a spectator, though, she had some sort of role to play in this particular scenario, a situation totally unfamiliar to her. She made an effort.

"Adrienne, I am so sorry for what has happened to you. But Charlie is not here, won't be back for some time. You had better forget her."

Adrienne stared at her in disbelief. She had tried to make this stranger share her suffering, she wanted commiseration, physical comfort, hugs and kisses, someone to say 'Darling, how awful! How you've suffered! What a pity!' Instead she was confronted by this ice-block.

"God! You are just like Charlie. Heartless, quite heartless!"

It was not the first time the word had been used about Anna, and probably wouldn't be the last.

"You'll get over it." How could she utter such platitudes? Yet what else was there to say?

Adrienne rose unsteadily to her feet.

"Only death can relieve this pain!"

Another cheap line? Or did she mean it?

The exit line had more effect.

"One can see, Mademoiselle, that you have never suffered. Please God you never will."

She was gone.

Anna sank into an armchair and closed her eyes. Suffered, yes, she had, in a grim insidious way. She would not, could not, express it. She had hated Robin's power over her, his absolute need for her. She had not given herself willingly, like Adrienne, their sexual relations had been a battle in which they both were deeply wounded. Her wounds were not healed, and for Robin, to use Adrienne's words, only death relieved his pain. She envied Adrienne her ability to live with such ease, to give herself to the moment so completely. All her life Anna had been detached, not quite at one with her surroundings, waiting to be elsewhere. There had been carefree moments in her youth, moments of pure happiness shared usually with her sister, Betsy. tomorrow she would write to Betsy. She remembered an outing they had on a nearby lake when they landed on a little island. She could almost hear the sound of their laughter as she drifted off to sleep.

Charlie found settling in more difficult than she had imagined. She hadn't lived in Finborough Place for so many years. She made frequent trips to London, spent at least three nights a week in Brighton dining with the theatre crowd. She and George met for lunch every so often. She had made a package of some of Toby's possessions she thought George would like and Toby would want him to have. She was fond of Toby's lover, who had been patient and sensitive during Toby's many crises. Indeed, as they talked about old times over Dover sole, they were more like parents consoling each other for the loss of their only son. George still refused to come home with her. For him the big house and all it stood for was the source of Toby's problems. He himself had run away from his family in Brixton at the first opportunity, which was when a much older man fell for his cheeky grin. George never ceased thanking his lucky star that he happened to be loitering in Bond Street when a silver haired gentleman emerged from an outfitter's shop carrying a precarious stack of parcels. George instinctively caught one as it slipped off the top.

"Thank you very much," said the gentleman. "I suppose I ought to have had them delivered." George took some of the other parcels and they looked for a cab together. The gentleman invited George to come back with him for a cup of tea, a tea-time that lasted ten years until the gentleman died of a lingering illness, during which period he was cared for devotedly by George, who loved him like a father. So George inherited a house in Chelsea and a comfortable income. (Distant relatives had tried in vain to contest the will.) For a while he went wild, mixing with a dubious bunch who came down to Brighton every so often to take over certain hotels for long weekends. It was on the occasion of one of these weekends, after a licentious night he could hardly remember, that he sat down at a seafront café, taking a table next to Toby and Charlie. He was intrigued by what he took to be two young men, very alike, in close conversation. There was something about the more delicate of the two stopped George's heart. He was like a tragic angel. When Charlie moved her legs from under the table, George saw the skirt. Were they brother and sister? Toby took out a cigarette, thereby giving George an opportunity he was hoping for.

"Excuse me, do you have a light?" If they hadn't been smoking he would have asked the time.

For both of them it was their first experience of passionate love. Charlie approved. George was so much more experienced than Toby, although younger. He taught Toby to open himself to pleasure, whilst protecting him from any kind of exploitation. With George Toby blossomed, but whenever he went back to Finborough Place he closed up again.

"I'm so glad my dad worked in the building trade," pronounced George, as he toyed with a crème brulée.

Charlie didn't bother to unravel the innumerable implications of this remark. It wasn't entirely true, she knew, mainly it was a statement about the damage created by being the heir to an estate.

"I can't see how you can take all this on. It's not you, is it? I mean your life is in the city. You're a city person."

Am I? thought Charlie, for the hundredth time.

"Why don't you sell the whole damned lot?"

Oh no, anything but that. Oh no, not sell.

"It's no use to you, is it? What use is it?

It wasn't a question of use. It was her land, her father's land, his father's before him.

"When you're gone, forgive me for being blunt, when you're gone, you don't know what will happen. It will get sold anyway, split up into bits and pieces. Wouldn't you feel better if you could choose who had it?"

He meant well and there was some truth in what he said, but he could never understand why his suggestions were impossible.

"Please, George. I don't want to discuss it."

"All right. Just think about it. By the way, I'm having a party next Friday. There'll be lots of people you know. You will come won't you? You can stay the night. A few days if you want. A weekend in Chelsea will do you no end of good."

It probably would. She might well take up the invitation.

Driving along the narrow road towards Finborough village, she decided to turn off along a track beneath the beech trees. She would park at the edge of the field then walk to the cliff and down a steep path leading to a narrow creek. The way lay partly across her land, partly across fields owned by Violet's family, so hardly anyone knew about it. It was late afternoon, the countryside was green and gold, with the gorse in full bloom, and the sea and sky an astonishing azure. At the cliff's edge were patches of deep pink thrift. Rabbits scampered for cover, hearing her light steps; the sheep stood their ground chewing nervously. Were they her sheep or Violet's?

The tide was well out leaving swathes of brown seaweed strewn across the pebbles. Long narrow rock pools led like furrows to the water's edge. As a child, Charlie had spent hours exploring these shallow troughs, never finding anything more exciting than sea anemones; as an adult she preferred combing the beach for strangely shaped pieces of driftwood polished and white as bones. Today her purpose was simply to sit for a while on the margin between sea and land. Eyes closed, she listened to the gentle drag of the water on the stones, punctuated by the occasional mewing of seagulls, until the calming rhythm was interrupted by the harsher sound of feet tramping in her direction. She could hardly believe it! Nobody came here, nobody had ever come here except herself, Toby and Violet. Violet!

"I saw your car. I came to find you."

Violet dug herself a comfortable hollow to sit in. Charlie was amazed at her presumption, the familiarity which Charlie herself was far from sharing.

"Isn't your friend coming back to stay?"

That was Violet, straight to the point.

"Which friend.?"

You know, your glamorous French friend."

"If you mean Gaby, no, she isn't."

"I thought you and she . . ."

"Did you? No, we're not."

During the ensuing silence Violet raked through the pebbles, making an irritating rattle.

"Don't do that, Violet. It's very annoying."

It was almost as if they were ten years old again, when Charlie always took control. Violet stopped.

"You know I came here to be quiet."

Violet picked up an oddly shaped flint, which she

examined minutely without a word. Charlie stared out to
sea, wondering whether she could make Violet go away.
Even if she moved out on to the rocks, the other's presence would impinge on her consciousness.

"So you'll be on your own, then?"

Charlie found the words oddly upsetting.

"Not exactly. I'll have people to stay. I plan to be away
a lot, in London, visiting friends in other parts of the
country."

"I miss Toby terribly. After your mother died we spent
every day together."

She's going to cry, thought Charlie. That must be prevented.

"You ought to have a holiday. Get right away from
here. See a bit of the world."

Violet stared at her with a puzzled expression.

"A holiday?"

Didn't the woman know what the word meant?

"You could afford to travel round Europe, France,
Spain, Italy, Greece."

"Why would I want to do that?"

Charlie felt defeated. Violet's world was Sussex, the
Sussex countryside. Even Brighton was too much for her.

"I can call on you, can't I?"

Charlie had a memory of a childish voice lisping, "Can
I play with you, Charlie?" But Violet was not a child any-
more. If she started calling on Charlie too often she'd be
playing with fire, didn't she know that? Or was that what
she wanted?

"Should I call on you instead? Will your parents invite
me to tea?"

This was mischievous. She was all too aware of Violet's
parents' heavy disapproval. Mr. and Mrs. Doderill's present sorrow was increased by the fact of the estate falling
into Charlie's hands. They had successfully avoided meeting her since she left home, until Mrs. Langham Price's
funeral, when they were forced to offer their condolences. Their abruptness on that occasion, their inability
to look her in the eye, had wounded her, in spite of her
tough shell.

"They're going to find it very hard, having me next door, aren't they? I might get a horse, take up hunting. How will your father deal with that?"

Mr. Doderill was the leader of the local hunt.

Violet threw the flint as far as she could, which was a surprising distance. Anger gave her extra strength.

"You can't blame them, Charlie They're not sophisticated like you. They're just farmers."

Farmers, stockbreeders, producing healthy males to service healthy females, thought Charlie. How could they have condoned Toby as a husband for Violet?

"I don't blame them. I don't care; it's not important, they aren't important."

"I'm not important either, I suppose?"

Charlie took a long time to answer this question, staring into the distance, wondering what Violet wanted from her, what she could give, should she want to give anything at all. She turned to the anxious face, tried to read the expression.

"You aren't . . . unimportant."

She realised the ambiguity of this so she continued.

"We have been friends, underneath we are still friends. But you don't know me any more, Violet. You'd best keep away."

"But we both loved Toby. We've both lost him. That makes us close, doesn't it?"

"Violet, you just don't understand."

"I must be a nuisance, I do understand, I do."

You don't, you don't, thought Charlie.

"If I came for tea sometimes, we could talk about the old days. And I could tell you about Toby, what he and I were planning. You were away, you don't know everything. I might surprise you."

Perhaps. It was certain that Charlie would surprise Violet, should she choose to.

"You mustn't live in the past. You have to find another husband, for God's sake. You're not cut out to be an old maid."

"I can't. Not yet. You can help me, you've got to help me, Charlie."

Although normally the words, 'you've got to' would have roused instant opposition in Charlie, she was disarmed by Violet's misery.

"Look, you can come round next week. What about Thursday afternoon? I'll tell Mrs. Branson to make a lemon cake. It was always your favourite, wasn't it?"

"Yes, it was. Fancy you remembering!"

Maybe that was a mistake.

"It mustn't become a habit. It's not the way forward for either of us. I'm going back to the car soon. You'd better go separately. You don't want your parents to see us together, do you? If they believed you were having secret assignations with me, they'd lock you in your room."

Violet obeyed meekly. She wanted to hug Charlie in gratitude for the life line. She refused to acknowledge that gratitude was not the real reason for her wanting to hug Charlie, to put her arms around her, to feel her strong body with her own, to rest her head on Charlie's shoulder, be stroked by her hands. She remembered the hands moving down her back. She didn't want to remember, though. She didn't want to admit that Toby's hands never thrilled her in the same way. Charlie and she would be best friends again, like they always had been before that day when things had changed. Well, they'd change back now to an age of innocence.

'You are being very silly,' Charlie told herself as she drove into the garage. 'You know how vulnerable Violet is. Why did you give way?' Unlike Violet, she recognized the impossibility of return to an age of innocence. This afternoon she had been tempted to draw Violet to her, give and take the pleasure they both yearned for. 'That woman is taboo. She would bring nothing but trouble. Do not touch!' she sternly decreed as she went into the kitchen where Ms. Branson had just baked a batch of scones.

Chapter 7
The Walthams

Betsy was overjoyed to receive a letter from Anna. She had missed her sister terribly and was very anxious about her state of mind and health. Betsy's husband, Alan, assured her that Anna was tough, that she'd always be all right, but then Alan's feeling towards Anna had always been ambivalent, especially after Robin's death. Alan had loved Robin, had dreamed of a closeness between the two which neither would achieve with any woman. He realised that Anna was not responsible for Robin's final act, she had merely been a catalyst for the noble suicide of an irrevocably damaged soul. Robin's deathblow had been dealt the day he provoked his younger brother, a lesser horseman than Robin himself, into taking a jump of unusual height. The horse and rider fell and Robin's brother died from a blow on the side of the head. On the surface he appeared blessed – the owner of a large cotton mill, strong, handsome, adored by his mother and sisters – underneath his emotions were withered. As Robin's only friend, Alan had tried to reach into the darkness of his heart. Robin's attraction to Anna when Alan was in love with her sister seemed to offer the possibility of a sort of salvation. The four of them had fitted together so well. Would Robin have fallen for Anna if she hadn't been the sister of Alan's beloved? Alan had asked himself this question often in a fruitless attempt to analyse the complexity of the knots which tied the four together. He talked of this to Betsy, but didn't want to upset her too much by revealing his obsession. The two of them settled down to life in Derbyshire; a happy couple now expecting their first child. Since Betsy had no idea of Anna's whereabouts she couldn't tell her the glad news. Now sitting in the kitchen of their pretty stone cottage, she re-read Anna's clear artistic script.

Dearest Bee,

I'm sorry I haven't been able to write to you until now. The last two years have been strange, things have happened to me as if I were another person. I suppose you could say I'm successful, because I've become quite famous in Germany and I've made a lot of money. But it's all so meaningless! It's just what I wanted, you know that, it's what I dreamed about since we were little, so why aren't I glad and proud? In case you're wondering, I'm not with anyone, a lover I mean. I'm living here in the house of an English playwright, a very odd person who is well known in what they call here the 'tout Paris'. She had to go back to England for family business, so I have the house to myself. I don't know how long I'll stay, until I get the urge to move on I expect, perhaps to America. Can you imagine me in America? I do have some contacts in Boston and New York. It won't be soon, though. I'm tired, so I should just stay put. Anyway, I have a good studio here and the house itself is comfortable. I had a wild sort of visitor the first night, an actress, the spurned lover of the owner (yes, my dear, my landlady likes women). I don't think she'll be back. Oh, darling Bee, I have missed you. I'd love to see you, but I'm not ready to come back, especially to Derbyshire. I might run into one of Robin's family and I'm sure they all hate me. I don't suppose you could come to Paris, with or without Alan? I'd rather without, but I expect you'd rather with. You must be happy, you adore him so much. I have to admit that you are good together, although he's a bit too pompous for my taste. I hope he's taking good care of you, for you are an absolute treasure, a gift to any man. I must say he was the best thing around, even if he was not at all my type.

Forgive me, forgive me for my silence. Don't tell mother and father where I am. Come and see me if you can. You might enjoy my exhibition,

Your ever-loving sister, Anna.

Betsy was four months pregnant, feeling very well and looking radiant. Everyone said she must take after her mother, Clara, who, having borne her numerous children with no trouble at all, still looked good. They were about to begin the school holidays, which meant that Alan, a teacher, would be free to travel. They had planned a quiet few weeks at home, refurbishing the cottage which they had recently moved into, tidying up the garden, taking excursions into the dales. They could easily find time for a trip to Paris. Although Alan had been there several times, of course, since he had travelled on the continent, Betsy knew very little of Europe altogether. This would be a great opportunity before the birth of the baby took all her time and attention. They could afford to stay for a few days in a cheap hotel, she was sure. She'd heard that Paris was hot in August, something she would look forward to as July in the Midlands was proving to be rather cool and rainy. She would have chance to wear the light summer clothes which still fitted her before she grew too big.

She told Alan about the invitation when he came in for dinner, after a morning spent looking for garden furniture. He was harder to persuade that she had imagined, for he had already been looking forward to a restful few weeks. Also the excitement about the baby had filled him with an optimism which was dispelled by the mere mention of Anna's name.

"I don't know if it's good for you at this stage," he argued.

"There's no danger, Alan, honestly. I've never felt better in my life. It's such a perfect opportunity."

"It's typical of Anna to completely ignore us for two years, then expect us to drop whatever we're doing because *she's* decided she'd like to see you." Betsy didn't need to show him the letter for him to be aware that Anna had no particular desire to see *him*.

"Don't be mean. It's been awful for her."

Alan wondered if Betsy would ever understand how awful it had been for him too.

"It would mean so much to me."

Alan was sensitive enough to catch the warning note. Standing between the two sisters would store up trouble.

"All right."

"Oh, darling, thank you!" She came into his arms, all warmth and love and tenderness.

If I'd said no, mused Alan, would she have made my life intolerable?

Betsy wrote her reply that evening.

My sweet,

How good to hear from you at last! I have been angry with you sometimes, very angry, and terribly worried. You're all right! More than all right, you're successful! I am just so delighted for you. Now I have news for you too – I'm expecting a baby! So you'll be an aunt. Actually, you already are since Tessa gave birth to a baby girl a year ago. She got married to the father, although mother was very understanding and said it didn't matter if Tessa didn't want to. Father made a great scene as you might expect, but nobody takes much notice of him. Tessa said the only thing she wanted to do in life was get married and have children and she loved the father (a local boy who used to taunt us at school for being stuck up) and he loved her, so the sooner they got married the better. I would have written to you about all this, if I'd known where you were, it was quite a scandal.

Naturally Alan won't have our child baptised, or I would ask you to be godmother. You could be a non-religious godmother, perhaps? I can hardly believe that in a few months we will be parents. We will have a party, even if we don't have a christening, so you'll come home for it, won't you?

And we will come to Paris. Soon. Alan is arranging it. He has to come to look after me, he thinks, though I'm fit as a fiddle. I'll write again soon.

Your own,

Bee.

It was very strange to Anna to read this letter from another world she had left behind. Even whilst she was staying in the large family house in a moment of respite after her life in London, she was not really there, only biding her time until she should take off again. Tessa, Kate, Billy, Celia, Arthur, and the rest of her siblings formed an amorphous mass, from which her older sister stood out as a twin spirit. Yet Betsy had settled near her parents, had married and was now expecting a baby. They had grown up surrounded by babies, watching their mother Clara become transformed into an earth goddess, rapt in her fecundity. Anna had never wanted this for herself, the mystery she sought was not to be found in the creation of new lives. She couldn't bear to imagine Betsy losing herself in motherhood, leaving her alone, drawing closer to Tessa, to her other sisters, to her mother, because they were all involved in the great life-cycle. Wasn't there already something ordinary in her words, a suggestion of setting for what everyone else had, an acceptance of the way things were? The older girl had been so brave, so defiant of convention until she met Alan, who tamed her by his intellectual domination, so that she became a contented wife.

Anna would not return to England after the birth, although she quite liked the idea of having a special relationship with the child. She doubted whether Alan would agree to this since he would be bound to consider Anna a bad influence. Betsy seemed to have ignored what Anna had written in her letter concerning her inability to face Robin's family or even her own. There had always been tension between their father, Ernest, and Betsy in the past, this must now be resolved, so he would turn his anger on Anna, Miss High and Mighty, too good for those who had brought her up, paid for her to go to school. "Come home," Betsy had written as if her sister was attached forever to the villages she felt to be so alien. It was not 'home'. And yet, some part of her felt that it was.

Once Alan had accepted the fact of the journey he made arrangements quickly, booking into a pleasant little hotel on the Left Bank not far from the Sorbonne, in order to be in the thick of the Latin Quarter. They stayed overnight in London, with one of his old friends who knew Anna too and was glad to have news of her. The short crossing from Dover to Calais was fortunately calm, the sun warm enough for them to spend the whole time on deck, Betsy exclaiming with delight at the beauty of the sun and shore. They lived in the very centre of England, so visits to the seaside were quite rare. Betsy could scarcely contain her excitement when a school of dolphins appeared beside the boat, to accompany them most of the way. She was immensely grateful to her husband for giving way, therefore she resolved to only spend a short time with Anna, using the rest of their holiday visiting places which had a special meaning for Alan.

When they checked in at the hotel, the porter handed Betsy a note, welcoming them and inviting them for lunch the following day.

"You must go alone," said Alan, "I shall go to the Place des Vosges and wander round the Marais." These names meant nothing to Betsy but she was glad he would not be there at that first meeting. They spent the evening strolling along the riverside, occasionally cutting along streets they found most interesting, not noting the names because they could always make their way back to the quays to find the hotel. Although Alan had known Paris well in his youth, he was taking time to become re-orientated.

"Look, my dear, oh look," cried Betsy, suddenly. She had stopped in front of the window of an art gallery.

"Look at the poster in the window. Oh, my goodness."

Anna had not given them the address of her exhibition. She hoped to take them to see it the following day, to watch their reactions.

She had chosen the most daring, most frightening of her paintings for the poster, after a long argument with Elisabeth, who thought the sculptures would be more attractive. Betsy was stunned, trying to reconcile what was before her eyes with what she knew of her sister.

"She certainly has moved on," said Alan.

The gallery was closed but they could see some of the works though the glass.

"Do you like them?" asked Betsy, eventually.

Alan shrugged. "I don't think liking comes into it. They are surprising. Actually, I must admit that from what I can see they are really rather good."

"I think they're horrid," announced Betsy, firmly.

"What is horrid about them?"

"They're ugly. The colours clash. Everything is fighting with everything else."

"Not a bad description," smiled her husband.

"Then why do you say they're really rather good?"

Alan sighed. He didn't want to give a lecture on Modern Art right now. He had been searching for a typical bistro when Betsy had brought them to a halt.

"I'll come with you when the gallery is open and we can look at them properly, then I'll explain."

In Betsy's opinion if a piece of art was ugly, jarring to the senses, it was bad. Good meant harmonious, uplifting. She was about to express this to Alan, but he was already on the other side of the road, reading a hand-written menu and beckoning to her.

Alan came with Betsy in the cab as far as the gate of the villa in Passy. He still had no intention of meeting Anna, at least, not yet, although he had been most intrigued by the vibrancy of her work, which Betsy still found slightly repellent, even after all his patient explanations. He would walk in the Bois de Boulogne, making his own way back to the hotel on foot, whereas he gave his wife firm instructions to take a cab from door to door.

It was with some trepidation that Betsy rang the bell. Would Anna be as fierce as her paintings? Would she have turned into some disordered bohemian, a savage-eyed harpy? Her letter had seemed quite sensible which was reassuring. She heard light footsteps then the door opened.

"Bee, my dear, dear Bee!"

Betsy had almost forgotten how beautiful, how elegant Anna was. Almost breathtaking.

"Oh Anna, you look wonderful!"

The sisters were in each other's arms, clinging fast, letting go, embracing again, until Anna remembered that

Betsy was pregnant and that she shouldn't hug her too hard. Holding her affectionately round the waist she led her through to the garden, where the table was laid most attractively with a fine lawn cloth and napkins to match. In the centre was a silver bowel of apricot coloured roses interspersed with sprigs of honeysuckle.

"This is perfectly lovely," cried Betsy.

"Sit down here, in the shadiest spot, and I'll bring out lunch. Where is Alan?"

Betsy saw that three places were laid.

"He wanted us to have time alone. You don't mind too much?"

Anna certainly didn't mind. She had been so nervous about seeing him that she had hardly been able to sleep. When she did finally close her eyes Robin's face came to haunt her for the first time since she had moved. Much as she longed to see Betsy, she regretted re-awakening the memory of the last moments they had spent in each others' company after Robin's death. She would take them back beyond, to the summer before it all happened, when they were truly happy, wondering about their future. Betsy must have been of the same mind, for when Anna brought a tray of cold prepared savoury pastries and little cakes, such as only the French provide, she clapped her hands and said, with a broad smile, "This reminds me of our picnics beside the lake.

They talked, in between mouthfuls, for more than two hours, without mentioning their last meeting, nor Anna's life between then and now. It was very curious for Anna to be given a description of life in Derbyshire, of her siblings, as if she was being introduced to a host of fictional characters. She scarcely recognised her parents in this account – was her mother really so wise, her father so equable? What did these places, these people, matter to her? Yet she listened eagerly, finding nourishment she had been lacking.

"Tessa's little girl looks like you. She's called Margaret Anna. Tessa always had a tremendous admiration for you, did you realise that?"

She was amazed. Tessa? What could she possibly have

meant to Tessa? The bond between the two oldest Waltham children excluded the rest, of whom Tessa was the first, being three years younger than Betsy.

"She has taken lessons in carpentry from father and she has made some pretty carvings. She's given Alan and me the cradle she made for her baby. It's decorated around the edges with a border of different kinds of leaves. Father says she has a gift. I'm pleased for her, because she never did well at school. You remember?"

Anna didn't. All three had, nonetheless, been to the same High School. She tried to fight down a growing feeling of jealousy.

"I'll take you to my exhibition later, Bee, if you're up to it."

"Alan and I went this morning."

"Did you like it?"

Betsy knew the expected answer was 'yes.' She hesitated.

"It was awfully interesting."

She has no idea, though Anna. She can only appreciate silly little carvings of leaves and flowers. In spite of herself she countered, "Most of them are sold."

"So I noticed."

"Even Picasso found something good to say."

Betsy didn't care for Picasso's work.

"Alan liked it very much. He knows a lot about art."

"Alan knows a lot about everything, doesn't he?"

Betsy looked sharply at her. The light tone made it difficult to detect whether the remark was sarcastic or not.

"Please don't be mean about Alan. He's the most intelligent person I've ever met. He's very sensitive, I have to treat him carefully."

He's an opinionated bore, thought Anna. There was a widening gap between herself and Betsy, which she was anxious to bridge.

"Bee, I am so glad you're happy, that you have found your soul-mate."

"I have the best of husbands, who will be the best of fathers to our child."

Betsy wanted to look round the house as well as the studio. She asked Anna many questions about the owner. She found the answers disquieting.

"Don't you feel odd living in a place belonging to a decadent?" she asked.

Anna felt very good, on the contrary.

In bed that night with her husband, Betsy confessed her fears that Anna might be affected by her environment.

"Who did you say it belonged to?"

"Charlotte Langham Price. She writes under the name of Charlie Price."

"Charlie Price! I've seen one or two of Price's plays. I always thought the author was a man."

This wasn't reassuring to Betsy.

"What were they about?"

"Oh, you know, affairs. They're rather clever, although I thought the last one I saw was a bit tired." Of course he hadn't been to the London theatre since their marriage.

"I wish Anna could meet a good man." Betsy snuggled closer to her husband.

She already did, thought Alan, and she killed him.

The couple left Paris without a meeting between Anna and Alan. All three found it better that way. Anna had refused to allow her to give her address to anyone else, or talk of their meeting. It had all been a disappointment for the sisters, each of them having hoped for the renewal of a friendship they had formerly relied on to reinforce their difference from their surroundings. They had mocked their parents, shuddered at the ugliness of the rows of red-brick houses, believing themselves to be superior to a community they purported to despise. With Alan by her side and a child in her womb, Betsy was able to take her place in this community, whereas Anna's separation from it had become all the more obvious. Each was sad to find the other changed.

Adrienne never called again since she had taken up with a new lover. Anna regretted this in a way, for the intrusion had provided a diversion from her own pre-occupations. She made a great effort to improve her French so that she could begin to understand more of the subtleties of the language. She went to Charlie's play again and was amused to compare the character played by Adrienne with the real-life woman, if indeed the person she had met that night *was* a real-life woman and not a character. She began to think more about theatre, which had not previously concerned her. She went to other plays, sometimes with Elisabeth, or some of Elisabeth's friends. She was adamant about not having a male escort, she did not want that kind of complication. She became a regular attender at Mabel and Belle's Saturday nights, flirting with Mabel when Belle wasn't looking. She dined with them several evenings during the week, finding their company stimulating and liberating. Frequently there were eight or ten people round the table, but Anna liked it best on the few occasions when there were just the three of them. She felt safe enough to tell them something of her past, and they were shrewd enough not to push her to reveal more, although, like all their friends, they were curious about this aloof beauty. She was working well, developing the flower theme, increasingly confident about the way she was using colour and form to communicate essential reality. Her exhibition came down with hardly any piece unsold. Charlie wrote to ask if all was well, she replied that things couldn't be better.

At the beginning of September she received a short letter from Betsy.

Dearest Anna,
I have to tell you that father is very ill. It appears that he has probably been sick for some times without realising it. It's awful, a dreadful shock for us all. He is going to die soon, the doctor says he only has a few months at most, maybe even a few weeks. There's nothing can be done. He looks terrible and mother is distraught. Father insists on working – not teaching of course, but his own

*carving. We keep telling him he won't die yet, that he'll
live longer if he rests, but he won't listen. I'm looking after
mother, who is like a sleepwalker, unable to do even simple things. The others take their turns at helping.*

*I'll write to you again. I think you should come home
when it's the end.*

Take good care of yourself, my darling,

Yours,

  Bee.

There was so much meaning in that short line 'You should
come home when it's the end'. She 'should', should she?
Was this authoritative demand from Betsy or the whole
family? 'Come home.' Betsy had been quite deaf, then, to
Anna's assertion that she didn't have a home. 'When it's
the end.' It's never the end, there's always a continuance,
waves of aftershock, which she wanted no part of. Her
father was not an old man, he was fifty years old and
had always seemed fit. Clara her mother was 49, their
youngest child was 11, a girl Anna hardly remembered.
Anna was to be the older sister, the maiden aunt free to
be her mother's support as long as necessary. How long
would that be? There were others to take this responsibility, Tessa was married with her own home but the next
sister, Kate, was still living with her parents, wasn't she?
Anna tried to remember what Betsy had told her of Kate,
Billy, Arthur etc. So many of them, so many to stare at
her and say, 'Look, here's our Anna. After all this time!'
Their voices would grate on her, the underlying rough-
ness in the men, the conciliatory whine of the women,
which even Betsy had not quite suppressed. Ugly sounds
in an ugly brick house, considered to be a cut above the
rest in Blackford where detached houses were rare. The
meanness of the streets, the antagonism of the workers'
wives as the Waltham girls picked their way over the cob-
bles had always made a rawness in her soul. It was only
the nearness of the countryside made life tolerable.

She wrote back to Betsy straight away, although it was
hard to find the right words.

Dearest Bee,
I am so sorry about father. He has been so solid, the cen-
tre of the family. He is a good man. It must be especially
difficult for you at this time, I do hope it won't affect the
baby. Please don't let mother know you've written to me,
or that you know where I am. And please don't think too
badly of me if I can't face a death and funeral. I can do
nothing to help, my presence will only disturb everyone.
You're much better off without me.
*   I love you, you must believe that. I suppose I love father*
and mother, I'd be a monster if I felt nothing at all for
them, yet I'm very confused about what I do feel.
*   Always yours,*
*   Anna.*

A reply came two weeks later.

Dear Anna,
This is not the time to be selfish. We do need you, I need
you to be beside me when it happens. There has been a
decline since my last letter. He is feverish, unreachable,
determined to wear himself out. You know how he and I
have opposed each other's wills – it is even worse now.
Mother is equally stubborn. I am very tired. I can't bear
the thought of you being absent. Prepare yourself – if he
doesn't rest the end will come sooner rather than later. It
will be better.
*   If you do love me, as you say you do, come home.*
*   Betsy.*

There's nothing wrong with being selfish, was Anna's
immediate thought on reading this. It was necessary to
survive. Her parents were selfish to have so many children, weren't they? It really didn't matter to them whether
one of their brood had flown the nest never to return,
about that she had no doubt. Betsy's need was more
important, though; in a way Anna found it gratifying. If
anything could pull her across the channel it was Betsy's
helplessness, even though it might be moral blackmail.

She was hardly sleeping at all. She had been invited to soirées at Pauline's where she had tried smoking opium, which was a disaster, plunging her into a nightmare world from which there seemed no escape. 'La belle Anglaise' was much sought after on these occasions, her air of mystery, her remoteness, encouraging the attentions of the more predatory habituées. Once she met Adrienne who entertained them all with theatrical anecdotes, some of which concerned Charlie. Anna's French had improved enough for her to recognize the malice both in the narrative and the laughter it gave rise to. There was also gossip about Gaby, who had given up attending these suppers. Anna suspected there would be malicious gossip about her too, as she appeared so untouchable. It was inconceivable that she would be celibate, so she must have a secret lover. Often celibacy was an affliction for Anna herself, the prospect of the continued frigidity threw her into a state of melancholy. If she stayed in Paris long enough she may be forced to take a lover, either man or woman, to avoid complete isolation.

She was painting all the daylight hours, for then she existed in the only place she wanted to be, a place of light and colour where nothing else mattered. The sun rose later and set earlier, she must do as much as she could before autumn. She would allow no visitors before evening. She stopped sketching in the parks – her inspiration was here, nowhere else.

The letter she had been dreading arrived in the middle of September.

Dearest Anna,
Father has at last taken to his bed. It will be soon. Please, please come. I beg you, do this for me.
Your desperate,
Bee.

With a sense of impending doom Anna began to make arrangements for the journey. She wrote to Charlie.

Dear Charlie,
I'm afraid that I must leave Paris for a while for family
reasons. I will pay your housekeeper to sleep in while I'm
away , if you agree, and, of course, I shall continue with
the rent. I shall lock up my work in the studio and leave
the key hidden because I don't want anyone to see what
I've been doing until I'm ready. I do hope these arrange-
ments will be convenient for you, since I am so happy in
your house and plan to return to it very soon,
  Very best regards,
  Anna Waltham.

A sympathetic note came by return post. There would
be no problem, perhaps she would let Charlie know her
English address, in case she needed to contact her for
any reason. Charlie would most likely not be in Paris
until next spring.

Anna packed some warm clothes. It would be cold in
Blackford. At first she chose less startling colours, then
she threw these out and filled her case with greens, blues,
purple, and yellow, bold statements her father hated.
Why should she make concessions? She would take a
couple of sketchbooks, some coloured crayons, for she
must find time to draw. She wondered whether she
should take gifts, but decided against it. When it was all
done, the housekeeper called a cab to take her to the
Gare du Nord. Anna's heart was thumping wildly.

Chapter 8
Sussex Life

Violet came to tea each week at the same time and always Charlie took care to have an engagement in the evening, so that teatime was strictly limited. It was a fairly formal situation with Mrs. Branson's daughter Emily serving them in the dining room. It was all rather ridiculous, and frustrating to Violet, who wanted hours of cosy chat. Every quarter of an hour Emily would come in to ask if they wanted more tea, winking at Charlie behind Violet's back. She was an intelligent, good-humoured girl, in whom Charlie had found an unexpected ally, since neither Mrs. Branson nor her daughter had been looking forward to working for Violet, who thought the way to treat servants was to be haughty. These farcical afternoons were intended to put Violet off completely, but she was not to be deterred. Charlie began to think that, if this woman was incapable of finding herself a husband, she should be helped. Sussex society had been waiting for Charlie to make a move, so she organised a party, with a guest list of about fifty people, including Violet and her parents. She didn't know whether she was expected still to be in mourning, but that wasn't her way and she must make it known that she would not be bound by any convention. It would be a relatively subdued affair, dinner with no dancing. Violet would help her with the guest list.

"As many young people as possible," said Charlie. "Especially unmarried ones. They'll be more fun. You'll have to do the seating plan. I'll be at the head of the table, naturally, but find me interesting people to be either side."

"It will have to be men."

"Will it? Do you think I'll be wearing a dinner gown?"
Violet considered this.

"Actually, Charlie, it would be a good idea."

Emily nearly dropped the plate of scones she was about
to place on the table. She hurried, hand over mouth,
back to the kitchen where she could give way to hysterical laughter.

"That girl is most awfully rude," said Violet crossly.

"Violet, do you think I even possess a dinner gown?"

"You could buy one. You'll need it for other occasions."

"I'd rather buy one for *you.*"

That had slipped out without thought. She continued
hastily, "Honestly, I don't have the figure for gowns. Bare
shoulders and décolleté would make me look like a scare-
crow. Now what you have to do is go home and write
me a list. You can bring it round tomorrow if you like.
If you don't think two teas in one week is too much.
Come earlier, I have to catch a train to London from
Brighton at six o'clock."

It was a task Violet enjoyed. She followed Charlie's
instructions in concentrating on the young as far as possible. There would be those who would decline so she
had to invite more than the fifty Charlie had stipulated.
Keeping the numbers equal was a challenge; there would
be a reserve list of both sexes so that if at the last minute
another man was needed one could be called upon. She
was disinterested in her calculations for she did not regard
anyone as a suitor for either herself or Charlie.

For her part, Charlie sought the 'below stairs' view of
the local gentry from Emily, sharing with her the intention
of pairing Violet off. Less generous than Charlie in her esti-
mation of Violet's marriageability, Emily suggested that a
somewhat boring lawyer from Alfriston, whose parents
had died the previous year leaving him a large farm, would
be a match. The gossip was that several other women had
already turned down his proposals, because they could-
n't bear the thought of listening to him at meal times.

"He wouldn't be my type," said Emily. "He has a

droopy face already, so I think he'll look like a blood-hound when he's older. I'll tell you though," she looked round to see if her mother was within earshot; as she wasn't she continued, "my cousin Lily, who works over at his farm sometimes, had a moment with him in the barn, and she said to me, 'Don't worry about his face, he's more that all right where it counts!'" She raised her eyebrows and nodded knowingly.

Violet explained her choices carefully, the bloodhound from Alfriston being included and as a single male Violet supposed he should sit next to Charlie.

"He's very learned," she said. "You'll want someone intelligent to talk to."

"Where will you be?" asked Charlie.

"Towards the other end, with my cousin Peter on one side and my second cousin Patricia's husband on the other."

Neither of them a prospective partner, thought Charlie.

"Couldn't you sit nearer to me, the other side of the bl.. that lawyer from Alfriston?"

Violet was irritated, to change one person would mean to change the whole lot.

"It's only provisional. We don't know yet who can come. I just wanted to give you a vague idea."

"Who do you plan to put on my left if the lawyer is on my right?"

"Don't call him the lawyer. His name is Roderick. Roderick Harding." On your left I thought Colonel Fitzjames' son, who's just back from a trip to South America, I hear. He's an explorer."

That sounds more fun, thought Charlie. With any luck she could leave the man on her right to his other neigh-bour. The whole thing was tedious, reminding Charlie of what she disliked most about her parents' life. She was-n't going to do it often, she would put up with having to entertain maybe once a year. Fifty guests meant thirty or forty return invitations, which was an unbearable prospect. Always the same faces round the table, give or take a few. It was best not to depress herself thinking about it.

With skilful manipulation, Violet managed exactly 25

men and 25 women. Mrs. Branson rose to the challenge with a menu which would be the talk of the county for months afterwards. Three other village women besides Emily were recruited to help with the cooking and service. Charlie began to worry about what she would wear. She wanted to be on good terms with her neighbours, she sought acceptance for what she was. She must avoid shocking them by an appearance which would immediately set her totally apart. There was nothing in her present wardrobe that would do. She would go to London, look for something in black, take George to give honest advice.

George asked nothing better than to escort her to expensive store after store, until Charlie was on the point of giving up. George was sure they would eventually find just the right thing. After two days and twenty shops they settled for a crêpe de Chine blouse and skirt in velvet silk. They only needed a slight adjustment in the skirt to fit Charlie's lean body. There was little decoration apart from three rows of satin piping ribbon round the hem.

"Now that is just out of this world," was George's verdict. "I could fall for you myself." This was an entirely satisfactory response, indicating to Charlie that the outfit was androgynous.

George's next concern was accessories. He insisted they shop for a necklace.

"I'd love to buy you something special," he said. " A final touch."

Charlie only accepted to please him, for she had no interest in jewellery. She was dismayed by his choice, not because she disliked it, but because the broad band of diamonds and jet, with simple matching earrings, were very expensive.

"What I like best to do with my money is to spoil my friends," said George at home in Chelsea the next day, when the altered clothes were delivered, and Charlie tried them on. "I knew the necklace would be just right with that blouse. Darling, you look so good in black, perhaps you should always wear it."

Indeed Charlie did look so good in black that her guests scarcely recognised her. She aroused universal admiration, although no one knew what to make of her. She took Violet's breath away, she looked so much more striking in her severe elegance than if she had been wearing the required dinner gown. As she passed amongst the crowd with a tray of champagne, Emily whispered in Charlie's ear, "Oh Miss Charlie, you are a stunner!"

Colonel Fitzjames' son, Simon, turned out to be as boring as the bloodhound from Alfriston. They both vied for Charlie's attention, trying to engage her interest by equally mundane accounts of their lives.

Violet, I'll get you for this, vowed Charlie. She looked around the table in search of, if not a kindred spirit, a potential friend, examining each person until she came to Violet who blushed and looked away self-consciously. Her cousin Peter on her right Charlie had last met when he was an awkward adolescent. He was an embarrassment to the family on account of his refusal to do anything useful with his life. Being the only child of very well-to-do parents, he didn't need to earn money, so he had bought himself a fishing boat and fished regularly for fun out of Newhaven. Violet's disapproving account of a way of life incompatible with his social station had interested Charlie. Was he the kindred spirit she was seeking? She liked the look of him.

Although the food was exquisite Charlie longed for the meal to be over. With course after course it seemed interminable. When at last they all rose after desert Charlie steered Simon the explorer towards Violet.

"I don't believe you two know each other very well," she said. "From what Simon had been telling me" (Could she even remember what Simon had been telling her?) "I'm sure you have a lot in common."

She turned to Peter.

"I believe you are a fisherman? I used to go fishing." She took his arm. Were ladies supposed to do that to gentlemen they had only just met? He didn't seem to mind, as he smiled at her.

"Do you smoke cigars? I have some in the library, perhaps you'd care to join me?"

Ladies were definitely not supposed to do that.

"I don't smoke cigars, I smoke a pipe, but I'd love to join you in the library for any reason whatsoever."

"But Charlie . . ." Violet began.

"Shut up Violet and mind your own business."

Violet gasped, went pale, so that Charlie was instantly contrite and remembered she was in polite society.

"I'm sorry, that was very rude. I didn't mean it. You have done such a good job getting us all together like this, I'm truly grateful. And you look lovely. I just want the chance to discuss mackerel with your cousin."

"Mackerel?" asked Peter quizzically, watching Charlie as she sank into a leather armchair and lit her cigar.

"It was just something to say. I oughtn't to speak to Violet like that, but she shouldn't try to tell me what to do. I won't have it."

Peter was fascinated by the way she was smoking, it was in contradiction with her appearance. At least, to a certain extent. The clothes were feminine, the way she wore them was not.

"What's your boat called? So I can recognise it when I'm at the harbour."

"Lady Louise. Do you often go down to the harbour?"

"Yes. It's a different life down there, takes you out of yourself."

Different life, very different people, thought Peter. The poverty amongst some of the fisherfolk was striking.

"Why Lady Louise?"

"Someone I used to know."

There was a silence.

"Look, any minute now someone will come looking for me. Probably Violet. I'll come straight to the point. Can we be friends?"

A long time ago Peter had wanted to make friends with Toby and Charlie, when he spent holidays with Violet. They hardly noticed him, or so it appeared, which made him feel awkward and resentful. They were so sophisticated, their communication with each other so deep, so subtle, he had no way to break into their fortress. Now here was Charlie, asking if she could play with him.

Should he rebuff her, pay her back for the way he was excluded? He decided that would be unfair, she had no idea what she had done to the adolescent boy, so the grown man should take her on new terms.

"There aren't many amongst that lot," she gestured towards the big hall, "I can be friends with."

I'm sure that's true, he thought. There weren't many who were his friends either. He was not exactly beyond the pale, simply on the margin. He sympathised with Charlie, was inclined to be her ally against 'that lot', but he wasn't going to yield too quickly to her natural arrogance, which gave her the air of conferring a favour instead of asking for one.

"Don't tell me a good-looking woman like you doesn't have lots of friends already."

Instinctively he knew this would not only displease her but warn her that if they were to have a relationship she would not necessarily be the one to dictate the terms. His games and Charlie's could be quite different.

Charlie stood up.

"I'm sorry. I'd better go back to my guests."

It was not the reaction Peter had intended.

"No, I'm sorry Charlie. Wait." He wasn't exactly sorry, because Charlie had to be reminded that she *was* a good-looking woman, albeit in a disturbing way.

"I really didn't mean to offend you. It was a stupid remark. Please do come and see me in the harbour. I go out very early most mornings now, so I'm back by 10 o'clock."

Charlie stubbed out her cigar. A portrait of her grandfather above Peter's head reminded her she was a Langham Price.

"I don't think it is a good idea after all."

She left Peter in the library telling himself he was a fool.

The following day Violet called after breakfast as previously agreed, in order to talk over the success of the evening. Almost her first words were "You shouldn't get too friendly with Peter. He's a bit of a bad lot."

These were the same words Emily had used when Charlie had asked her about him that morning. "He's a bad lot. I'd be careful of him, if I were you, Miss Charlie."

When pressed to explain what she meant by it, she had replied, "They say he's put one or two in the family way. He lived with a Frenchwoman for a bit in Newhaven town. Very fiery temperament, they say. She left him after a big row, screaming and shouting she couldn't stand England any more. My friend Dolly lived next door, heard every word. Some in French she couldn't understand."

Charlie wondered if she would hear the same story from Violet.

"What do you mean, 'a bit of a bad lot', Violet?"

"He has no sense of responsibility towards the family."

Charlie liked Emily's version much better.

"Then why did you invite him?"

"He is one of us, after all. He's a single man, he helped even up the numbers."

The subject was closed. Instead Violet prattled on about characters in whom Charlie had no interest, until Charlie interrupted her to ask, "Did you like Simon?"

"Yes, he was most agreeable. I found his descriptions of the Andes fascinating."

That's because she didn't have to spend the whole meal listening to them, thought Charlie.

"Might you see more of him?"

"See more of him?"

Sometimes Charlie thought Violet was half-witted.

"Will he call on you?"

"Oh no, I don't think so. He'll probably call on you, though."

Charlie was not at all pleased.

"I'll invite you at the same time. Would you like that?"

"That wouldn't be appropriate."

"Why not?"

"He will want to see you, not me."

"That's not appropriate either, is it, just the two of us alone? I'm out of touch with how to behave, Violet, I'd rather you were there too if I am to receive young men."

Would Violet go along with this feeble argument? If Charlie Price didn't need a chaperone, it was just possible that Miss Charlotte Langham Price did. If it weren't for the fact that she wanted to marry Violet off Charlie would never have entertained the thought of male callers.

Violet hesitated between the fear of being *de trop* and the desire to spend as much time as she could in Charlie's company.

"All right. This first time."

Is he planning a second time already, wondered Charlie. She had tried her best the previous evening to make it plain that she was not open to matrimonial advances. Her fortune made her a good catch for a man in need of funding for his expeditions and Simon had told her in detail of his projects for the Upper Amazon. She was actually quite prepared to give him some funds, he might as well spend her money on something useful. If that was what he was after, she would tell him straight away. How about promising to pay for the whole trip if he married Violet?

"Charlie . . ." Violet was seeking the right words.

"Yes?"

"I didn't have chance to tell you - how absolutely beautiful you looked last night." Violet finished in a rush.

"As a matter of fact I was very uncomfortable in that damned skirt and blouse. Not really me, you know."

"Oh, but they were perfect. They suited you so well." Pause. "You are really very . . . handsome."

"You looked a picture too, Violet old girl."

Charlie felt she had to lighten things up, she didn't like the gleam in Violet's eye. The sooner she fixed this woman up the better.

"If you'll excuse me, I have a lunch date in Brighton with an old friend of Toby's. See you the normal time next week."

George was dying to hear how successful his choice of outfit had been. When they met at English's Oyster Bar to talk over the dinner party, Charlie confided her misgivings about Simon's intentions.

"He must have heard about me, so it can't be sex he's after," she said.

"Is he one of us?"

"I don't think so, I don't know. Why should he be?"

"He could be. A bachelor who goes off on long trips with other men. Introduce me, I'll soon tell you."

"What would he imagine he could offer me in return, then?"

"Respectability. Children"

"Children!"

"Some of us can, you know. No problem. Just enough copulation to plant a few seeds then off to the real thing."

"I don't want children."

"He doesn't know that, does he? It could be convenient. Both of you put up with each other in bed for as long as it takes, then each to his or her own. You give him money, he gives you heirs."

Charlie experienced rising panic contemplating this new proposition.

"I hope you're wrong."

"Believe me, there are a lot of married men out there who'd rather have another man in bed with them than their wives. I know." He greedily swallowed his remaining oyster.

Driving home, Charlie vowed to herself to give the jet necklace and earrings away at the first opportunity. Not to Violet, that would be asking for trouble. Black didn't suit Gaby, who would otherwise have been the obvious recipient. Maybe the skirt and blouse could have a different effect if worn separately. She would put them away in a drawer for the time being. Because it was a cool, windy day, she was now wearing her tweeds and one of her favourite cravats. She was in a bad mood, so preoccupied that she narrowly avoided running into another motor car round a bend in a lane near Newhaven. She braked, swerved and ended up with two wheels in a ditch. She was furious, even more so because it was entirely her own fault. She clambered out cursing under her breath. The other motorist, who had stopped his car at the edge of a field, was coming towards her. He looked familiar.

"Miss Langham Price! I didn't recognise you. Can I help?"

Peter stood there, in old clothes, reeking of fish. "I was on my way home to change. I smell vile, I know."

You may smell, but you look a lot better in a sweater than a dinner jacket., thought Charlie, taken by surprise. "I seem to be well and truly stuck," she said aloud. "Thank you anyway."

"I have a friend not far away with a couple of dray horses. They would do it. If you can bear to sit here for an hour I could fetch them for you." The offer was almost chivalrous.

"Thank you. I don't know what else to do. Thank you Peter. Please call me Charlie."

"Right you are Charlie. I'll be as quick as I can. I hope the horses aren't out working somewhere. These sorts of accidents are a great bore, aren't they?" He smiled sympathetically.

"It hasn't happened to me before, I'm usually a very careful driver." She hated being beholden to him.

"It would probably be safe for you to leave it here and come with me, if I wasn't so stinking." This smell is quite hard to get rid of when it gets on your clothes and yours are very fine." He looked her up and down impertinently.

"I'll be all right. Take as long as you want. Please do go home and have a bath first."

"I'm not usually this bad. I've been working all day in the shed gutting fish. I like to give a hand when it's needed. There's a couple of the women off having babies."

The picture conjured up of Peter amongst the fishwives was extraordinary.

"Anyway, see you soon." He climbed into his car and disappeared down the road.

Charlie jumped over the ditch to go through a gap in the hedge into a field of wheat. She skirted the edge, astonished at the number of wildflowers. There were still poppies amongst the yellowgreen of the ripening grain, and cornflowers and corncockle, but the hedgerow was a tangle of vetch, campion, scabious, umbrellas of cow parsley overshadowing it all. She walked on into a field of clover where she stood for a while, drawing in deep breaths of the sweet air. She always thought clover had a special fragrance when it was near the sea. Below her, the harbour was peaceful, the nets pulled up and drying ready for the next morning. The ferryboat lay patient until the crossing. Once again she was struck by the smallness, the meanness, of Newhaven compared with historic Dieppe, hoping that it didn't represent the cultural divide between England and France. She thought about Peter's oddity in choosing an inappropriate lifestyle, going native Sussex-style, she thought about her own deviant individuality and supposed that these were what the French might see as British eccentricity. She and Peter were alike in their defiance of what was expected from them as members of their social class, yet they had not entirely escaped from the bonds of convention, if they had she would not have given such a dinner party, nor would he have attended one. She tore a handful of hawthorn leaves to chew, an action which had its roots in childhood. The leaves were too old, she spat them out and sucked on a stem of grass instead. She was not sorry to be forced into idleness in the no-man's land between Brighton and Finborough Place, on English soil gazing towards France. She sat down on a stile, enjoying the soft colours on the gently rolling hills, until she heard the sound of hooves in the distance.

She reached the car as Maisie and Molly came into view, led by Peter and their owner, a short wiry man. They were magnificent creatures, tall chestnut shires, used to pulling brewery carts piled with heavy barrels of beer. Their muscled rumps looked powerful enough to pull a locomotive never mind a car.

"We'll soon have you out of there, Miss Charlotte," said the wiry man. Did she know him? She didn't recognise him.

"My mate Dan works for you. He tells me you're a good sort, so I'm happy to be able to help you out of a spot. Get in, will you?"

Charlie got in whilst the horses' harnesses were attached by rope to the front bumper.

"Carry on now, gals, gee up!" shouted Dan's mate.

Maisie and Molly geed up, and Charlie's car came out of the ditch as easily as a cork from a bottle.

"Oh bravo! Well done! Thank you so much!" Charlie was so taken with the shires that she was sorry to see them unhitched. It would have been fun to have them tow her home.

She offered money, which was refused.

As she started the car Peter came to speak to her.

"I've been thinking about what you said about being friends. I really would like to, unless I said something so unforgivably stupid you don't want to have anything more to do with me." The smell of fish had begun to wear off. She noticed his eyes were an interesting light hazel and their present expression was serious.

"It was offensive to me. I suppose it would have been a compliment to most women you know. You have to realise I'm not like them."

And you have to realise that the only way most men will be able to deal with you is to pretend you are simply a woman like all the others, thought Peter. He said, "Would you join me for a drink at the Fisherman's Rest? It's at the entrance to the harbour. Would you come tonight, at nine o'clock?"

For a moment Charlie didn't know how to reply. Apart from the occasional glass in the Finborough Arms, she wasn't used to drinking in pubs. Certain bars in Brighton, yes, but a regular tavern would be a novelty.

"It's the most peaceful watering hole. The others are a bit rough. Or would you rather not be seen in a pub?"

Although it wasn't intended as a challenge, Charlie took it as one.

"Nine o'clock you said? I do know where it is. I know all the pubs. See you there then."

At once she regretted allowing herself to be provoked. A night out with Peter was practically the last thing in the world she would choose to have.

You have to be careful of this man, she told herself, leaving him waving to her in the deepening shadows, he has a way of getting through to you.

Hearing her trundling up the drive, Dan left off working in the rose garden to meet her and garage the car, which he liked to do.

"She looks a bit muddy," he commented. "Where've you been, Miss Charlie?"

"In a ditch. A friend of yours helped me out. Brought his horses, Maisie and Molly."

"Ah, Tom Tapper. A good sort, Tom"

He didn't ask for details, for he would find them out from Tom later.

"Don't put the car away, Dan. I'll be using it." She hoped that Dan and Tom didn't drink at the Fisherman's Rest.

As she entered the hall she was accosted by a giggling Emily.

"You've got an admirer, Miss Charlie, that's for sure. The Colonel's nephew came round this afternoon with a big bunch of roses. Fancy bringing roses here! With a sweeping gesture she indicated the numerous bowls and vases of flowers on every available surface. "I could hardly find a pot to put them in. They're on the table in the library. He was very put out that you weren't here. Asked me to be sure to tell you he'll be back at four o'clock tomorrow and hopes you'll receive him. If that's not serious, I don't know what is."

Yes, it's serious, though Charlie grimly. It was precisely what she would have done herself if she was in pursuit. She was a past master at hunting and bringing down her prey. But then she never wasted time if there was no chance from the beginning, which is what Simon was doing. Not only had she not been encouraging, she had been pointedly cool, abandoning him to Violet. The note he left with the flowers underlined his insensitivity. It read:

Dear Charlotte,
I think after last night, we are on first-name terms, are we not! I so enjoyed talking to you, finding in you a rare interest in the esoteric customs of the Indian communities. I would like an opportunity to share more of my exciting experiences with you, so I'll take the liberty of calling again. Thank you so much for the most pleasurable evening I have spent since my return to these shores,
Yours respectfully,
Simon.

Charlie was not a good actress, so she was unable to conceal boredom. If Simon had been unaware of her glazed expression he must be dim-witted or short sighted. She wrote a quick note and rang for Emily.

"Would you take this round to Violet's before you go home, please? Tell your mother I said you could leave whatever you're doing to go on an errand for me."

"Yes ma'am." Emily occasionally behaved like the archetypal maidservant, especially when Charlie spoke in the tones of the archetypal mistress.

It had not been a good day. Charlie had the impression that she was not in control of events, a new situation for her. So much was new about the present circumstance that she had the urge to take off back to Paris, run away to her own kind. But that would be cowardly, she had to reinvent herself to face all this. She dismissed the notion of standing Peter up and retreating to her bedroom with a book. She'd already made up her mind that she would wear her knickerbockers for this assignation, pass for a man, incognito if possible. There were to be no more comments about her being a good-looking woman. Was she being trapped between Violet, Peter and now Simon? Trapped by a house, trapped by duty? She had been convinced that she could rise above it all more easily than Toby. For the first time she had an inkling of his dilemma. Of course she was stronger, she always had been. She would dictate her own terms. Yet she had already given way, with unintended consequences. She must pull herself together, make sure she recruited Peter as the ally she needed.

The Fisherman's Rest was a comfortable place, with small tables and oak settles in corners where you could hold a quiet conversation. Peter was waiting in one such corner. His eyes widened a fraction and his lips twitched very slightly as he caught sight of Charlie's attire.

"Hullo, Charlie, glad you could make it. What'll you have?"

Charlie didn't know. She looked at Peter's pint of bitter, hesitated.

"They do a good draught wine here. That's one reason I suggested it. Strong contacts with the continent."

"Thank you, a glass of red wine would be nice."

"How about claret?"

"Yes fine, thank you."

The landlord had already examined her curiously, as had all the other men in the bar. There were no other women, so she was very glad not to have chosen a skirt. There was no one she recognised and if her disguise was effective no one would recognise her either. She tried to imagine what she looked like to them; an effete young aristocrat she supposed. Had Toby ever drunk here? How would he have appeared? She became aware that a sturdy weather beaten individual, to whom Peter was talking, was staring at her. She looked away. Was Peter discussing her, revealing who she was? She felt vulnerable, although the atmosphere was in no way hostile. She changed her posture, sat squarely on the bench, legs apart, elbows on the table. She lit a cigarette; a cigar would have been ostentatious.

"I hope you find this is to your taste."

Peter put down a large glass of claret and a pint of ale for himself.

"Alfie over there had certain ideas about you. I put him straight. Well, not entirely. I just told him to keep off, you weren't for him. Nor for me. Don't worry, your secret is safe. I said you were a friend of my family, visiting. My family's a bit of a joke to these people."

Which means I am a bit of a joke too, thought Charlie. Next time she and Peter met, if there was to be a next time, it would be on her territory in Brighton, where he would be the one out of place.

"Did Toby ever come here?"

"Toby? I shouldn't think so. I didn't see much of him, except with Violet. He didn't strike me as the sort who'd go looking for rough trade."

"Is that why you come here?"

"Rough trade? No, I only sleep with women. Like you."

There was the hint of a question rather than a definite statement.

"Like me, yes." She raised her glass. "To your good health!"

"Santé," replied Peter, raising his and drinking deep, before taking out his pipe.

There was a silence while he went through the lengthy procedure of filling and lighting it. Charlie watched. She envied his masculine assurance in this setting. He was at home here, in spite of the fact that there was something about the refinement of his looks which set him apart. When he leaned back to look at her, she was startled to recognise a pain which was similar to her own.

"Why are you here, Charlie? What do you want from me?"

Such a simple question, so difficult to answer.

"I'm not a suitable friend for you. I'm a bit of a disgrace, not mentioned in the best circles."

"Do you mind?" She was grateful to be given the opportunity to ask a question, to avoid explaining her confused motives.

"Only sometimes. What can you expect when you break out, refuse to accept their narrow boundaries? You can't do that sort of thing, you know, if everybody went around just doing what they fancied where would Britain be?" Mockery was his defence against rejection. However, there was no mockery in what he said next.

"I'm an only child, you see, the son and heir. It's always been up to me to keep up the side. You had Toby to carry that burden whilst you escaped."

This was an accusation Charlie had not anticipated. It caught her off guard. Was he implying that what she had always considered to be the courage to stand up for herself was in fact cowardice? But it was surely the reverse; it was Toby who didn't dare to admit what he was!

"That's not fair, I .." Oh god, she was going to cry! She stopped, swallowed hard, breathed deeply.

"I'm not blaming you. I would have done the same. And my parents are still alive, still hoping I'll mend my ways, get married to a county girl, good stock."

Charlie sipped her wine, calming down. This was proving to be worse than a waste of time, forcing her to acknowledge new truths. And she hadn't managed to say anything yet, put her point of view. She must speak.

"I'm good stock." Had she really said this?

"What?"

Now she had taken them both by surprise.

"I'm good stock."

It was a good few seconds before he began to laugh. "Charlie, you are surely not asking me to marry you?" Of course she wasn't.

"Peter, I like you, I don't know why. That doesn't matter. Please listen to me will you?"

Peter liked Charlie too, always had if she did but know it. He would listen to her.

"I did escape, but I'm caught again. I'm caught between what I am and what I'm expected to be. I have to get Violet away from me. She's infatuated, and to be honest, there's a sexual magnetism between us which she won't admit." She ignored Peter's raised eyebrows and continued. "The whole purpose of last night's stupid dinner was to shift her attention to someone else. I thought she and Simon, that explorer chap, would suit each other. But he's got designs on me now. He's already sent me flowers. Believe me, Peter, I gave him no encouragement."

Peter believed her. No encouragement as far as she knew. A handsome, intelligent woman, listening, or seeming to listen, to a man talking about his passion, is an encouragement.

"He's invited himself tomorrow afternoon, so I've asked Violet to be there too. I don't think that's enough protection, though."

Peter began to see where she was leading.

"Aren't you with anyone Charlie? Isn't there a woman who has your heart?"

No there wasn't. This admission gave rise to a number of feelings in Charlie, sadness, inadequacy, even guilt.

"Are you with anyone, Peter?"

"Not at the moment. There was a woman who had my heart, I'm trying to get it back. She's gone out of my life forever. I'll tell you about it some time."

The Frenchwoman, wondered Charlie, Lady Louise,

enshrined on a fishing boat?

"Do you think you could pretend to pay court to me? I mean only pretend. A courtship of convenience. We'd both be able to do what we wanted really. It could get me out of a hole and suit you for a bit."

Oh Charlie, thought Peter, life's more complicated than your plays.

"We'd have to spend a lot of time together to make it convincing. Would you mind that?"

"No. Would you?"

"No."

No he wouldn't. It could be fun. He needed fun. The loss of Louise had shaken him to the core. This game Charlie was proposing would end badly. When the marriage didn't take place, there would be vengeful fury from his family. So what? He could never satisfy them, never bring home a suitable bride, so a breathing space of feigned respectability might be a good thing.

"All right. What do you want me to do?"

Charlie found this an odd question.

"Whatever you would do when you court a woman."

"Excuse me, but you're not a normal woman." The mockery was back.

"Well, I'll have to imitate one."

"I look forward to that. And I'll try to behave like a normal man. Except when we are alone," he added hastily, catching her warning look. He lifted his pint pot.

"Here's to a happy couple, Peter and Charl. . .otte."

"Here's to Peter and Charlie."

They stretched arms across the table and drank from each other's glasses.

Chapter 9
Anna goes home

It was a long journey to Blackford and Anna chose to make it even longer than necessary, by spending a night in Rouen to look at the cathedral, a night in Dieppe because it was a town beloved of artists, on account of its lively harbour surrounded by cafés and restaurants. She liked the sea, so the four hour ferry crossing was preferable to the Calais-Dover route. She sat on deck until the French coast had completely disappeared, only going below when the breeze became a brisk cold wind. There were few passengers that day, so she was able to relax comfortably at a table next to a window, where she could watch the patterns made by the sun on the wrinkled water. She went outside again as soon as she caught a glimpse of the Seven Sisters and Seaford Head. She had booked into a hotel in Brighton for a night rather than travelling from Newhaven straight to London. She wanted to pass through London as quickly as possible, for fear of seeing people she knew. She had stayed in Brighton on a few occasions, in a quiet hotel just off the seafront. She found the town an exciting mixture of fashionable and seedy, the kind of liberated place that would make England palatable. She would settle into her room then go to a restaurant she knew of for a good meal in a convivial atmosphere, to relax her and give her a good sleep before she caught an early train to start the final stage to the Midlands.

She had just ordered her meal when a group of three arrived to sit at the reserved table opposite. One of them looked familiar. Her heart stopped when she realised it was Charlie. A more relaxed Charlie, somewhat fuller in the face, hair a little longer around the nape of her neck, laughing with the two men who sat one on either side. She was more striking than Anna remembered. Both men were agreeable looking, one slighter, more delicate than the other. She shrank back into her corner, hoping to avoid notice. This was most unfortunate. She hadn't forgotten that Charlie lived in Sussex but she didn't expect to see her in Brighton, and that she should be here now was an unimaginable coincidence. With any luck she would be too preoccupied with her companions to bother to look around.

It was certainly true that for a while after the trio settled down they only paid attention to each other and the menu. They appeared to be in playful mood, almost flirtatious, in a triangular relationship rather than a couple and a single. Anna watched them in fascination as they kept the balance of energy going from one to another with fond concern. How they all seemed to like each other, she thought, and how vibrant they were together, lighting up the dining room.

Whilst they were waiting for their first course, the waiter arrived with Anna's lemon sole. The eyes of the trinity followed him as he placed it in front of her and poured her a glass of white wine. He moved off and they all stared at Anna.

"Anna?" said Charlie. She knew who it was for she remembered Anna's every feature, but she had to have confirmation that it wasn't a mirage.

"Hello, Charlie." Anna had blushed a deep rose colour.

"Anna, what on earth are you doing here?"

Charlie's companions looked from one woman to the other.

"Charlie, aren't you going to introduce us to the delicious young lady?" asked George.

Peter said nothing.

"I'm sorry. It's just such a shock. Anna Waltham, my tenant in Paris, a painter, George a . . . socialite, a friend of my brother, Peter . . . a fisherman."

"How sweet of you to describe me as a socialite, darling. How do you do Miss Waltham." George stood up and bowed.

"How do you do, Miss Waltham." Peter half rose, inclined his head. "Please don't let us divert you from your dinner. A fresh fish like that should not be allowed to go cold."

"Wouldn't you like to join us?" asked Charlie. "It's a shame to eat on your own."

As she spoke the waiter brought their order too, so Anna was persuaded to move across. She would really rather have stayed where she was, the whole situation being extremely embarrassing. They had been so happy together, now she was introducing an element of formality which had been totally lacking.

"So, what are you doing here?" Charlie asked again.

"Breaking my journey to the Midlands. I came over on the Newhaven ferry."

"Of course, you're off to your family." Charlie had almost forgotten Anna's letters. "You did tell me where they live, didn't you? Somewhere in the North wasn't it? You sent me the address."

"The Midlands," Anna repeated. She realised that for these Southerners Derbyshire would be the North. Not the far North either, the brave border country, but the industrial landscape which they would consider totally alien territory.

"It's rather romantic, isn't it, all those pit tips," was George's fantasy. "Those miners are so earthy, so elemental, aren't they?"

"You can tell he's a Londoner, can't you?" said Charlie. "Really George, you haven't a clue."

Peter said nothing. He felt sympathy for the young woman sitting there discomfited, delicately removing her fishbone.

"I did know a Kentish miner once," persisted George. "He had the most beautiful body and he was really strong."

"I shouldn't think Anna has anything much to do with miners and coal mines." Charlie stated this as a fact.

"She's an artist."

"Well, if I were an artist I would have wanted to paint my Kentish man. He had such soft white skin, would you believe, and fine muscles. Actually he looked a bit like you Charlie, except he had very black hair." George was on the verge of nostalgia. "Do you ever paint people, Miss Waltham? Have you painted handsome miners? I should think it would make a good picture, with one of those wheel things in the background." He was not as naïve as he sounded. It was sometimes his way to affect a kind of superficiality to make others feel more at ease. He wanted to give Anna a chance to present herself. In this instance it was not a fortunate strategy, stirring up anxieties she was trying to quell. She wished they would just ignore her and get on with their own meal.

"Distant cousins of mine have property in the East Midlands," said Peter. "I visited them once. The countryside is lovely. Their house overlooks a wooded valley beside the River Derwent. Excellent for trout fishing. Not that fishing interests either of them very much. He's an M.P. and she's a sort of Bohemian. Their father, my great uncle, is scarcely ever there. Do you know the Derwent Valley, Miss Waltham?"

Anna was startled. Yes, she knew the Derwent Valley. She also knew a brother and sister who fitted his description.

"Where do you cousins live?" she asked.

"Near Cromford. Just up from tiny village called, let me see, er .. Whatstandwell. Are you familiar with that stretch of the river?"

She was.

"I think you may be talking about the Montgomeries at Upton Hall."

"You are acquainted with them?"

"Yes. I've been to Upton Hall. The house is delightful and the grounds are very unspoilt." That will stop the conversation about miners, she thought.

"I believe my sister and her husband go there quite often. They are good friends of the Montgomeries."

Crestfallen, George concentrated on his shellfish. Once

these country gentry got into the 'Do you know' mode, he was well and truly out of it. He and Toby had existed in a world apart, where this network of social relations had no place. When Charlie had introduced him to Peter he was reserved at first, not being sure how to deal with him on any level. In his view Charlie was playing with fire pretending to be on the point of engagement to this man. However, he overcame his misgivings out of his affection for her, finding Peter quite easy to get on with after all, in his openness, his acceptance of Charlie and her friends. Well dressed and refined though she was, Anna had not seemed to him to belong to the same social class as the other two. He was sorry to be proved wrong.

Anna disliked Gertrude Montgomery, considering her to be superficial and affected. They had artistic friends in common in London, which was one of the reasons Anna and Betsy had been invited to a house party at Upton Hall. Gertrude made a show of finding them charming, but could not conceal her condescension towards women who taught in a local school, the daughters of a schoolmaster.

"Fancy you knowing Peter's cousins," said Charlie. "Waltham. I think my mother used to talk about Derbyshire Walthams near Bakewell. Are you from the Bakewell Walthams?"

Oh dear, thought Anna. This was almost as bad as being associated with coalmining.

"No. My family were farmers on the Nottinghamshire/Derbyshire borders."

Her family! Her purpose in spending the night in Brighton was to continue to deny her family. Where her ancestors were born, what they did, was of no importance whatsoever. Why should she be categorised in this way? What was Manor Farm beside Upton Hall? And who was this so-called fisherman, whose accent belied that description, who was a distant cousin of Gertrude? Why did they make her feel inferior, how could they still make her feel inferior when she had been admired so much?

"On my father's side they were farmers, my mother is Ukrainian." There! She had retrieved herself, reasserted herself as something other, from a vastness beyond the British shores. There might be anything there – princes, counts, generals, making her elusive. The subject of her background was closed.

"I'm sorry you didn't tell me you were taking the Newhaven boat," said Charlie. "You could have come to stay with me, or if you'd rather, in my Brighton house. Much nicer than a hotel. Will you be returning the same way?"

"Probably."

"Do you know when?"

"No. Soon, I hope."

"Then do let me know. It would be fun to show you Finborough Place. And there might be a few things you could take back to Paris for me. Small things. Will you do that?"

"I can't say."

She couldn't say what she would feel like, whether she would want to escape as quickly as possible. The conversation became desultory after that. Anna excused herself as soon as she had finished, claiming exhaustion after travelling.

Just before dawn, Anna got up and walked along the beach. She wanted to watch the sun rise over the sea before she caught her train, to start the day with a vision of beauty. As the rim of the great, gleaming disk appeared on the horizon she vowed to hold fast to her uniqueness through the trials to come.

She took a cab between Victoria Station and St Pancras, seeing on the way what she supposed was essential London – Buckingham Palace, with its impassive, bearskin hatted guards, the Mall, St James' Park, Trafalgar Square, then St. Pancras Station itself, an improbable redbrick gothic fantasy. In spite of her determination to keep calm she began to be very nervous when she checked the time of the Derbyshire train on the departure board. In a little over two hours she would alight to face – who? Who would meet her? Betsy hadn't been sure who it would be.

She chose a seat in a Ladies Only compartment. It was

completely empty until just two minutes before the train left, when two elderly ladies, breathless and sweating, slid open the door of the corridor and fell into the nearest seats. Anna stared fixedly out of the window, ignoring them and trying to be ignored.

"Ay up, Aggie, we're going!" said one woman to the other.

The sound of her voice at once took Anna into that world from which she hoped to have escaped.

"Good job we ran," said Aggie. She rummaged in a bag which she had placed between herself and Anna and produced two packages one of which she handed to her friend. "Here you are, my duck, here's the sandwiches our Jessie made for us. We might as well eat them now."

Aggie took her package, began to unwrap the contents. "What did she put in them?" she asked, peeling back the wrapper.

"Potted meat, I think. They're both the same. She might have put some bloater paste in as well, I'm not sure. Is that all right?"

"Very nice, thank you. She's a good girl, your Jessie. It was very nice of her to invite me with you. She made me real welcome."

"She's always been good to me. 'Mam,' she says, 'you'll never want for ought whilst I'm alive.' She'd never let me come down to London all by myself."

"Her Ken seems a good lad."

"I told her she'd picked a good one there. He's a worker. He's always seen me right." She reflected for a few seconds. "It's a shame they live in London."

Aggie nibbled a corner of a sandwich.

"This one's bloater paste."

"Is it all right?"

"Lovely, thank you. Do you think they'll move?"

"Oh aye. As soon as the right job comes up for Ken, they'll come back home. They don't like it down South."

"No, they wouldn't." She tried a second sandwich. "This one's potted meat."

"Is it nice?"

"Very tasty." She took another bite before continuing. "Well, they wouldn't, would they, like it down South. It's not what they're used to. Folks are different aren't they?"

"Oh, aye. They're not so friendly, are they? I don't like them Cockneys. A bit too sharp. Ay up, we're going through a tunnel."

They were silent in the dimly-lit darkness as if cowed by a primitive fear.

"I'm glad we're out of that," said Jessie's mother, as they shot out into the sunlight. "I don't like tunnels, do you?"

"No, I don't," answered her friend. "Just think if we got stuck in one!"

"I'd have a fit," declared Jessie's mother. All at once, she took notice of Anna.

"I'm sorry, duck, I should have asked you if you wanted a sandwich. There's plenty." She held out her package.

"No, thank you, I'm all right." She heard her accent sliding towards theirs.

"Are you sure? They're very tasty. Good fillings, not cheap."

"I'm fine, really. I had a very good breakfast." That wasn't true, she'd eaten hardly anything. However, she had never been able to stomach either potted meat or bloater paste.

Oh dear, now they would include her.

"Have you got relations down South, then?"

"No, no I haven't." The questioning faces demanded a fuller explanations of her presence on this train.

"I've been working in Paris."

"Have you, my duck? Paris, fancy that! Paris, Aggie, she's been working in Paris, fancy that!"

"Fancy that," said Aggie. "Fancy working in Paris."

They digested this extraordinary information. Then Jessie's mother asked the obvious question.

"What kind of work?" The glint in her eyes showed that for her Paris was a city of sin. "Are you a dancer? You look as if you could be. You've got a nice figure."

"I'm an artist. A painter and sculptor."

"Are you, by guy! Well, I'll go to Trent." This latter

was an expression of surprise Anna had not heard for years. She supposed its use was confined to those who lived near enough to the River Trent to get to it without too much effort.

"My niece does a bit of painting," volunteered Aggie. "She's ever so clever. She copies cards. I've got a picture she did of a cottage with roses round the door on my bedroom wall. I don't know how she does it. It must be a gift, to be able to copy something like that. Is that what you do?"

"No," said Anna. "I do something different." It would have been useless to explain.

Jessie's mother and Aggie recognised that this line of enquiry had reached a natural conclusion.

It was Aggie who made the next approach.

"I expect your mam and dad miss you, when you're all that way away."

Anna was taken aback.

"Yes, I suppose."

"Of course they do." Jessie's mother joined in. "You're going back home now, I expect."

"Yes, I am." Oh no she wasn't. Home was Paris. For the time being.

"I miss Jessie. She comes home as often as she can. And she pays my fare down to London to see her. She's paid for Aggie, as well. She's a good girl, she does what she can, but it's not like having her at home. I always thought she'd be able to live near me when she got married, but she can't."

"She will, though," Aggie chipped in. "As soon as Ken can get a job near home."

"I know. But I do miss her, though." She wiped away a tear. "I cried my eyes out at her wedding."

"It's such a long way away, Paris." This seemed like an accusation from Aggie. "Couldn't you get a job as an artist in Derbyshire. I'm sure there are plenty of artists in Derbyshire. Couldn't you work there?"

"Now stop it, Aggie." Jessie's mother had regained her composure.. "Happen she's got a sweetheart there." She nudged Aggie, slyly. "She's not going to tell us that, is she?"

This is too bad, thought Anna.

"You see, she's blushing!" A cry of triumph from Jessie's mother. "Don't worry, duck, if you've been swept off your feet by a Frenchman, that's your business. I hear they're a bit cheeky, them French, lots of ooh, la, la." The pair of them burst into raucous laughter.

"Excuse me," said Anna, stiffly. "I have to go to the lavatory."

"I'm sorry if we've upset you. It's just a bit of fun. We don't mean any harm. Livens things up, passes the time." Jessie's mother watched appreciatively as Anna squeezed past her. "You are bonny, though. You must have a sweetheart tucked away somewhere."

In the corridor Anna closed her eyes, laid her forehead against the glass of the window. She had felt like a victim in there, a mouse being played with by two cats. If only she could have shouted "No I don't have a sweetheart. I don't want one. My parents don't miss me, they have lots of other children. I have every right to live where I please." They would have been terribly shocked. To them the conversation was unimportant, everyday chatter. To her each remark was an offence. She shouldn't take it all so seriously, she told herself. She used not to mind being teased, what other people said and thought slid off her surface, hardly touching her inner calm. She had been much teased, by her schoolmate and her siblings, all of them provoked by her dreaminess, the impression she gave of always being somewhere else, wanting to get through to her even if only to make her angry, which they rarely did. The girls at the High School made fun of her for doing so badly in lessons, her teachers constantly berated her, Betsy, the conscientious, studious Betsy, pestered her to make more effort; she responded with a vacant look or a half-smile, as if not understanding why they should bother, since she was quite content. When her talent for painting and drawing became obvious the blame turned to praise, what had been condemned as stupidity or obstinacy was now perceived as the outward sign of the powerful internal world of the creative artist, which dominated external reality. Anna responded to adulation in the same way, so that in the end no one bothered to comment any more.

It was Robin who had disturbed her infuriating tranquillity. When she met him she had been ready for a lover, but the qualities that drew her to him, his energy, his corrosive passion, nearly destroyed her. Since then an emotional numbness had replaced her natural imperturbability. Standing watching the fields flash past in the inevitable progress towards her birthplace, she was afraid that numbness was beginning to wear off, leaving her sore and unprotected.

The train slowed down, pulling into Derby station. It was the only stop before Blackford. She took her seat again and two other women joined them. They were young and smart looking, radiating health and optimism. After a quick smile at the other occupants, they became totally engrossed in each other, recounting what had happened to them in the last twenty-four hours, discussing what they were going to do when they met their friend, with whom they were going to spend a few days holiday. Working girls who'd managed to have unusual time off together. Jessie's mother and Aggie started up a rival conversation out of politeness, though they were fascinated by the girls' stories. Anna took out her sketch book to absorb herself in what they looked like rather than what they were saying. They became slightly self-conscious when they saw her drawing, but they soon forgot her in their excitement. All too soon they reached their final destination.

Anna waited for the others to get out first. She unloaded her luggage onto the platform, looking round for a porter. The smoke and steam from the engines in this enclosed space began to make her cough. She bent over, eyes watering. When she looked up two men stood before her, one much younger than the other.

"Ay up, our Anna," said the younger.

"Let us take your cases," said the other. "Welcome back." Alan tried to sound as if he meant it. This first meeting after Robin's death was as nerve-racking for him as for her.

118

"Thank you, Alan," she said.

She turned to the younger man. "Billy?"

Her brother threw his arms round her to give her a great hug.

"You've not changed at all," he said. "Still the same daft clothes."

Only two years and Billy had matured almost beyond recognition. He was broad-shouldered, fresh complexioned, a typical Waltham man, Anna thought. She was glad to see him.

"Haven't you had enough of those foreign parts by now?" he asked, carrying two of her heavy cases as though they weighed nothing.

Instead of answering Anna said "You've grown into a fine young man, Billy."

"So all the lassies tell me!" Where did that cheeky grin come from? Not his rather grim-faced father nor his mother, although she was a merrier sort of soul.

"Betsy thought it would be better for me to fetch you in my car and take you to our house first," said Alan. "Put the cases in here, Billy. Billy insisted on coming with me and I'm glad he did, considering how much luggage you've brought."

"Happen she's staying for good, with this amount of clothes." Billy sounded hopeful, looking sideways at his sister.

They didn't talk much as Alan's car trundled along the miles between the city and the cottage not far from Blackford, where Betsy and Alan had settled. Anna began to recognise the roads, feeling a slight thrill when they passed the familiar lake.

"We're going a longer way round," said Alan. "Otherwise we'll pass very near The Grange." He glanced at Anna to see her reaction. The Grange was Robin's family home, where his mother and sisters still lived. Anna was silent. She was grateful for what she took to be Alan's consideration. It would have been dreadful to meet any one of them.

Betsy was waiting for them impatiently by her garden gate. She had heard the noise of the car chugging up the sunken lane. She was proud of their little home, she wanted to escort Anna right to the front door.

"Oh my dear," she said. "You can't imagine how glad I am you decided to come home."

Chapter 10
The Confrontation

"You really have arranged everything beautifully, Bee."
Anna liked the way her sister had made the tiny rooms
comfortable and airy. The walls were whitewashed in different pale colours, which was not at all like the home
they had both been used to. The baby's room, in which
Anna was to sleep, for there were only two bedrooms,
was a delicate primrose with cream curtains, hand stitched
by Betsy herself. There was no bed, just a sort of couch,
long enough and wide enough to sleep on. In one corner, the cradle carved by Tessa stood ready and waiting.
There was hardly any furniture except a chest of drawers and a woven cane chair. When Anna opened the
drawers she found tiny nightdresses and exquisite little
knitted bonnets and boots in one and embroidered cov-
erlets in the others. Like many of the other windows, the
window of this room looked towards the garden and
beyond, to the fields and woods. The old stone building stood in its own space, no other houses near. There
were sheds where coal and garden tools were kept.

"We were lucky to get this place," said Betsy. "It was
a tied cottage, actually, part of The Grange estate. But
the old man who lived here died, his wife went to live
with her daughter and the family said Alan could buy it."

So this place had belonged to Robin.

"Of course it looks quite different with our own things
in it and painted in these colours. It was dark and dingy
before. I love it. I feel so at home here. And it's just
right for a child, don't you think? It reminds me of Ivy
Cottage, I loved Ivy Cottage, didn't you?"

Yes, Anna loved the house next to the church where

they had grown up, except that it was always full of people, full of children. How had they all lived there, eight children and their parents? How many babies would come to live here, she wondered.

"In fact, if the tenants had wanted to move out, we might have taken it again. Alan didn't like the idea, but I thought it would be very romantic. It would have been, wouldn't it, to go back to where we were born, to the house mother and father made their own?"

It would have been awful, thought Anna. Betsy, how could you?

"This is much nicer," she said. "I don't suppose Alan would have liked being next to the church, would he? And those trees made it rather gloomy."

The sisters chatted on in a desultory fashion. Alan and Billy had gone out again on some mysterious errand. The rays of the September sun slanted through the sparkling panes of glass, filling the living room with a gentle golden light. It was a restful, peaceful scene in which Anna began, at last, to feel somewhat at ease, until Betsy suddenly jumped to her feet.

"Look at the time! I'd better start getting tea ready. I forgot to tell you that Tessa's coming for tea with her husband and their baby. And Billy of course, he's round here most days. Alan's fetching them in the car. They'll be here at half-past five. Kate might call in too. She doesn't finish work until nearly six."

What work? Yet again Anna tried to remember what Betsy had told her, tried to recall this other sister only three years her junior. Tessa, Kate, Billy had only had a tenuous existence for her throughout her life, now she seemed to have obliterated them completely from her consciousness. As she helped Betsy to lay out the plates of cooked ham and salad on the pink damask tablecloth clearly being used for the first time, the image of two strong looking, loose limbed young women began to emerge.

"Celia is coming here from teacher training college this weekend. We thought it better she shouldn't interrupt her studies too much. She's been back most weekends. She'll collect Arthur from boarding school. You remember he's at school not far from her college."

No, she had forgotten that Celia was at college and Arthur at boarding school. Why wasn't he at the local grammar school, for goodness sake? Sending boys to boarding school was unheard of amongst their circle.

"Dolly's been wonderful. Such a constant help to mother. Her teachers have been very sympathetic when she's been too tired to concentrate on her lessons. Most of them know our family so well, they've taught us all. They're especially fond of her because she is the baby, and so sweet natured. You'll see her tomorrow."

When the table was fully laid Anna wanted to paint it. As well as the salads there were large plates of thinly sliced and buttered bread, a tall silver cake stand with currant buns and slices of flapjack, a bowl of cooked peaches and a large, iced cake with 'Welcome Home, Anna' painted on in cochineal. The teacups and saucers, with their small matching plates, were in fragile, hand painted bone china.

"Bee, did you make all this?" Anna never credited Betsy with culinary skill. "I have time to do those things now," replied her sister, modestly. "I'll just put the kettle on, I can hear the car coming up the lane."

Anna's heart sank again. Could she plead a headache, fatigue from the journey? Maybe she could pretend to be overcome by dizziness before they appeared, have to go to her room and stay there until they'd gone. No, she couldn't do that. The car engine stopped, the gate opened, the latch clicked, the door swung open, and there they were.

"Don't you think Tessa's little Margaret Anna is adorable?" asked Betsy later, as they sat by the fire. Although the days were warm the temperature soon dropped when the sun went down, so the three of them gathered round the glowing hearth when the visitors had gone. "And she does look like you, doesn't she? Apart from the red hair from her father's family. Hasn't he turned out just fine? Who'd have thought when he was pulling Tessa's hair all those years ago that they would marry. When we all went to the grammar school she didn't see him for a while of course, but then they met at a dance and that was it. She kept it secret that they were going out together because she knew father would want somebody better for her, with a profession. He has a heart of gold, though, and he already has his certificate from the University as a 'shot-firer'." William Stonely, Tessa's husband, was a coal miner, who earned very good money for someone so young. He had left school early and gone to work at one of the local pits as soon as he could, like his father before him.

"I'm pleased Dolly found time to call. She is so sweet and she was dying to see you." Betsy continued in this way, whilst Alan sucked on his pipe and Anna stared into the embers. She was determined that all would be well, that Anna would recognise that they were all good people who loved her and whom she loved. They were all from the same brood, after all, with deep blood ties, and those they chose to enfold within their clan must be lovable too.

Anna scarcely listened to her. She was worn out by the tension of the last few hours. There had been long silences whilst everyone looked at Anna trying to find something to say after the initial greeting. Most of the conversation, such as it was, revolved around the toddler, who wriggled about on her father's knee, snatching at pieces of cake, which she then threw on the floor. William was clearly besotted with his daughter, cradling her, rocking her and scolding her in tones so gentle that it was clear that 'Naughty girl' meant 'You're and angel and I'm mad about you.' The mother had looked on indulgently, every so often staring hard at Anna whilst the latter picked delicately at her bread and butter. Billy and William joked with each other, an easy camaraderie existing between them. There were occasional teasing remarks addressed to Tessa and Betsy, who smiled at them with the contented look of a mother-to-be. They even teased Alan a little about his impending paternal status. Anna was relieved to be ignored. She hoped their curiosity had been satisfied by simply looking at her. She didn't want to know what they thought of this outsider who was their sister. As they said their strained farewells, Tessa said, "I hope you'll come round to us and see what I've been making. I know you're a real artist and I'm not but I'd like to show you some things." For the first time that evening Anna looked into the girl's serious face. "Of course, I'd love to," she said.

The hour or so spent later with Dolly had been diffi-cult for different reasons. Once more, Anna had been left out, but the talk this time had been about their father's fast deterioration and their mother's increasing instabil-ity. Dolly was astonishingly calm and capable, apparently relishing the responsibility. She was discovering a talent for caring, an ability to maintain a sort of order when breakdown threatened. She was thinking about becom-ing a nurse, she said. Alan had asked her whether she thought that they should phone Celia to ask her to come the next day, pick up Arthur a day earlier than planned. Dolly had considered the question a long time before answering, "Yes, I think so." Her parting words to Anna as they lingered for a moment in the already frosty dark-ness were, "Thank you for coming. It's important."

Is it important? Anna doubted it. She ceased to hear Betsy's endless anecdotes that were an attempt to fill in for her all she had missed during her time away, to re-establish the severed connection. She lost herself in the red of the hot fire, the twisting patterns of the occasional flames as the coal shifted and dropped. She basked in the heat of the miniature sun.

"Anna must be very tired, and you shouldn't stay up too late, so let's all go to bed." Alan put an abrupt end to his wife's monologue.

"I hope you'll be comfortable on this couch." Betsy sounded truly anxious. "Tomorrow you can move into our parent's. There's a room ready for you. We'll take you over in the morning. I'm sorry if we've overwhelmed you. Alan says I rattle on too much sometimes but I just want you to feel welcome. You do, don't you?"

Anna avoided a direct answer. "You're very sweet, and I appreciate it. Goodnight."

Betsy frowned slightly. "Goodnight then. Sleep well."

The couch was not very comfortable at all. Anna didn't sleep again, exhausted though she was. The situation was made worse by the fact she didn't dare toss and turn too much for fear of disturbing the couple next door. She could hear them whispering well into the small hours, an annoying soft patter of sound, the words indistinguishable. When silence finally reigned, she got up, crossed over to the window, cursing the creaking floorboards as she did so. She drew back the curtains as quietly as she could. The moon was brilliant, almost full, flooding the landscape with its pale crisp light. She had lived in cities for so long that she had forgotten how many stars there were. She opened the casement, gulped in the cold air. As children she and Betsy together had gazed, bewitched, at the moon, thrilled by a mystery lacking to the sun. They had watched its light move across the bedroom, longing for the apparition of some nocturnal spirit. Now the clarity of the air was such that the pattern of craters on its surface was clearly visible. With the window open, Anna became aware of noises at the end of the garden, where a gate led out towards a grassy bank. She stood perfectly still. Was someone trying to break in and steal tools from the garden shed? She kept her eyes fixed on the spot where the noise was increasing, tramping and breaking of flowerpots. Noisy burglars! Then, out of the fruit bushes came a group of badgers, their striped faces matching the shadows cast by the moonlight. They wandered up and down, rooting in the earth, talking to each other in a high-pitched chatter. For half an hour she watched, unconcerned about the damage they were doing to the plants. Then they went away. She closed the window and hastened back to bed, burrowed, shivering, under the heavy eiderdown. When the warmth came back into her body and spread to her fingers and toes she was able to doze until Alan got up to go to work. Each step he took caused the old floorboards to creak. She heard him raking the fire and running water in the downstairs bathroom. He was light and graceful, making very little noise, but the floors and walls were thin so it was impossible not to be aware of activity wherever it was in the house unless one was heavily asleep. The oak door swung clumsily on its hinges and the latch clattered as Alan closed it behind him. If she hadn't been awake before she would certainly have been woken by the several attempts he made to start his car before taking off. She heard Betsy groan and turn over, clearly not ready to get up. She was conscious of her intrusion into the couple's living space, of her own distaste for this unaccustomed intimacy. There would be more privacy in her parents' large, solid home, she reassured herself, trying to find something positive about a move she was dreading.

Since both sisters were weary and anxious they got up late, had several cups of tea with lots of sugar, exchanging occasional remarks about nothing in particular, avoiding any mention of their father. Anna helped Betsy prepare vegetables for their dinner at midday, when Alan would return for his main meal with them before driving them over to their parents' house. Their mother had a nurse every morning to help her with the routine of the sickroom. The doctor came round every other day at nine o'clock to administer medicines which would dull the pain. The mother of one of their father's pupils was employed to do the daily cleaning and prepare a light meal which Clara could hardly eat. There was a quiet period between two o'clock and five o'clock when Dolly came home from school. It was therefore at two o'clock they were to arrive. Alan would drop them off and go back to work. Peeling potatoes, letting them fall one by one into a pan of cold water, Anna recalled the details of the grand dining room with its thick rush matting, its imposing fireplace, its big mahogany table where ten people could sit without difficulty. It was as big as the drawing room next to it. When they all moved there from Ivy Cottage they moved up into a different social order, into the life of the new leafy suburbs, as befitting their father's promotion. Now he is dying, the house will be without a purpose, thought Anna as she carried the potatoes from the table to the old-fashioned range Betsy used for cooking.

Betsy took Anna's hand when they drew alongside the

red house, feeling the palm cold and damp. "Don't worry, it will be all right," she whispered.

"I'm afraid I'll have to leave you," said Alan. "I'll bring Anna's things over this evening. You'll be staying here, won't you Betsy?"

"Yes. I'll see you this evening. Thank you my love." They exchanged the kind of kiss which Anna had never experienced, a tender kiss between true lovers.

Still hand in hand, the sisters walked up the black and white tiled steps. The front lawn had been neatly mown by Billy, the flowerbeds around the edge were still bright with carefully ordered rows of colour, white, red and blue. The front door was freshly painted in a pretty green which showed off the glass panels Anna had always loved. Even from the outside one could appreciate the skill in the depiction of birds and butterflies. The brass doorknob and letterbox gleamed with pride.

Betsy turned the knob, opened the door.

"Mother, we're here! Our Anna's here!"

She closed the door, crossed the hallway to the drawing room.

Anna didn't follow. Awkwardly she stood in the dimness looking up at the window above the first landing. In shape it was like the windows in a chapel, tall with a semicircle at the top. It contained a semi-abstract representation in stained glass of a vase of lilies. There was a double border of red and blue, through which the sun was streaming at this moment, with a vibrancy which took her breath away. She remembered her father was particularly fond of that window.

"Anna, where are you? Come on in, mother's waiting." Betsy returned to fetch her sister, grasping her firmly by the arm.

Like a duchess waiting to receive me, thought Anna.

But Clara was not like a duchess. She looked a poor, shrunken thing as she rose from the leather armchair to greet her daughter.

"Anna," she said. "I'm glad you've come." That was all, no embrace, not even a smile of welcome. There was a dull listlessness in her expression, almost a lack of recognition as if Anna were any woman come in off the street. Anna's immediate anger gave way to pity. It was she who took her mother in her arms.

"I'm so sorry about father," all of a sudden she found it difficult to speak.

"Aye," was all Clara replied, but a deep, shuddering sigh shook her whole body, as she clung to Anna for a brief moment, before sinking back into her chair.

"Shall I make us all a cup of tea?" Betsy was seeking a means of escape, of leaving them alone.

Why, wondered Anna, what was the use, what could they have to say to each other?

"Go on then. You might as well." No sooner had Clara consented than Betsy disappeared.

"You may as well sit down. You are staying, aren't you?" There was hardness in Clara's tone.

Anna perched on the edge of a chaise longue.

"You've made it very nice in here, mother. The walls weren't this colour before, were they?"

"Before what?" Anna recognised that this was not an innocent question.

"When I was last here."

"There's been a few changes since then, not that you'd care."

Anna let the remark pass. Clara studied her from head to toe, raising her eyebrows slightly.

"Is that the latest Paris fashion then?" She seemed particularly taken with the purple stockings.

"Not really. I have my own ideas."

"You always did. Always going your own way, no matter what." In that one sentence she reduced Anna to a self-centred, obstinate child. Clara had plenty of things she had to say on that subject, now was not the time to say them. Later she might give vent to the hurt and bitterness caused by her second daughter. She changed the subject.

"Betsy tells me you're doing well. Your painting is being admired."

"Yes it is."

"We didn't waste our money sending you to Art School, then."

129

"You knew I had some success even when I was living in London."

"We knew you kept company with some dubious friends. That's why we were so glad you came back to teach. You couldn't stick that for long though."

"I'm not a good schoolteacher. I hate the atmosphere in schools." Anna was trying to ignore the sneers, rationalising her behaviour.

"Because you have to accept the discipline, obey the rules?"

Oh, this was going too far. What did Clara know about discipline or rules? She had never needed to conform. She had never needed to earn a living either. She had lived as Queen Bee, with all of them as her drones. Did this haughty woman have any right to judge Anna, simply because she gave birth to her?

"Mother, I earn my own living, enough to pay you back every penny you ever spent on me, if you like, I am highly regarded in my profession and I work harder than any teacher ever worked. I have been painting from dawn until dusk, isn't that discipline?"

Clara changed the direction of her attack again.

"Aye, well, for all the money you may have, you're likely to end up a lonely old woman."

Fortuitously, Betsy brought in the tea. The last jibe had left Anna speechless, coming too near to her own fears. She crossed over to the window, stared out without seeing, reluctant to give Clara the satisfaction of knowing her shot had hit home.

"Is father sleeping?" asked Betsy.

"He's been asleep most of the day. You can go up and see at about four o'clock, if he's awake."

The spark that had ignited when Clara took Anna to task was extinguished again. Her voice was a monotone.

"Will you sit down and drink your tea, Anna?" Betsy gestured with the milk jug towards a chair. "Isn't this china pretty? We all decided to buy it for mother and father last Christmas. The old cups were getting chipped and several of the saucers were broken. Tessa chose it, since she's the most artistic one." Suddenly conscious of her slip she added, "apart from you of course. Don't you like it? It's very modern, the latest thing."

Yes it was the latest thing, the new art with its continental influence, very different from the traditional British flowers. Not what Anna would have chosen herself. "It's lovely," she said.

The three of them sipped their tea in silence. Then Clara put down her half-empty cup and announced. "I'm very tired. I'll go and have a lie down. Tell me if your father wakes up. You know where I'll be, on the couch in the study."

She trailed out.

"Would you like to come out into the garden? It seems a shame to stay indoors when it's so sunny."

Did Betsy think she needed to find things for them to do the whole time, wondered Anna. Although she had left her luggage behind she had brought a small leather satchel containing pastels and a sketchbook. As it was, indeed, sunny and unseasonably warm, she could have settled herself down to draw in some corner outside, regain her composure, as her heart was still beating too fast.

"Wouldn't you like to rest, Bee?" she suggested.

"I'm far too restless. Besides, mother doesn't sleep properly in the afternoons, she sometimes has bad dreams and wakes up very disturbed. She was all right just now but sometimes she becomes almost demented."

Anna had a sudden inspiration.

"Why don't we sit in the garden somewhere I can draw you? You are so beautiful, I'd love to do a portrait. We'll come in if you start to feel cold."

The back garden was a glorious mixture of exuberance and control. Planted fairly closely together the flowers had fought for space, growing into each other in their last burst of strength at the end of the summer. There was a little wooden seat against a west-facing wall, where the Virginia creeper was beginning to turn scarlet. Anna fetched a cushion to make Betsy comfortable, with a book for her to read. Since Betsy had come bareheaded she set her own straw hat on her sister's brown hair, its pale violet colour being striking against the red and green.

The composition pleased her mightily, the bent head, three-quarter view, the flow of Betsy's cream woollen dress over the arm of the chair.

"Keep as still as you can, Bee, and don't talk," she said. She fetched a wooden chair through the French windows into the dining room, placing it opposite her model, back to front so that she could sit legs astride the seat, leaning the sketchbook against the backrest. They stayed in these positions for almost an hour with no sound except the humming of bees. When the shade crept round to Betsy's face, she shivered.

"There's a nip in the air, though," she said.

Anna began to put away her pastels. She was satisfied with what she'd done. "Thank you, Bee," she said. "You can move now. Do you want to look?"

In spite of the fact that the face was partly covered, the drawing was unmistakeably Betsy.

"That's extraordinary! What a beautiful, beautiful picture. And it is so like me. To have made something so perfect in such a short space of time! My darling, you are so clever!" Betsy wanted to add, why don't you do this always, instead of those repellent things I saw in Paris.

"It's only a quick sketch. It does have something, though. Would you like to have it?"

"Oh could I? Do you mean it?"

"Yes, but you have to be very careful. Pastels smudge easily."

"I'll have it framed. Tessa will do it for me. She'll love it. You're so good at getting a likeness." Betsy paused. "I suppose you wouldn't want to draw little Margaret Anna one day?"

"You suppose right," said Anna firmly. "I don't draw children. We'd better go in before you get a chill." She felt she had found herself again, so she would have the confidence to face whatever might happen next.

"Should we see if father is awake?" Betsy sensed that her sister was ready.

They tiptoed past the study, up the sweeping staircase to the first landing, with its many doors. The first led to their parents' room. This door was always left slightly open in case of need. There was always someone near enough to hear, should the ill man be in distress. When Betsy pushed, it opened silently on well-oiled hinges.

Ernest Waltham lay in the middle of the large bed, so light and spare that he scarcely made a bump in the surface of the heavy eiderdown covering him.

How fine his face is, thought Anna. Almost noble.

His eyes, which had been closed when they entered, opened as they approached the bed. A loss of weight had drawn back the skin around the sockets which gave him a mad, wide-eyed stare, which he turned towards first Betsy then Anna, looking at her with uncomprehending fixity.

"It's Anna, father," said Betsy .

Ernest said nothing, his eyes not moving from Anna's face.

"She's come to see you."

"Anna." He pronounced the name as though it was totally foreign to him.

Betsy pushed her sister gently towards the bed.

"Hello, father," said Anna.

Ernest turned his head to Betsy. "Will you give me water?" he asked. His voice was faint, husky, barely audible. Betsy poured him a glass of water from the decanter on the side table.

"I'll help you sit up," she suggested.

Very gently she took hold of the sick man under his arms and lifted him whilst Anna piled up the pillows behind him. When he was propped comfortably in a sitting position Betsy held the glass to his lips, wiping his chin with her handkerchief.

"Anna," he repeated staring at her again. She felt unnerved, dumbstruck. There was a minute's silence.

"She's been away," volunteered Betsy.

"I know that," he retorted, with much more strength than he had shown hitherto, although he had a fit of coughing immediately afterwards, which gave way to painful wheezing.

Betsy drew up a chair beside the bed.

"Sit down beside him for a minute," she said to Anna. "I'll go and see if mother's awake."

Don't leave me alone, please don't leave me alone with him, Anna would have begged, had she been able to open her mouth. As she said nothing, Betsy smiled at her encouragingly, before leaving the room, closing the door softly behind her.

Ernest struggled to produce a hoarse sentence, incomprehensible to his daughter. She leaned close trying to read his lips. He made a supreme effort to articulate.

"Cat got your tongue?"

"No." She found her voice. "No, I thought you might want to be quiet."

"There's nothing but quiet here." The words came out slowly, painfully. "Talk to me."

What to say? What could he want from her?

"Would you like some more water?"

"No. Talk . . . to . . . me."

His pale long hand lay like a dead thing on the covers. Impulsively, she took hold of it. He didn't withdraw it. Perhaps he hadn't the strength.

"Father, I've just had an exhibition in Paris. They liked my work."

Why did she tell him that? At this moment it was of no importance whatsoever.

"Did they, my lass?" He was taken again by a wheezing fit, his thin flanks heaving. He continued, "You've done well, then."

She felt the slightest pressure of his fingers against hers. He closed his eyes at last. "I'm glad," he said.

His hand was totally relaxed again. His breaths were deep, shuddering, intermittent.

Betsy came back with Clara. The wife was wringing her hands, her face a grief stricken mask. She glanced grimly at Anna, who let go of her father's hand and got up from the chair. Immediately Clara sat in her place, took both the man's hands in her own. "Ernest," she moaned, "Ernest, don't leave me."

He struggled for air, drawing it in, holding it before releasing it.

"I want to be alone with him, go away, go away, both of you." It was the cry of a wilful child.

Downstairs the sisters sat quietly. Even though the bedroom door was closed the soft moaning seemed to fill the house. "Ernest, Ernest, don't leave me, Ernest."

"Dolly will be home soon," said Betsy. "Mother's calmer when she's here."

They sat for another fifteen minutes, as the moans became a ritual chant. They heard the front door opening, then a shriek from upstairs. Dolly ran in. "What's happening?" she cried, scared.

The three hastened upstairs together.

Clara lay sprawled over her husband's body sobbing, shaking his lifeless head from side to side.

"Mother don't!" Dolly spoke sharply. "Come away now. Let him rest in peace. Anna, Betsy, take her arms. And telephone the nurse to come and help me lay him out. You two stay with mother. I'll see to things here."

Clara struggled, but they managed to get her to the couch in the study where she sat rocking backwards and forward, ignoring Betsy's arms encircling her. Anna phoned the nurse, who, since she was expecting the call, arrived quickly, with an assistant. Clara watched them ascend the stairs then pulled herself roughly away from Betsy.

"I'm going to help them," she declared.

"No mother, you mustn't. They'll know what to do. They'll make him nice, you'll see." She was very much afraid Clara would make another scene and get in the way.

"I have to help." Clara was at the bottom of the stairs by now. The nurse turned.

"Do you think you'll be all right, Mrs. Waltham?" Her manner was kindly.

"Yes. I must do it. He's my husband."

"Come on then. But you'll have to do as I tell you."

"I will." Clara was all meek obedience.

The nurse winked at Betsy. "Don't worry. It'll be fine."

Clara refused to leave the bedroom all night. Dolly brought her a supper tray but she would only pick at the food. Arthur and Celia had arrived, upset to find that they were too late to say their goodbyes to their father. Tessa and Billy had both sat with him the night before so they felt they had paid their respects. They took it in turns to be with Clara who now sat nearly as still as her dead husband, looking almost young again in the candlelight. The only words she spoke were to Arthur, her last baby.

"Look at him. Look at your father. Isn't he handsome? He's like he was the day we married."

Arthur looked, scared and fascinated. Travelling home from boarding school with Celia he had told her all about his escapades, about the teachers he hated, those he loved, trying to share with her a world which was most meaningful to him. The sudden dramatic return, the announcement that his father had already died, left him bewildered, especially since the man on the bed looked quite different from the man he'd last seen.

William Stonely came to be with his wife. Their little girl helped make the evening more bearable, vital and 'demanding' as she was, as assertion of new life needing to be cared for. Around the supper table the talk was as much of her as of the circumstances which brought them all together. Of these all they could find to say was "it's a relief." "An end to his suffering." "It's a good job it didn't drag on much longer" and such like.

William, Tessa and child finally went home. Alan asked Betsy if she wanted to stay. As she hesitated Dolly assured her there was no need, there were enough of them to keep watch, she should have her rest, the baby's welfare was most important, etc., etc. So they left too, Alan's arm comfortingly around his wife's waist.

"Arthur, it's time you were off to bed, you must be tired." Although she was younger than Arthur, Dolly was playing mother. He looked at her in amazement, about to protest, but she had such an air of stern authority that he gave way. Age was clearly irrelevant to their roles in this unaccustomed situation.

"Did Alan take your luggage up?" Dolly turned her attention to Anna.

"I don't know. I'm not sure where I'll be sleeping."

"I'll show you. You're to have my room. I'll share with Celia."

Anna felt she ought to protest, to offer to share with Celia instead, but the idea of sleeping with any of them was anathema. Dolly's was one of three bedrooms overlooking the back garden. It was the smallest of the three, at the furthest end of the corridor from the parents' room across the landing. Next door was Arthur, with Dolly and Celia at the other side. Billy was opposite in a large room at the front next to the bathroom.

"If the four of us do a three hour shift with mother, then we can all have at least six hours rest. I'm not including Arthur because he's too young. So I'll sit with her now and perhaps you could take over next?"

This child is truly amazing, thought Anna.

With Arthur in bed and Dolly with Clara, Anna was left with Celia.

"How are you keeping then, Anna?" Celia's voice was almost identical to Tessa's. Physically the two resembled each other as if they were twins. It was as if Clara's body had run out of ideas after her third daughter, producing another baby almost the same model before taking off in a new direction with a boy. They were tough looking women, Celia having a particularly strong looking body. She took out a cigarette, offered one to Anna. The way she moved reminded Anna of Charlie.

"No thank you. I don't smoke."

There was a pause, whilst Celia lit her cigarette and inhaled deeply. She looked expectantly at Anna who remembered she'd been asked a question.

"I'm well." Out of politeness she felt bound to ask. "And you?" although Celia looked a very picture of health.

"I'm fine, absolutely fine. Now I'm away. I couldn't have stood being at home any longer. I had to get out somehow or other. I'm not really the studying kind, but going to college is a good way to escape. She smiled ruefully. "I'm not as brave as you. But now I've made a break, I'm not coming back."

How strange this was, thought Anna, finding an ally in a girl who had scarcely impinged on her consciousness.

"There were terrible storms when you disappeared," Celia continued. "Nobody forgave you for not coming to

Robin's funeral. They couldn't understand it. It was shocking. We were all thinking about your marriage then Robin was dead and you'd gone away. I was the only one thought you did the right thing. I couldn't stand Robin, he was arrogant, like his whole family."

"Why are you telling me this?" To her horror, Anna heard her voice tremble.

"To warn you. Be prepared for some scene or other. It hasn't gone away, all that, just calmed down a bit. I wanted you to know that I am on your side. You don't belong here, never did. Look at you! You're dazzling! And I might never see you again, we'll both live a long way away. So I wanted to say this now. I understand, I understand completely."

Impulsively she took Anna in her arms and a deep warmth of feeling passed between the two before she let go.

"Thank you," whispered Anna.

"I'm going to try to get some sleep now, before it's my turn to watch. I'll see you in the morning."

During the next two hours Anna busied herself sketching the more interesting corners of the downstairs rooms. She was particularly taken by a large carved piece over the fireplace in the study. She had never seen it before and supposed it was one of her father's more recent pieces. Mysterious feathered creatures, birds or angels, curved around an oval mirror. For years Ernest had been an important part of the life of the church next to Ivy Cottage, playing the organ and acting as caretaker. He had a natural inclination towards religious ecstasy, which was not entirely absorbed by his sexual bliss with Clara. Drawing the loving detail of these upward-reaching figures, Anna felt an affinity with the sculptor. A sharp pain of grief went through her. Perhaps, after all, they had been kindred spirits. Those last words "You've done well, I'm glad," were they his blessing?

When Dolly came to fetch her she had become so totally absorbed that she had forgotten her spell of duty was about to begin.

"Mother won't be any trouble," Dolly sounded weary.

"She's not asleep but she's not awake either. I like to imagine her soul has gone off to join father's before he leaves the earth forever. They say it takes three days until the spirit has properly departed, don't they?"

Do they? Anna wondered again at the strangeness of this child, as she followed her upstairs.

Going into the bedroom now was like entering a holy place. There were candles burning all round the bed. Apart from their flickering flames all was silent and still. Clara was like a statue, rigidly upright in her chair.

"Here's Anna come to be with you for a while," whispered Dolly.

Clara seemed not to hear, but as Dolly turned to leave, she sprang into life.

"No," she shouted. "No, I won't have it. Not her. I don't want her here. Get her out!" She was shaking all over.

"Hush, mother. Stop it!" Dolly spoke sharply, at the end of her tether after the long day.

"Get her out! It's her fault! She killed him! Take her away!"

Anna ran out on to the landing, where she stood leaning against the wall, panting, her knees weak. She collapsed on a chair. The others emerged, frightened, crowded round her.

"What's happening? What's the matter?" Celia went to help Dolly whilst the boys, still not properly awake, tried to comfort Anna.

"Come down to the kitchen, I'll make us all some tea," was Billy's way of dealing with the drama.

The kettle had just boiled when Dolly reported that Celia had taken over. Billy was to take a tray of tea and biscuits up to his mother and sister.

"If Anna can't take her turn then let me. I won't be bullied by you, Dolly, I can deal with death better than you think." Arthur took advantage of Dolly's exhaustion to defy her.

"Oh, all right. I don't care any more, it's all going wrong." Dolly was becoming tearful.

Billy decided to take command. "Dolly, take your tea up to bed. I'll do the shift after Celia and Arthur can go after me. Anna, you'd better take your tea up to bed as well. Get some sleep, you look all in."

Anna was in no state to object. She took her tea upstairs and sipped it slowly as she sat by the window, trying to regain control of herself. Her cases stood unpacked by the wardrobe. She wouldn't unpack them, she wouldn't sleep here, she would leave in the morning. Her anger rose against Betsy, for exposing her to this viciousness. How naïve to believe that rifts could be closed that easily! And she reproached herself for being led into a trap where she was pounced upon, lacerated by wicked teeth.

She lay on the bed, Dolly's bed, fully clothed, trying to work out her strategy. For the first time since leaving London she thought about Charlie. Hadn't Charlie asked her to let her know when she was leaving? That's what she would do. She would write to Charlie, stay with her for a few days if possible. She couldn't go straight back to Paris in this state, she needed a transition to set her right again. As soon as it was light she went down to the study to find writing paper. On the landing she met Arthur, who had just finished his watch. He gave her the faintest of bleary-eyed smiles, neither friendly nor hostile, simply neutral.

Betsy came round early, dropped off by Alan on his way to work. Dolly was asleep, having been persuaded to take the next few days off school. Clara was at last asleep too. All the curtains had been closed, the whole house was plunged into mourning. Celia had gone shopping and Billy had gone to make the funeral arrangements. The weather had changed, there was a light drizzling rain. Fires were lit everywhere except where the corpse lay in chilly shadows.

"I'm moving into a hotel for a few days," declared Anna, as Betsy was taking off her coat.

"Whatever for? There's lots of room here." She was strained and irritable. She wasn't prepared to tolerate capricious behaviour from anyone.

"There's no room at all here for me. I'm not going to argue about it, I'm moving out." Anna was unable to describe the night.

"Oh for goodness sake. Where? What hotel?" Betsy had no knowledge of hotels in the area.

"The nearest respectable one."

"Do you really mean it?"

"Yes."

"Well, Alan will take you, when he comes back here at dinnertime."

Anna would rather have taken a cab, found her own way, but it would be too difficult. Instead she took her sketch book and went walking, stopping to draw whenever the rain eased off. She left the others to explain. She was dripping wet when she returned to he house, to find her bags in the hall and Alan waiting for her.

"I believe you want to go to a hotel," he said. "I know a rather comfortable one not far from here."

They didn't speak as he drove her to a pleasant, ivy-covered place three streets away.

"Do you think this will do?" he asked when he'd pulled up outside.

Anna thought it would do very well. There was a vacant room at the back. It was all clean and comfortable. There was a cosy lounge and a dining room where she could have supper as well as breakfast.

"When are you coming back to the house?" asked Alan.

"I don't know."

"May I bring Betsy round this evening?"

Anna hesitated. "All right."

When he'd gone she sat in the lounge and took out her unfinished letter to which she added the address of the hotel. She put it in an envelope and took it immediately to the nearest post office.

The next few days she was in limbo. She kept away from her parent's house, spending time in the town or in her hotel room. Fortunately the sun came out again, making the days pleasantly warm, though the nights were frosty. She went once to the theatre, where a touring company was performing a translation of a French farce. It made her laugh and reminded her of the Parisian life she knew. Betsy and Alan came by to keep her up with the funeral arrangements. It didn't occur to them that

141

Anna might stay away. She was hoping that in the weeks that followed there would be a reconciliation. She was counting on Anna being near her when the baby was born.

Anna chose not to reveal her plans. As soon as she had a reply from Charlie, she would be off. As far as the funeral was concerned, she still wasn't sure what she would do. She didn't want to be there, yet she was afraid that if she didn't go she would add to the guilt she was already made to feel. In her rational moments she told herself this was unjustified, but she kept hearing her mother's voice shrieking "It's her fault!" Ernest was to be buried in the little cemetery next to the church that had been such an important part of his life.

When the appointed morning came there was as yet no word from Charlie. Anna dressed in black, walked to the house from where they were all to follow the coffin. The hearse arrived before she did, it was waiting at the gate with a series of cabs to take the family out to the country. She stood in the garden until the coffin was brought out and borne carefully down the steps. Wreaths of flowers were piled on top. She joined Celia, Billy, Arthur and Dolly in the second cab, leaving Betsy and Alan, Tessa and William to accompany her mother. After them came uncles, aunts and cousins.

The church was packed with friends. The service was simple, with a few of their father's favourite hymns. The vicar made frequent references to Ernest's contribution to the life of the parish. There was much quiet weeping, but it wasn't until they were at the graveside and earth was thrown on to the coffin that Clara broke down. It was what was expected. As the crowd dispersed Anna noticed a small group standing around Alan and Betsy. Her heart stopped. It was Robin's family. They were looking toward her, talking about her. She ran back to the cab, where she slumped in her seat until her siblings were ready to leave. She was aware of a slight figure passing by, stopping and staring through the window. She looked up. It was Robin's sister. The expression of hatred in the girl's face made Anna's blood run cold.

Anna felt sick travelling back. Upon arrival Celia and Dolly helped her into the house where they insisted she had something to eat and drink. She was surprised that this actually made her feel better. The dining room and drawing room were thronged with chattering guests. Every so often a stranger would come up and say, "Well, Anna, so you've come back." Much fortified, Anna eventually pushed her way to Clara, who was surrounded by well-wishers.

"Mother, I must speak to you in private."

Clara frowned. "Now?"

"Yes, now."

Excusing herself in her grand manner, Clara came with Anna into the study.

"What have you to say then?" she asked coldly.

"I am leaving to go back to Paris."

Clara raised her eyebrows. "What is that to me?"

Anna caught her breath. Clara could still deal her a hurtful blow.

"I thought I should say goodbye."

"Did you? There's no need. You already stopped existing for me."

Anna left the room and the house. A letter from Charlie was waiting at the hotel.

Dear Anna,
You sound as though you're having a very bad time. Please come to stay here. There are always spare rooms. I'll expect you any time in the next few days. Get a cab from Newhaven. See you soon.
    Charlie.

Anna caught the first train she could to London.

Chapter 11
Complications

Charlie was living a curious double life. The day after Charlie and Peter made their pact, Simon called as threatened. Violet came to tea, which was interrupted as usual by Emily constantly coming in to 'see if they needed anything else.' At one point Violet said sharply, "I'm sure we have absolutely everything we could want, Emily." The fact that Simon stuffed himself greedily with sandwiches and cake did not prevent him from going into detail about his forthcoming expedition. Charlie tried hard to look bored, although in fact she was becoming interested in the project. Violet listened open-mouthed, trying to understand why anyone should want to expose himself to the dangers of those awful countries.

'Oh good, she's looking suitably impressed,' thought Charlie.

Unfortunately Simon was fixated on Charlie, not Violet. His eyes were shining with an excitement Charlie feared was not only due to his enthusiasm for foreign parts. What kind of man could be attracted to her? Today she was dressed as severely as possible, she was smoking a cigar, despite Violet's pointed coughing and spluttering. Simon had refused one, saying he didn't smoke, which ought to have put him off her. His roses were tucked away in a corner, whereas vases of garden flowers were ostentatiously displayed.

When at last he stopped talking for a minute to finish his third cup of tea, Violet ventured timidly, "How marvellous!"

Politeness dictated that he should turn to her, if only for a moment.

"What?"

"Your expedition. It must be marvellous to travel, you learn such a lot."

He stared at her.

"Exploration is my absolute passion, Miss Doderill."

She was rebuked.

"Shall I clear away, Miss Charlotte?" Emily was back again, eyes darting from one to the other, assessing what had been going on.

"Yes please, Emily." She addressed her guests. "I'm afraid I have to go out now. I have an appointment with Peter who is going to show me his boat. She heard the faintest tutting of disapproval as Emily picked up the plate.

"May I call again?" He was too eager.

"I'm going to be busy. I have to go to London. If the weather is still good next week, perhaps you could come on a picnic with Peter, myself and Violet.

"It would be a great pleasure."

"Would you mind walking Violet home?" She could think of no good reason why he should do this, so she simply asked the stark question.

"Of course, I'd be delighted to escort Miss Doderill to her door." Anything Charlie wanted him to do, Simon was prepared to do.

Violet, on the other hand, was furious. She still felt discomfited from being treated as stupid. Besides, she knew as well as Charlie, that she was of no interest to Simon.

"Please don't bother. It's not far. I'm used to going alone."

"It will be nice to have company for a change, won't it?" insisted Charlie. "You could show Simon your garden. You'd enjoy that, wouldn't you Simon?"

"Oh, yes." Simon was not a gardener and scarcely knew a hebe from a hydrangea.

Charlie looked at her watch.

"Oh dear, I must run or I'll be late."

They rose awkwardly and took their leave.

As the front door closed, the kitchen door opened. Emily burst into the library, where tea was usually served.

"Miss Charlie, what are you up to?"

"Why nothing, Emily dear." It was better not to share too much with her maid, an inveterate gossip. "Peter and I have quite taken to each other."

"That was quick," said Emily disbelievingly.

"Only as quick as Simon's fancy for me," retorted Charlie, then cursed herself for bothering to enter into a discussion. "I'm going out in half an hour. Please ask Dan to bring the car round to the front."

Emily realised the subject was closed, but couldn't resist asking her mother's opinion. Mrs. Branson, who was more discreet, in the old-fashioned way of family retainers, told her to mind her own business.

Charlie was sensible enough to park her car some way from the harbour, so as not to attract too much attention. The alpaca overcoat with which she covered the oldest clothes she could find, she left neatly folded in the back seat. She wore a skirt and faded jacket, choosing to appear as a woman of modest means, for the time being at least. Since she hoped thereby to attract little attention from the women gutting fish and the men mending nets, she was surprised that they all looked up as the tall confident figure strode past.

"Why is everyone staring at me?" she asked Peter crossly, as he helped her climb aboard 'Lady Louise'.

"I can't imagine. Could it be that however you try to hide it, you look every inch an aristocrat?"

She didn't appreciate his teasing. He didn't look much like the other fishermen either, but he was accepted.

"It took them a long time to get used to me," he said, guessing her thoughts. "Well this is it. How do you like my Lady Louise?"

She liked the boat very much. Peter kept it in good order, making sure the paintwork was always fresh and bright. The nets lay dry and ready for the next morning, their glass floats glittering like so many Christmas decorations. The brass was polished, the engine room spick and span.

"Would you like me to take you out? It's very calm this evening."

Charlie would like nothing better. When they had

passed the harbour, she took a turn at the wheel making for Seaford Head and the Seven Sisters. They spoke little, overawed by the majesty of the white cliffs in the late afternoon sun. At this time of year they had a particular radiance, reflecting the luminosity of the sea below. Land and water shone together under a mellow, golden sky. They stayed out for a couple of hours, experiencing a particular ecstasy.

"Would you like to come back with me for dinner?" asked Charlie as Peter moored 'Lady Louise' to the quayside. "Mrs. Branson always makes too much for me."

"Why not? I ought to change though, don't you think? I'll be along in about an hour. Tomorrow night I'll cook for you, if you would accept to come to my little place. It will be some of the fish I will have caught that morning. After all, you do want us to see a lot of each other don't you?"

For the next few days they did indeed see a lot of each other, becoming more and more easy in each other's company. Charlie loved Peter's cottage overlooking the harbour, he was equally entranced by Vine Place. She had business to do in London over the weekend, when she would stay with George in Chelsea, giving her the opportunity to tell George all about their games, promising to set up a meeting between George and Peter as soon as possible.

The picnic with Simon and Violet was arranged for the following Tuesday. It was a glorious day, with not a breath of wind. Mrs. Branson packed a large hamper of food and drink which would have fed a very large family. Charlie drove them to a place she knew in Friston Forest, a clearing on the edge between trees and downs. She used to ride there sometimes. There was a convenient track near where she could park the car.

"I remember this place," said Violet, as they spread the red and white gingham cloth on the grass.

Charlie had forgotten that she and Violet had ridden here together sometimes when Toby was busy with other things. Reminded of it, she wished she had chosen somewhere else. Too late now.

"I remember feeling really happy here," continued Violet. "We had some good times, didn't we, Charlie? We used to race with each other," she explained to the men. "We could both ride better than poor Toby."

"Violet, will you cut up these roast chickens, please, and put them on our plates? Simon, will you open the wine? Oh look, there's some of Mrs. Branson's home-made chutney and pickles. What's this? A plum tart! And a little pot of cream to go with it! Oh, she is a darling!" Charlie was determined to put a stop to more reminis-cences.

Violet shared the plump birds. "Charlie, would you prefer leg or breast?" she asked. Charlie looked up from her explorations of the rest of the contents of the hamper, caught Peter's eye. She turned, very straight faced, to Violet. "Well, breast actually, if I have a choice." She looked back at Peter and both looked away to hide a smile.

Instead of paying attention to Violet, which Charlie had intended him to do, Simon attacked the food with single-minded concentration, until he was quite replete, when he addressed Peter exclusively, pumping him on his knowledge of geography. As an attempt to demonstrate his own superiority it was a failure, since Peter was very well informed. In his turn he asked Simon some pertinent questions about the flora and fauna of the Amazon basin, which Simon was unable to answer.

'I wish he wouldn't try so desperately to show off,' thought Charlie. 'Does he still think he has a chance with me?'

Evidently he did. Abruptly he changed tactics by being solicitous to Charlie and, as an afterthought, Violet. If he couldn't do well in competition with the man, he would look after the ladies, make them feel good.

'If he goes on like this, even Violet will think he's overdoing it!' Charlie was dismayed at the turn of events. She would have to raise the stakes a little.

"Peter darling, do come and sit beside me."

All the other three were surprised at the sudden familiarity, but Peter obeyed as if it were the most natural thing in the world.

"Violet, you know these woods, why don't you take Simon to the pond where we used to fish for newts? There are at least two varieties there, and caddis flies and all sorts of other things. It's not the jungle, Simon, but there's plenty to interest you."

Although Simon was quite ignorant about the wildlife of the English pond, he was sensible enough not to say so. He would count on Violet being equally ignorant to make up something convincing. He was reluctant to leave Charlie and Peter alone, but what could he do? As for Violet she was greatly distressed by the sight of her cousin settling down so close to Charlie that their bodies almost touched. She sat rooted to the spot until Charlie's meaningful glance stirred her into action.

"Show him the badger set," commanded Charlie.

"That's the other side of the forest," objected Violet.

"It doesn't matter, we have all afternoon," was Charlie's riposte.

Peter remarked that Simon was indeed very keen, as he and Charlie packed up the picnic things. He suspected that at that very moment Violet would be encouraging Simon not to give up, since he, Peter, was a most unsuitable match for any respectable woman.

"She'll be telling him that one day soon you'll realise what a cad I am, so he should hang around." He folded the tablecloth and napkins.

"You don't think she'll fall for him herself?"

"No chance." He buckled the hamper. "I don't sense any magnetism between them, do you?"

Charlie didn't. The magnetism was definitely elsewhere.

"You have to shake the two of them off. We'll be pretty convincing."

"We'll do what it takes. If you're still willing."

What will it take, wondered Peter. How far was she prepared to go? How far was he prepared to go, for that matter?

"Calling me darling was a good start. A few more of those would be an excellent thing. Perhaps even the occasional 'my love'."

That wouldn't trip as easily off Charlie's tongue. She

would save it for a critical moment.

"Leave the hamper here and we'll go for a walk – in the opposite direction from Violet. I'll tell you about my old friend George. I'd like to introduce you."

Thus Charlie set up her two lives. She, Peter, Simon and Violet became a regular` foursome, visiting local beauty spots, dining in country restaurants or in Eastbourne or Hastings, always avoiding Brighton, where she and Peter met George at least once a week. Peter was invited to stay at George's in Chelsea, after the opening of Charlie's play in London, but he declined since the theatre was a part of Charlie's world he couldn't enter. George was pleased to have Charlie to himself for once.

It was on her return from the success of the first night and the excess of the party following that Charlie found Violet waiting for her.

"She's in a bit of a state," warned Emily, waylaying Charlie in the hall. "I told her I didn't know what time you'd be home. She wouldn't go way. She's in the garden."

Charlie's good humour was replaced by apprehension. What was the matter now? Of course Violet was disappointed that the teatime tête-à-têtes the two women had were over, there was no time for them any more. Still she seemed to have got used to the new regime. Charlie looked at her watch.

"It's past tea time. Perhaps you'd better ask your mother to prepare supper for two."

She went out into the garden. Violet was nowhere to be seen.

"Violet! Violet! Where are you?"

After wandering round the rose garden and shrubbery, she heard a cry from the maze.

"Charlie, Charlie, I'm lost."

Silly woman, muttered Charlie. She and Toby had played at losing Violet in the maze when they were children.

"Just stay where you are, don't move!" That's what they always said when they were tired of tormenting her.

She was not far from the centre, which she had never succeeded in finding on her own. She was shaking when Charlie found her.

"What are you doing in here?" Charlie was unsympathetic. "You know you always get lost."

"I thought you might be hiding in here."

"Why should I be? Why should I want to hide from you at all? Come on, idiot, this way." She took Violet's arm. When they were near the exit, Violet grabbed her, pulled her to her with surprising strength, pinning Charlie's arms to her side.

"Oh Charlie, Charlie," she moaned. "I love you, Charlie."

Charlie struggled to break free.

"Violet don't! Stop it! She managed to push Violet away, but the girl was immediately back again, arms round Charlie's waist, head against her breast.

"I can't help it! I keep thinking about you all the time."

This was just what Charlie had been trying to avoid. She grabbed Violet's shoulders, held her at arm's length, looking sternly at her pleading face.

"You don't love me. It's an obsession because of Toby. You would have been happy to marry Toby, I would never have entered your head. You must get over it. I don't love you."

"You could, you could love me, I know you could."

She was so desirable, offering herself in this way. Charlie couldn't love her, she could take her, though, then and there. Violet read her expression.

"You want me don't you? Just kiss me. Kiss me like you did before."

If Charlie was tempted the last words were a warning.

"You were ashamed of our kisses before, you'd be ashamed now. For heaven's sake, your parents consider me to be an unnatural freak."

"They needn't know. We could have secret assignations."

Simple, innocent Violet. Desperate to have her flesh come alive.

"Don't be silly. I've asked Mrs. Branson to make a

meal for us both. Wipe your face, Emily's already dying of curiosity to know what's going on."

"I hate that girl," said Violet fiercely, taking out her handkerchief.

"Don't let her get under you skin. Try to behave normally or I'll have to send you home without any dinner."

Violet made an effort, calming down as they walked back to the house. Charlie gave Emily strict instructions to leave all the food on the sideboard then go home, so they could be quite alone in the dining room. Violet was then able to talk about why she had been so anxious to speak to Charlie at this particular moment. Yes, she found it increasingly difficult to contain the growing intensity of her feelings but she might well have kept silent, if disruptive events had not taken place over the weekend. On Saturday Peter's parents had come with several other members of the local hunt to dine at the Doderill's. They had stayed behind after the other guests had left to discuss with Violet's parents their anxieties about Peter. The latter had not as yet revealed the extent of his involvement with Charlie, nor had he brought her to his parents' house, which would have been a very public statement of intent, and was being saved until deemed necessary. Nevertheless, there had been much gossip in local society about the fact that Peter and Charlotte seemed to be 'walking out together'. It had also been observed how often Violet and Simon were in their company, so Violet was required to give an account of what was happening. Since her grasp of the situation was somewhat confused, this account was garbled. She had always been afraid of her parents, particularly her father, a man of strong views and limited understanding. Her incoherence was such that he accused her of lying, of trying to protect Peter and Charlie in some way. There followed an angry scene in which all the Doderill's venom against Charlie spilled forth – she was a menace to decent people, an evil influence, a spoilt brat who should have been horsewhipped when she was young, to keep her in line. Any man prepared to marry her would need his head examined. Peter's parents were dumbfounded,

Violet was shocked at the depth of the prejudice. Even her mother laid down the law to her sister, Peter's mother, declaring that she should insist that her son break off all relations with Charlie. Peter's mother didn't think it was worth replying that she and her husband had long since ceased to have any influence over their son's actions. Nor would it have been wise to point out that compared with the dubious French woman Peter had been with before, Charlie would be quite a catch. They had almost given up hope of a respectable match for him. Whatever Charlie had done or been in the past, her association with Peter might indicate a change of mind.

When this last proposition was voiced, Mr. Doderill exploded.

"Don't trust that woman an inch! If you can call her a woman. She's a monster, an aberration. Should be put down! Change of mind! She doesn't have a mind like us. Believe me, get him out of it before it's too late. And you," he turned to Violet, "you keep away from her in future."

Violet had fled to her room where she lay sobbing into her pillow.

Charlie was silent during the story of these happenings. When Violet stopped speaking and attacked her lamb hotpot with some appetite, Charlie said, "What are you doing here? I believe your father capable of taking his horsewhip to you, if you disobey him."

She made no comment about her own designation as evil and unnatural. She did not want Violet to see how deeply shaken she was.

"I don't care. I hate him." This was a new, defiant Violet.

"Does he know where you are?"

"Of course not. And I won't tell them where I've been either. I shall come and go as I please."

"You can't do that, Violet. You'd have to leave home."

"Then I will."

She wouldn't, thought Charlie. How could she? She had no money, nowhere to go.

"I'll go to London, work."

"What work can you do?"

"Anything," said Violet vaguely. "You could help me, you have friends in London."

Charlie began to feel as though she was living in a bad dream. Violet was fast becoming her responsibility. Should she help her to change her life completely? Would any help be completely misconstrued? The one thing she was certain of was that she should not allow Violet to seduce her, which would be difficult since she found Violet's present vulnerability charming. Charlie's instinct was to take her to bed, caress her tenderly and give her the moments of rapture she had been waiting for. Instead, she looked at her sternly.

"Violet, you have to be very grown up about this."

Violet opened her dewy eyes wide.

"Grown up?"

"I could help you. I have friends who would find you somewhere to live, even find you a little job, but I can't believe that's what you really want. You've never worked, you have no idea what it would be like. You've never lived anywhere except at home."

"I can't live there any more. I have to get away. They treat me like an infant. You said I have to be a grown up person. I *am* grown up. I won't be told where I can go, who I can see. Oh Charlie," her eyes filled with tears again, "it would all have been all right if I'd married Toby."

Oh no it wouldn't, thought Charlie, although she understood that Violet had been counting on the marriage as her salvation.

"I can't go on living there with them for the rest of my life, I can't." She was beginning to cry again.

"No you can't. You have to find a husband. Almost any husband. What's wrong with Simon?"

"Nothing except that he's in love with you. All he talks to me about is you. And the jungle."

"Can't he see I'm not interested in him? I would have thought I'd made that quite clear."

"He won't give up until you announce your engagement. It's no good, I'm not his type."

"You have to try harder. If you offered yourself to him like you do to me, he wouldn't refuse. Men are simple, Violet, it's easy to make them want you."

"I don't love him. I love you!"

Charlie began to feel angry.

"Well, I don't love you, and there's an end to it. You're, you're," she struggled to find a suitable metaphor, "you're like a beautiful ripe fruit, luscious and tempting. I would like to pick and eat you and be finished. I would make you very unhappy."

"I'm unhappy now."

"Believe me you'd feel far worse if I slept with you and threw you aside. Listen. You have to stand up to you parents. Tell them you are going to do as you please in future. You can spend the night here if you like, there's a bed made up in the red room." The red room was the other end of the corridor from Charlie. "In the morning you go home and face the music. It's the only way to change your life."

They sat for another half hour, discussing what Violet could possibly do to earn a living, should she decide to cut loose. Then Charlie showed her to the red room, where she left her to review her situation.

The night was long for both of them. Charlie sat smoking by her bedroom window. There was no moon, so the stars were even brighter in the cold, clear air. The window was wide open, so she could hear every little sound from outside. A dense, dark silence surrounded the house, as not even the slightest breeze stirred the foliage, and even the friendly owls were not to be heard. Charlie strained her eyes to make out the edge of the shrubbery, half expecting Mr. Doderill to emerge with a shotgun. During the lonely vigil she tried to establish some order in the confusion of her thoughts. To add to existing problems she now had another perhaps even bigger one.

This wasn't really her fault, she argued. It was Toby's fault. He should never have agreed to marry Violet in the first place. Couldn't he see that this wasn't a solution for either of them? Her anger with her brother gave way to a wave of grief stronger than she had yet experienced.

How she missed him. She shouldn't have let him go through with this charade. It was her fault, then, after all. Instead, she was busy with her own petty affairs. What was a play compared with real life? She should have left Paris; taken her brother by the shoulders and said "Don't do this." She had abandoned him. If she was lonely now, it was nothing to the loneliness he experienced that fateful night. She even fantasised that he had thrown himself into the channel to be nearer to her, but that was ridiculous. Anyway, he was a grown man, she had always looked after him, he had to look after himself, make his own decisions. It was his mistake not hers, and now they were all suffering – Charlie, Violet, Violet's parents, all suffering because of Toby. She, Charlie, had been honest, whereas he, Toby, had trapped himself in a web of lies. A web of lies, she realised with horror that she was in the process of constructing just such a web. There was nothing honest about her present scheme.

So it went on until first light, when she went down to the kitchen to make tea and toast for herself and Violet. She always made her own breakfast these days. None of the Branson family came on duty until 10 a.m. Violet must be gone before then with the red room restored to pristine order. As it happened the bed was unruffled, Violet having spent the night, like Charlie, sitting in a chair by the window, fearful of her father's sudden apparition. She was pale, dark circles around her eyes.

"I've been thinking about what you said Charlie." Violet was drinking cup after cup of hot sweet tea to warm her up. "I'm not fit to work. London terrifies me. I tried to imagine what it would be like, living in a city amongst strangers. I couldn't"

Thank heavens for that, thought Charlie.

"But I'm so frightened of going home. Will you come with me?"

"Don't you think that will make matters worse?"

"You're brave and strong. I'm not."

"You've already taken the first step by spending the night away." At least she'd done that, the first act of rebellion in her life.

"I'm not going to stop seeing you."

"Good." Another act of rebellion. She was making progress.

"I don't care if he beats me."

"Violet, has you father ever beaten you?"

"No."

"Then I don't think he'll start now."

There was a ring at the door. Both women were startled. It was only 7.30 in the morning. The bell rang again insistently.

"Oh no, it's him," Violet began to shake.

Charlie went to the front door. There stood Violet's mother.

"Is Violet with you?" she asked.

"Yes." There was no point in lying.

"I'd like to speak to her." The tone was not aggressive.

Charlie considered. Looking at her, Charlie saw how like Violet she was. She had a similar vulnerability. She was expecting to be opposed.

"Come in," said Charlie.

Violet was on her feet, hostile, defensive. She had been prepared for her father. She and her mother faced each other for a minute before Mrs. Doderill opened her arms wide.

"I'm sorry," she said.

It was enough. Violet was there in an instant, and the two of them wept, holding each other tightly.

"Don't go, Charlie," Mrs. Doderill begged.

They all sat down.

"I expect Violet's told you what happened." This was a statement rather than a question.

"Yes."

"It's all been too much for us, you know. Toby's death, the wedding cancelled."

"There's no need to explain. I understand." Charlie wished she'd go, taking Violet with her.

"He shouldn't have lost his temper like that. I told him. I said you'll drive your only daughter away. He's not a bad man, really."

157

That's a matter of opinion, thought Charlie. He was certainly a bully. She remembered that both Mrs. Doderill and her sister were considered extremely lucky to have found wealthy husbands, coming themselves from a family of modest means. Their looks were their fortune, since they were far and away the best-looking women in the county. Their glamour made them a status symbol, as they grew older they were afraid of losing their power, becoming more and more acquiescent to their husbands' demands.

"He's calmed down now." She turned to Violet. "He's promised to forget the episode when you come back home."

"I'm not going to stop seeing Charlie," declared Violet.

Mrs. Doderill was embarrassed. "No, well, we'll talk about that later."

"I'm not going to stop seeing Charlie. She's my friend. She's my only friend now Toby's dead." Her voice didn't falter, even on the last phrase.

"Yes I know, dear. You all played together all the time, when you were children." The 'when you were children' relegated the relationship firmly to the past. "We need to have a long talk, you and I. There are things we must discuss."

"I'm not going to stop seeing Charlie, and there's an end to it." Violet was exceptionally definite.

Mrs. Doderill looked appealingly at Charlie. It was a look she must have used on men many times. Could she really expect Charlie to explain why she was a pariah? All right, she would.

"Violet, what your mother means is that I have such a reputation for my disgraceful conduct that any woman who associates with me will be contaminated. No man will ever want you, no man will ever trust you. You will be doomed forever to lonely spinsterhood. Isn't that it, Mrs. Doderill?"

Mrs. Doderill blushed scarlet to hear her fears put so succinctly. She was unable to look Charlie in the face.

"And now, if you don't mind, I have affairs I must attend to. Mrs. Branson will be here soon and I would

rather not discuss personal matters in front of my staff."
This was Charlie at her haughtiest. Deviant she may be,
she was still on the highest rung of the Sussex social
ladder, looking down on the Doderills far below. Violet
and her mother were dismissed.

As she escorted them to the front door, Charlie added,
"Don't worry, Mrs. Doderill, I have every reason to believe
your daughter's virtue is still intact. Violet, remember that
we had organised an outing with Peter and Simon for
tomorrow. I shall understand if you stay away. Good
morning." And she closed the door behind them.

As soon as they were all out of the way, she drove
down to Newhaven harbour. Peter would return from his
morning's fishing about 10 o'clock. She needed to know
his version of events, if he even had one. She parked
her car in the usual place, called good morning to Peter's
friends, who smiled and waved back. It was a grey, misty
morning, with a damp chill which struck through to the
bones. The sea was flat, featureless, the horizon line invisible. Charlie sat on the quayside, shivering slightly, until
'Lady Louise' came into view.

"Charlie, you look frozen," was Peter's comment, as
he moored the boat. "Here, have a swig of this." He took
a flask of rum from his pocket. She found it very strong,
but it was true that it was instantly warming.

"Here's the door key," said Peter. "Go up to the house
whilst I deal with the fish. It was a great catch today.
Make up the fire, put the kettle on. I'll be with you
soon."

Charlie was glad of the warmth of his cottage. The
embers were still lively so she added a good shovelful
of coal. When Peter saw her by the cheerful blaze, the
teapot warming and the kettle singing on the hob, he
grinned broadly.

"How comforting to return home to 'la femme au
foyer'!" Louise was never prepared to be 'la femme au
foyer', the woman in the home. He was teasing Charlie
again, she couldn't have looked less like a housewife in
her tweeds, holding a cigar.

"Have you had breakfast?"

"Some time ago. With Violet."

"Ah!" was his only response to that information. "I'll wash and change, then you might be hungry enough again to join me in some bread and cheese."

When he reappeared, fresh and clean, Charlie found she was quite ready to eat a chunk of the crusty bread. They sat easily together, until Peter pushed his plate away.

"I hope you had a good weekend," he said. "With people who have their priorities right."

"I wouldn't say that." Charlie remembered some spiteful scenes at the first night party. "They just have different reasons for being jealous and vindictive. I take it your parents had a go at you?"

"Sort of. They left me a note whilst I was out, saying they urgently needed to see me. I guessed it must be something to do with you, so I went for Sunday lunch. Very good it was too. I don't bother with such things myself, but once in a while roast beef and roast potatoes and the rest are a treat. But I guess you don't want to know about the food." He took out his pipe, began the long process of separating the tobacco, packing the bowl. Charlie waited patiently. He lit up, sucked hard to get it going.

"As you know, I was already given up for lost. So any kind of marriage to a girl of the right class, especially one with land and money, is good news rather than bad, even if that girl's behaviour had been even more scandalous than mine." The pipe went out. He went through the process of lighting it again. Charlie took out another cigar. "They aren't stupid, my parents. They guess Mr. Doderill is furious that your enviable estate is coming to our family not his. Damn this pipe, I don't know what's the matter with it." He knocked out all the tobacco and started again. "You see, Charlie my love, it's as much about money as about morals."

Was that what it was? In her complete financial security Charlie had never considered cupidity to be the primary motivations for public posturing. Nor had she and Toby ever experienced the kind of sibling rivalry Peter was suggesting between his mother and Violet's. So her estate was more important than her lifestyle? She felt somehow disappointed, as if her individual stand counted for nothing in the end. The only thing that mattered now, it would seem, was who she married, not who she had been to bed with. And who she married was only about which lucky family won her land.

"So, do you want to have done with this pretence, or shall I take you to meet the parents?"

Charlie realised they were at a turning point. To proceed further along the road of engagement would raise the stakes considerably. To announce that she and Peter were just good friends would open the door to other suitors, convinced they might have a chance.

"The decision is yours. But whatever happens, I don't want to lose your friendship." Peter spoke with unusual emotion. Charlie was touched. She needed to know someone close by was concerned for her. To others Peter might seem a bad lot, to her he seemed a good man, a man she could trust. If she were ever to marry, it would be a man exactly like Peter. It would be Peter! She had grown increasingly fond of him. They understood each other. She frowned.

"I think our friendship is the only thing that makes my life here tolerable."

They had begun to talk to each other about other friends, past loves. It was a comfort to him to describe parts of his life with Louise, whom he still missed, it was an immense relief to Charlie to take him to Brighton, to know he enjoyed George's company. They needed each other, they supported each other, respected each other's difference. An engagement would mean even more time spent exclusively together. It was an agreeable thought.

"Would it be too terribly unfair to get engaged?" asked Charlie.

Peter shrugged. "Engagements can last a long time. They can be broken honourably. Not without disappointment, of course, but it happens."

"Then take me to meet you parents."

Peter smiled. "That's what I hoped you would say."

They were both inexplicably very happy.

Peter's parents were charmed by Charlie and surprised by the affection the couple displayed towards each other. They presumed that all wild oats had been sown, that the defiant pair had grown at last into responsible adults, that both were aware that the production of an heir should not be left much longer. They offered to give an engagement party, which would be an impressive affair. Perhaps the beginning of November would give them ample time to organise the event and for their guests to order presents. The mention of presents made Charlie feel guilty, but she supposed they could all be given back. Peter's mother took her son aside to show him an elaborate ring in rubies and diamonds, which was her grandmother's. She had looked at Charlie's hand with her slim fingers and thought it would fit. His father had serious talks with him about estate management, assuming, quite rightly, that Charlie would rather leave these matters to someone else.

Having done his best to prevent the union, Mr. Doderill accepted defeat. Violet had screwed up her courage to tell him that she would continue to be friends with Charlie, which after all appeared quite natural if Charlie was engaged to Violet's cousin. Mrs. Doderill gritted her teeth when she congratulated her sister on her news. The official announcement was to be made at the party, but the county grapevine ensured that everyone knew long beforehand. Charlie wanted George to be added to the guest list, but he was horrified at the idea.

"Are you sure you know what you're doing?" he asked anxiously, over a so-called celebratory supper at Wheelers.

"No," replied Charlie, "But we'll make it fun."

George looked questioningly at Peter. He was far from sharing Charlie's complete trust in this man.

"You won't hurt her, will you? She's very precious to me."

"Hurt her!" Peter looked offended. "No, I won't hurt her. She's quite precious to me too."

"And I'll try not to hurt him, either," chipped in Charlie.

"Nobody's going to hurt anybody, George."

George didn't pursue the matter, but at home alone, he remembered Toby telling him of his engagement to Violet, which George had condoned. The three glasses of whisky he drank before going to bed failed to keep the nightmares at bay.

The trio's meeting with Anna in Brighton had taken place shortly after Charlie's introduction to Peter's parents, during a period of time when everyone seemed relatively happy. Peter was enjoying an approval his parent s had not accorded him for years, the Doderills held their peace, Violet began to entertain a hope that she and Charlie might have a better chance of a secret affair, even Simon took comfort from the fact that Charlie and Peter were both interested in his next expedition to the point of offering generous financial support. When Charlie received Anna's letter, contrasting her own situation with that of the young artist, she was immediately sympathetic. She would give Anna a break, take her out of herself. Here she might even create a confluence of the two streams of her existence by persuading George to join them all on an outing or two, to keep Anna company, thereby extending the usual foursome, which was becoming rather boring, and bringing George to Finborough Place. She put the proposal to him in Chelsea, where she was staying overnight after a discussion with the director about a possible rewrite of a scene in her play. The evening had been irritating, Charlie had refused to rewrite, since the play had worked very well in Paris. Other things were more important at the moment, she turned all her powers of persuasion on George.

"If you join us, Anna will be more comfortable, not so much an outsider," she argued.

"I don't want to come to Finborough Place and I don't want to meet Violet." George was, nevertheless, beginning to find the proposition interesting.

"I won't introduce you as a friend of Toby's, just an old friend of mine. Oh do come, please. You're such good company and Anna could do with cheering up, poor thing."

George contemplated her seriously, before smiling mischievously.

"All right. For you darling, just for you. I would do almost anything you asked, except do not, do not ask me to be your chief bridesmaid. I don't look good in frills."

"You are an idiot! And I'm not getting married!" Charlie laughed.

Aren't you? thought George.

For the first time, on the train back to Brighton, Charlie imagined what marriage to Peter might be like. They were very harmonious. She saw them sitting in the library, smoking, talking, enjoying a companionable silence. The bedroom was another matter. They could have an arrangement, give each other latitude to have sexual adventures. She shook herself. For goodness sake! She was not going to get married.

Chapter 12
Anna comes to Finborough

Anna didn't have the courage to go to Finborough Place right away. Arriving in Brighton in early evening, she went straight to a hotel, where she went to bed immediately and slept for twelve hours. She woke much refreshed but still with a persistent headache. Not having eaten the previous evening, she ordered a large breakfast, which she found she could hardly touch. The first mouthful made her slightly nauseous. She began to have misgivings. After all, she hardly knew Charlie, to accept her invitation had been clutching at straws. In this frame of mind, she wandered aimlessly around the streets, along the promenade. Finally, she spent a couple of hours sketching the pier, until the thickening clouds made her feel cold. Walking back to collect her luggage, the smell of fish and chips turned her stomach.

She was too weary to take a tram or train to Newhaven. She had enough money for a cab all the way. The driver, who was not familiar with Finborough Place, had to ask directions when they arrived in Newhaven Town. The wind had risen as they drove along the cliffs bringing darker clouds and driving rain.

"It's a mighty big place you're going to," said the cab driver as they left Finborough village and turned into the drive through the park.

The sight of the imposing building did nothing to calm Anna's fears. If she hadn't been so cold and tired she would have asked the driver to take her back to Brighton. He piled her cases on the doorstep, she paid him and he drove off highly satisfied. She rang the bell. Emily opened the door.

"Good afternoon. I'm a friend of Charlotte's. I think she is expecting me." Anna hoped this was true.

"Oh yes, miss. There's a room ready for you. I'll get my brother to take your luggage up. Come on in, you look frozen." Emily was, of course, curious to know exactly who the newcomer was.

"Miss Charlotte is in London today. She said she wouldn't be back until later, but there'll be some supper for you."

"Thank you, I'm not hungry. I'm a little unwell. Would you mind showing me straight to my room? I need to lie down for a while." The headache had become worse.

"Yes, miss. Just a minute." Emily disappeared into the kitchen where Anna heard her talking to her mother. She reappeared.

"Mum's going to tell Dan about the luggage. She'll bring you some soup up."

"No thank you. I couldn't eat anything." She was feeling giddy.

It took a great effort of will to follow Emily to the violet room, one of the prettiest rooms in the house. When the maid returned to the kitchen, Anna collapsed onto the bed, her teeth chattering. She drew the eiderdown around her and closed her eyes.

For some hours she drifted on the borderline of consciousness. Unable to lift her head, she was dimly aware of people coming in and out of the room, of whisperings, or maybe she imagined it all. A clearer voice called her name.

"Anna, Anna, are you awake?"

Painfully she turned her head, half-opened her eyes. There was a nightlight burning on the dresser, her cases were standing by the wardrobe and a figure was leaning over her. Where was she?

"You look awful." A hand was placed on her brow. "You're very hot. You must have a fever."

Who was this person? One of her sisters?

"Mrs. Branson tells me you've had nothing to eat or drink."

Mrs. Branson?

"I've brought you a drink she prepared. Some old country recipe made from roots. It's probably disgusting but it will do you good."

This was said with a briskness which suggested a nurse. Did she need nursing?

Charlie realised that anxiety had made her sound brusque. She said more gently, "Do you think you could sit up, old thing?"

Anna closed her eyes again and turned away. She most definitely couldn't sit up.

Charlie was nonplussed. She wasn't much use in a sickroom. She had been surprised to find Mrs. Branson still in the kitchen when she came home late. Upon learning of Anna's condition she asked her housekeeper if she could possibly spend the night at the house. Mrs. Branson, a sensible soul, had already foreseen that eventuality. She had taken the liberty of asking Emily to fetch her nightclothes.

"You could sleep in the room next to Anna's, if you don't mind," Charlie had suggested. "Do you think I should call the doctor now?"

Mrs. Branson's opinion had been that they should wait until the morning, but that meanwhile, if Anna could take a drink, it would help her.

Charlie sat cradling the steaming bowl, gazing at the patient. This was not what she had planned. The flushed cheeks, the dark hair tumbling over the pillow, called to mind a dying heroine of a romantic novel. Surely Anna didn't have consumption? She had looked healthy enough in Paris.

"It really would be better if you drank even a little." Charlie's tone had recovered its firmness. She put down the bowl, placed one hand under Anna's head and with the other pulled up the pillows. She picked up the bowl again, leaned over, drew Anna's head towards her and placed the bowl to her lips.

"Just a few sips."

Anna swallowed with difficulty. However, she made an effort to finish the drink because the feel of the hand behind her head was inexpressibly comforting. In spite of the dizziness caused by being raised at all, she was sorry when she was laid back down.

"Good girl. I'll leave you to sleep now."

Sleep she did. When she woke in the morning and tried to sit up, the nausea and dizziness returned, but her mind was clearer. In the early morning light the room looked dove grey. Sick though she was, she appreciated the tasteful harmonies of soft pinks and mauves chosen by Gaby, when she took the redecoration in hand. This was Charlie's home! She remembered driving in the cab, being shown up here. Oh how unfortunate, how humiliating to fall ill! She wished she could get up and go away. Charlie probably already had a poor opinion of her, now she would think she was totally useless. Her eyes prickled, tears began to run down her cheeks. She had a vision of herself and Betsy, small girls in bed with a chill, with a fire burning and Clara sitting reading to them, all tender concern. She wanted her mother! The tears rolled faster. She wanted her mother, but her mother had pushed her away!

There was a gentle knock on the door. Anna held her breath. Clara! Clara had come to care for her after all. The door opened, and a plump, middle-aged woman smiled down at her.

"I'm Mrs. Branson, Miss Charlotte's housekeeper. How are you this morning?" Her expression changed, looking at the tearful face. "Oh there, there, dear. Nothing's that bad!" She wiped Anna's cheeks with a corner of her apron.

"I'm so ashamed," whispered Anna

"Ashamed! Nonsense! Would you like some porridge?"

The thought of the grey, glutinous mass made Anna's gorge rise. She shook her head, which increased the pain between her eyes.

"Well, if you've a fever you'll need to drink. I'll make you some herb tea. You ought to get out of those clothes and into a nightdress. May I look in your cases?"

Without waiting for permission she searched through Anna's luggage until she found two or three lawn gowns.

"Aren't these pretty! You must have got them abroad. Come on, I'll help you change. Oh my, your clothes are wringing wet! And the sheets. I'll have to fetch fresh ones. You can't sleep in those."

She left Anna on a chair, a woollen blanket round her shoulders, whilst she went to find clean linen. Anna wanted to say "Can't you see I'm dying? Leave me alone." Instead she obeyed as far as she could, without resistance.

The bed remade, Anna was helped back in. The new sheets smelled of lavender. She was grateful for their crisp coolness. Whilst Mrs. Branson was off to make the herb tea, her patient drifted into a doze, which was disturbed when the tea arrived, brought not by Mrs. Branson but by Charlie. The colour of Anna's already flushed cheeks deepened.

How fragile she looked, was Charlie's first thought, seeing her guest more clearly than she had in the candlelight the previous night. So easily breakable.

"Charlie, I'm so sorry, forgive me." The tears came into her eyes again.

"Nothing to forgive you for. We'll soon have you right as rain," was Charlie's cheerful response. "Here, Mrs. Branson says you must drink this. I'll call the doctor this morning to have a look at you. Can you sit up?"

Anna suddenly remembered the hand behind her head.

"I'll try."

"I'll help you."

Again Anna experienced the special quality of Charlie's touch, perhaps the gift of healing. She allowed herself to be lifted gently and held whilst she drank Mrs. Branson's concoction. The well-being which flooded through her more than compensated for the nausea. When the drink was all gone, she looked into Charlie's eyes and gave her a smile of incredible sweetness.

"Thank you."

Charlie's heart stopped still. She became acutely aware of the soft roundness of the shoulders cradled in her arms.

"It's a pleasure," she said, gruffly, as she cautiously withdrew her support.

The doctor's opinion was that Anna was suffering from a bad feverish chill, brought on by cold and exhaustion. It could easily have turned into pneumonia, if it hadn't been caught in time. He prescribed lots of fluid, light food when she felt better, warmth and rest. There would be no need for him to come again unless there was an unforeseen crisis. He approved of Mrs. Branson's herbal remedies, recommending that they should be administered morning and evening. He assumed that Anna would be able to stay at Finborough Place for two or three weeks.

"She can stay as long as she likes," Charlie assured him.

Anna was appalled.

"I only meant to stay for two or three days, not weeks," she protested. "This is an awful imposition."

Nevertheless, she was also relieved to be resting in a place where she would have to do nothing, amongst people who would make no emotional demands. She was still prone to weeping for no apparent reason, her body lacked strength and her mind was unable to concentrate for long.

It was Emily who unpacked her clothes and hung them in the wardrobe, with exclamations of surprise.

"Oh my word! Isn't this fancy? And what about this? It's got a bit of the old ooh, la, la, about it, hasn't it?" She was fingering a fitted blouse in purple satin and lace, which Anna had added at the last minute, hoping to shock her family by wearing it one evening. Used as she was to serving at grand dinner parties, Emily had seen nothing like it in her life.

"Are you an actress?" she asked.

"I'm a painter."

"I thought you must be theatrical." Emily knew a painter, the wife of a Brigadier who lived in Alfriston. The lady in question didn't look like Anna, nor did she ever dress in such clothes.

Charlie explained that unfortunately she had previous commitments which would prevent her from spending

as much time with Anna as she would like. She hoped
that as Anna grew stronger she would be able to join
her and a group of her friends for outings together. She
debated with herself for a long time about what to tell
Anna with reference to the engagement. She would have
to say something. Should she pretend it was for real or
tell the truth? She guessed Anna would have heard lots
of stories about her in Paris. So she prevaricated until
the patient was well enough to get up and eat downstairs. To celebrate this step forward Charlie asked Mrs.
Branson to prepare an especially light and delicious supper, to be eaten tête-à-tête.

"This is lovely!" cried Anna.

Not as lovely as you are, thought Charlie. Indeed, Anna
had taken great care with the way she dressed, after
spending so much time in nightclothes. In her turn, Anna
found her hostess extremely handsome. She must paint
her!

"By the way," she said as Charlie helped her to a plate
of chicken consommé, "A friend of yours called on me
just after you left Paris. Adrienne."

Charlie spilled a little soup on the tablecloth.

"Oh, yes?"

"She refused to believe you weren't there. She rushed
into the bedroom before I could stop her."

"I'm sorry. She shouldn't have bothered you." This was
annoying. Charlie certainly didn't want to spend the
evening talking about Adrienne.

"She didn't bother me exactly. It was interesting.
Especially as I'd seen her only a few hours before in
your play."

Charlie was surprised. "Did you understand it? The
play, I mean."

"Not at first. More and more as my French got better.
I saw it several times."

This was even more surprising.

"Adrienne is very pretty. Very . . . " Anna searched for
the right word, "vivacious."

"Highly strung," said Charlie, briefly. "Let's talk about
something else. Adrienne is my past."

Anna digested this remark. This was Charlie's past. What was her future?

"I'm getting engaged," said Charlie, very suddenly.

That was not the future Anna would have imagined.

"I was with my fiancé." Her voice faltered slightly over the word, "when you met us in Brighton."

Anna remembered the two men clearly. The fiancé would not be the one who talked about coal miners.

There. Charlie had said it. As if she meant it.

"It's not official yet. We're announcing it at a party in November."

This is unbelievable, thought Anna.

"Congratulations," she said.

Charlie was startled. Anna was the first to use that word, doubtless many others would repeat it. What did it mean? Did it mean, well done, she had achieved every woman's aim, secured a man to be hers for life? Anna had responded knowing nothing about Peter, he was a man, any man, a husband to be. This was not a matter for congratulations. She should be congratulated on writing a successful play, perhaps in seducing a very desirable woman, but not on hooking a man.

Anna was thinking that in the end like paired with like. What she knew of Peter from the one meeting was enough for her to put him in the same stratum as Charlie. He was a relative of Gertrude's after all. She was sad, disappointed. Her manner changed from teasing to reserved.

"Will it be all right for me to continue renting your house in Paris?" she asked.

"Of course, why shouldn't it be?"

"You might want to give it up if your life in Paris is over."

"I didn't say that."

"I thought that's what you meant."

"Not at all."

Charlie would not give up her life in Paris. Even if she were to be married, which was not the case, she couldn't be confined to Sussex, to England.

They continued their meal in strained silence, except

for the odd polite remark from Anna about the excellence of the food. When they had finished Charlie suggested they adjourn to the library where Emily had lit a fire. Anna could concentrate more on reading now, so she could browse through the books. However, she excused herself, saying she was tired. So Charlie was left on her own, feeling rather flat.

Anna's gradual recovery of strength put Charlie in a dilemma. It would be rude to abandon her guest for too long, on the other hand she did not want to neglect Peter with whom she had been spending an increasing amount of time. Until Anna felt ready to go out then Peter might come over to Finborough Place more often. Usually the two of them preferred to relax in his house or Vine Place. She put the idea to him. He hesitated, more conscious than Charlie that he would have to play the part of lover, not good friend, in front of this stranger. With Violet and Simon the need was no longer as imperative, although Simon still harboured a lingering hope that until she was actually married, Charlie might change her mind. As time went by he nevertheless paid more attention to Violet, who was beginning to blossom as a result. A sharp-eyed newcomer would detect a lack of passion in Peter's attentions to his so-called sweetheart. In fact, he did love her and she was beginning to be very fond of him. She was careful never to present herself as she had at the party when they first met, even when she met his parents she looked severe rather than feminine. So the deepening affection was that of soul mates, not lovers.

"If I come to tea with this woman, will you hold my hand, even kiss me?" he asked.

"Is that necessary?" Charlie opened her eyes wide.

"I believe that's what lovers do, isn't it?"

"I'll hold your hand. I'm sure that will be enough. You don't want to kiss me any more than I want to kiss you."

I wouldn't mind, thought Peter. He didn't insist.

Mrs. Branson took the opportunity to spend a whole day baking, for this was no ordinary teatime. Violet,

Simon and George were all invited. Peter was to fetch George, so that they would arrive together. He understood George's reservations about the house that had dictated the pattern of Toby's life.

"I hate this place and I'm sure it hates me," said George, upon their arrival, staring at the grand façade. It was more frightening than he had imagined.

"It's only a pile of stones," said Peter, taking him firmly by the arm, but the day was overcast so the pile of stones was a forbidding grey, solid with the weight of establishment, frowning down upon a flighty upstart, who was quite outside its tradition. George would have fled without Peter's vicelike grip.

Once inside the entrance hall he felt better. Charlie and Gaby had replaced the sombre furniture and rugs with something brighter, more adventurous. There was lightness, colour and risk. Also as soon as he and Emily set eyes upon each other, there was an immediate rapport – he winked at her, she responded by ever so briefly sticking out her tongue.

Simon and Violet were already waiting in the drawing room where tea was to be served. Charlie had gone to fetch Anna, who had been sketching the view from her bedroom window. Peter introduced George as one of Charlie's London friends.

"Ah, Miss Doderill," said George as he took Violet's hand. "You were to be married to Toby, were you not? I met him. He was a charming man. I'm so sorry."

There was something in his tone made him instantly antipathetic to Violet. His manner towards Simon, on the contrary, was such that the latter experienced an immediate attraction.

"I hear you've already met this woman who's staying with Charlie." Violet addressed Peter.

"Briefly."

"What's she like?"

"Divinely beautiful." It was George who answered.

Violet gave him an 'I'm not talking to you' look.

"Rather reserved." This was Peter's view.

"A bit bohemian, I expect," continued Violet.

"Aren't we all darling!" George knew he shouldn't have said that. Simon put his hand to his mouth to cover a smile.

"Unusual, I would say," replied Peter.

At that moment Charlie came into the room with the topic of their conversation. Unusual indeed. Anna was still sensitive to cold, so she had a woollen shawl adorned with enormous flowers of red, green and purple thrown over a plain dove-grey blouse, tucked into a purple and green striped skirt just long enough to show her ankles clad in red stockings. Her slippers were Turkish leather. Violet's jaw dropped, George clapped, Peter raised his eyebrows appreciatively and Simon was transfixed.

"This is Anna," said Charlie.

Emily stopped in the doorway. She was about to ask whether she should serve tea. Instead, she uttered a strangled gasp and ran back into the kitchen where she proceeded to have hysterics. She couldn't go back into the drawing room, she told her mother, she just couldn't, so Mrs. Branson herself waited on them, being of a more phlegmatic disposition than her daughter.

It was a very odd occasion. Conversation was stilted, most of the cakes and sandwiches were untouched, as Simon was the only one with any appetite. In fact he devoured the rich gingerbread slices with such rapidity and gusto that Charlie asked him if he would like to take some home with him. He was tempted to say yes, though he realised she was being sarcastic. Violet couldn't stop staring at Anna, who she thought was the most extraordinary female she'd ever laid eyes on. Peter had been right, she was beautiful, but she had no dress sense whatsoever, and Violet was glad that she herself was wearing a beige dress she had recently bought in an exclusive shop in Eastbourne. Peter, too, was mesmerised. There was a compelling contradiction about this woman - her outrageous self-presentation, combined with an unmistakeable warning not to touch.

"Charlie tells me you had a grim time in the Midlands," he said sympathetically.

"It was difficult." She was not going to be drawn out on the matter.

"I thought the Midlands were grim anyway, aren't they. Potteries and factories and things?" This was Violet.

"I know some Midlands cities. Birmingham, Coventry, Nottingham, for example. Nottingham's quite an industrial place. Lace making and bicycles. And of course all the coalmines around." Simon spoke with confidence.

Oh, not coalmines again, thought Anna.

"Emily's christening robe was Nottingham lace," was a totally unexpected intervention from Mrs. Branson as she cleared away. Violet was scandalised. But then, the housekeeper wasn't used to waiting at table, so she wouldn't realise that servants were always invisible and never, never joined in a conversation.

Anna wished she had pleaded a bad headache, to avoid what seemed to be a tedious waste of time. Charlie had described the others to her before she met them; Anna now realised they were as boring as they sounded. And they stared at her as if she were an exhibit in a zoo. She decided to ask some questions of her own, dispensing with the formality of surnames.

"Do you know Paris, Violet? No? What a pity! You've never been out of Sussex? Now that's a shame, there's such a lot of world to see. Simon, I understand, on the contrary, that you'd rather live with savages than in civilised society? Sorry, did I get that wrong? Peter, are you going up to Derbyshire for Gertrude's birthday party? You could take Charlie with you, Gertrude would just adore her." And so on. All she said to George was "I'm pleased to meet you again," sensing that in some ways he and she were two of a kind.

At six o'clock the party broke up, with the usual parting formalities. They would all go on a trip to Rye together at the weekend, if Anna was well enough to go out. Simon walked Violet home, not before agreeing to meet George in Brighton, to talk about George's newly discovered interest in South American culture. As he waved goodbye to Simon from Peter's passenger seat, George caught a glimpse of Emily's brother Dan standing near the shrubbery. The handsome youth gave him food for thought.

"Are you worn out? Won't you come into the library for a while? We would be much cosier." Charlie searched Anna's pale face with some concern.

"Just a short time. Yes, I am rather beaten."

Stretched out on the library sofa, she scanned the rows of leather bound volumes.

"I suppose these all belonged to generations of your family."

"Most of them, yes. All the interesting ones are in my room."

"You have some extremely interesting books in Paris." She smiled as she said this. Her French had improved enough for her to understand some of Gaby's more titillating descriptions. "Don't you miss Paris? It's so different here." She paused. "*You* are so different here."

Charlie shrugged. "Do you like Peter?"

Anna considered for a time before answering. "Yes, I do. Is he a good lover?"

Charlie was shocked at her directness. Yet Anna had first met her in a milieu where such questions were normal. She tried to be nonchalant.

"Of course. I wouldn't be marrying him otherwise, would I? Doesn't he look as though he'd be a good lover?" It was a question she had never asked herself.

"Yes," Anna sounded unsure, nevertheless. "He's handsome."

"So you approve?"

Anna said, "Does Gaby know you're engaged?"

"I haven't corresponded with Gaby for a while. She's busy with her new husband."

"Husbands, especially new ones, demand a lot of attention. Have you told any of your Parisian friends?"

"No. It's all very recent?"

Charlie was distracted. Anna's shawl had fallen off and her head was thrown back, emphasising the long line of her delicate white throat. Her hair was loosely knotted at the nape of her neck, stray dark tendrils around her brow. The grey of her shirt accentuated the deep blue of her eyes, almost violet in the soft, diffused light. She was languid, open.

"Isn't Violet rather a bitch?" was Anna's next remark.

"She's unhappy. She was my brother's fiancée."

"Oh!" Anna sat up. "You didn't tell me. You just said she was a neighbour."

"I didn't want to confuse you with details before you met her."

It was hardly a detail, thought Anna. So far, Charlie had told her very little of the circumstances of Toby's death and Anna didn't press her.

"He died the night of their engagement party."

"How dreadful!" There were beginning to be terrible resonances in Anna's mind.

"It was a bad scene." Charlie was looking down at the table. Her voice was unsteady. In spite of this she went on. "He fell off the cliff. I suppose he was drunk." She turned right away, eyes still lowered.

All Anna's preconceptions about her hostess fell away. In front of her sat not a wealthy landowner, nor a successful writer, but an orphan, all alone in the world, without even her brother. She rose from the couch, knelt beside Charlie, enfolding her, laying her head on Charlie's breast, whispering, "Oh Charlie, oh my dear Charlie." An instinctive gesture of comfort that came from way back when her siblings were small and hurt.

Charlie felt the warmth of Anna's body against hers as an electric shock. "Don't!" she cried. "Don't! Don't feel sorry for me!" She pushed Anna away and walked towards the window.

Anna was shaken. The embrace had been so spontaneous when her heart went out to Charlie's wretchedness. She stood up quickly, white-lipped.

"I'm sorry." She picked up her shawl, drew it tightly around her shoulders. She was humiliated. It was so rare that she would reach out in that way. Charlie's expression was closed against her, as Clara's had been. Her head began to swim, everything went black and she fell in a faint. Charlie caught her before she hit the floor.

The blackout lasted only a few minutes. Charlie had managed to lay her back on the couch. When she opened her eyes again Charlie was looking down at her with an expression Anna found unreadable. "I've poured you a glass of brandy," she said. "If you sip it slowly it will make you feel better. Then I'll ask Emily and Mrs. Branson to help you upstairs. I expect it was all too much, all at once."

She didn't say she was sorry, nor did Anna apologise again. She took a couple of sips of her drink and shuddered.

"I think I'd better go up now, if you don't mind.

Charlie rang the bell.

"My goodness, what's the matter with you both? You're as pale as death!" Emily looked from one to the other. Anna's clothes no longer made her laugh.

"Please ask your mother to help you to take Anna upstairs."

"Yes, miss." Emily was back almost instantly with her mother.

"Oh dear, I hope it isn't anything you ate! It was all fresh."

"No, I'm just not very good yet."

Charlie watched the two women almost carry Anna away. Her mind and body were in a turmoil. She paced agitatedly up and down, before deciding to go out for a walk. She asked Mrs. Branson to stay until she returned, then set off along the cliffs, down to the beach, only starting back when it was almost dark.

Chapter 13
Confusions

Anna spent the next few days in her room. She had another visit from the doctor, who recommended quiet and rest. Nervous exhaustion was a serious matter, he said. Being wise and experienced he diagnosed her troubles as having deep roots, making recovery more difficult.

"Keep warm," he said. "Sleep as much as you can, eat well and avoid any kind of agitation."

Mrs. Branson and he discussed a suitable menu and he approved her recipes for soothing herbal drinks to be taken at bedtime. His parting words to Charlie were: "Take very good care of that young woman. She has a strong, healthy body, but I'm afraid there is some sickness in her mind." Then, because he was a man who believed in God, he added, "or perhaps a wounded soul."

A wounded soul, how can I take good care of that, wondered Charlie.

Especially as she was afraid she may have inadvertently touched that wound. Maybe the best way to help Anna heal was to stay away from her, as she was disturbed by her own responses. So she chose books for Anna to read, sat and chatted about nothing for an hour or so, which was as much as either of them wanted for the time being. Anna read, sketched and slept – a deep, mercifully dreamless sleep, most of the time. Only once, the night after the tea party, did she wake sweating from a nightmare in which Robin's destroyed face turned into that of her father, who became her mother, who jerked upright like a jack-in-the-box, laughing spitefully.

Having lunch with Peter and George, Charlie wanted
to know what they made of her guest, after a second
meeting.

"She's a winner," was George's verdict. "Bring her up
to Chelsea. There are lots of my friends I'd like to introduce her to."

Peter was more guarded.

"There's something about her that is very . . . provoca-
tive," was all he said.

"But that Violet – what a little madam!" Naturally,
George saw nothing good about Toby's fiancée.

"She'll have you into bed with no bother if you don't
watch out, darling," he warned Charlie.

"I do watch out, all the time."

"Now Simon, well!" He dissected his lemon sole and
removed the bone. "Definitely to be had."

"Look, I'm trying to fix him up with Violet."

"Waste of time, my love. Oh, this muscadet is excellent!" George drank deeply.

"He's been pursuing *me*, so there's nothing to stop him
trying with her." Charlie was annoyed at the categoric
classification.

"Isn't there? Look at her, look at you!" He gave a meaningful glance at Charlie's cavalry twill jacket and cravat.

"You're the nearest thing to a man he could hope to
marry. After all, you are supposed to be in the marriage
market, and he probably thinks he would be a more suitable husband than Peter. He might even fancy you in
bed, which, let's face it, Peter wouldn't do." The friendship between them all had reached the point where he
could be honest. "Would you?" he challenged.

Peter was trying to decide how to respond.

"If Charlie and Violet were standing naked in front of
you, which would you go for? It would be Violet made
you stand to attention, wouldn't it?"

Don't be too sure, thought Peter. Aloud he said, "This
is not a conversation I want to have in front of a lady,"
which he knew sounded absurd.

George wanted to riposte 'That's no lady, that's my
best mate,' but Charlie was looking surprisingly uncom-

fortable, so he simply said, "Oh pardon me," and attacked his chocolate pudding.

Charlie's discomfort was caused not by what George had asked but by another image the question brought into her mind – a picture of Violet and Peter standing naked in front of her, Charlie. She would envy Peter's lean form, his hard shapely muscles, but Violet's soft fullness, the gentle curve of her belly . . . Charlie drained her glass. "It's time to go." It sounded like an order.

Anna not being well enough to take part in the planned excursion, George suggested that if she liked he would keep her company that day. He didn't mind coming to Finborough Place, once the ice was broken by the first visit, but he had no desire to put up with Violet for long, and he was wooing Simon in private. There was an innocence about the young explorer he found appealing, so he was treading carefully. Anna was beginning to be bored. It wasn't warm enough for her to sit outside, otherwise she would have found plenty of inspiration for drawing in the grounds. The prospect of an afternoon with George was therefore welcome, he would be a breath of fresh air in an atmosphere which was becoming oppressive. The coolness between her and Charlie made her sad. Since she didn't understand the cause, she could do nothing to change it. The violet room was her retreat, a place that was beginning to look like a studio, with piles of sketches and some half-finished detailed water colours. There was a large table, several chairs and even a small sofa as well as the bed, so she asked George to come up to her corner of the house rather than going down to the library.

"Isn't this delightful!" he cried, looking round appreciatively. He took in every detail of the furnishing, nodding his approval. "May I?" he stretched a hand towards Anna's sketches.

He didn't know what he'd expected but he was surprised by her obvious skill. He spent a lot of time in London galleries and had a large collection of bold works. He was particularly impressed by the studies Anna was intending to use as the basis for oil paintings. He asked her questions which revealed his own knowledge, so that she in her turn was agreeably surprised. As they talked they discovered common acquaintances on the London art scene. Next time Anna was in London, she should stay with him in Chelsea, George insisted. He would like to see more of her work, perhaps he would visit her in Paris, which would be an adventure, as he'd never crossed the channel. Conversation ran on easily, they felt totally at home with each other.

"I'm so glad Charlie bullied me into coming up here to meet you." He paused. "It has helped me a lot."

Anna waited for a further explanation. None came.

"I suppose you met Charlie through the theatre," she said.

George wondered how much he should tell her. Seeing her friendly, sympathetic expression, he decided to be honest.

"No. I picked her and Toby up in Brighton. I was Toby's lover."

Anna began to understand.

"I'll never love anyone like that again. I was totally swept away. He was so beautiful, so good, so . . . well, I can't describe him. He was Toby, that's all." He turned away.

"Violet," asked Anna gently, "what about Violet?"

"He didn't love her. He just felt he had to marry her."

"Charlie has only just told me about that awful accident."

"Accident? Charlie knows it wasn't an accident."

His round, boyish face was drawn, haggard, the hurt in his eyes was unbearable. Without thinking she might again be rebuffed, Anna took him in her arms. She too desperately needed that embrace. They held each other, rocked each other, making inarticulate soothing noises, for George sensed her pain too. When they pulled apart they still held hands.

"Stay as long as you can, Anna," said George. "I think we need you."

Returning from a tiresome trip, when everyone seemed on edge, Charlie found the two who'd stayed at home quietly absorbed in looking at a volume of reproductions of Fra Angelico's frescoes. She was unreasonably put out by their closeness.

"Not too worn out, Anna?" she asked. "I'll take George home now."

"I feel refreshed," asserted Anna. Her appearance bore this out. Her cheeks had more colour, her eyes had more sparkle, than when Charlie left.

"Peter's downstairs, he's staying for supper. I don't suppose you'd care to join us, in that case?"

"Why not?" Anna was anxious to become easy with Charlie again. She had learnt so much that afternoon.

"Of course you're welcome to stay too, George." This was a polite, rather than pressing invitation.

"No dear, I'm already a bit late." He would have taken the hint, even if he hadn't arranged to meet up with Simon and some friends later.

"Peter's in the library. I won't be long." Charlie wanted Peter and Anna to get to know each other better.

As it happened, Charlie was stuck behind a herd of cows for at least half an hour before she even reached Newhaven. She and George didn't exchange many words, since he was always wary of her when she was in a grumpy mood. She cursed the innocent beasts wending their way to be milked, especially since she had to get out and crank the car before it could start again. George's attempts to pacify her being met with a snarl, he lost himself in a reverie.

Peter had mixed feelings about being left alone with Anna. He didn't find her easy, as they appeared to have very little in common, apart from his cousins, whom he had always considered rather odd. At the same time he was totally fascinated. This afternoon she was softer that he remembered. There was no hostility. Her smile had warmth, her movements expressed no tension. She sat opposite him in a dark blue woollen dress, the exact colour of her eyes. She was the loveliest thing he had ever seen. He was tongue-tied.

It was Anna who made the opening remark.

"Did you have a nice afternoon? I'm sorry I couldn't join you. Perhaps next time."

"I hope so. We missed you." This was sincere. "You would have brought new interest. We don't have much to say to each other any more. I don't mean Charlie and me, we are very happy on our own."

"Of course. You're in love." As she said this, she looked at him and saw the desire in his eyes. "You're going to announce your engagement soon, aren't you?" she added.

"Yes, I'm afraid there's going to be a big do to celebrate it. You will still be here in November, won't you?"

"Good gracious, no. I shouldn't have been here now. I must get back to work."

"What kind of paintings do you do?"

Anna sighed. The usual unanswerable question. "Recently flowers. And people." She knew that would bring to mind delicate watercolours, but so what?

"My lover, Louise, liked to draw. She drew me sometimes, but she always said it was no good. I never saw the results, she threw all her sketches of me away. Tore them up and burned them, in fact." He remembered their agonising battles before she left.

Anna studied his large head, his compact body. He was sitting with easy grace in a large armchair. "I don't think you'd be too difficult to draw," she said. "Would you like me to try?" She had a sudden urge to show him what she could do. Her afternoon with George had restored her to herself

He accepted the invitation gladly. He didn't mind sitting still, he was like an animal, relaxed when at rest, ready to spring into action whenever necessary. Anna moved around him, sketchbook in hand, to find the best point of view. "Turn round to look at me," she ordered, drawing up her chair. She liked the twist on his body and the angle of the jaw. He watched her quick, deft movements, the way she tilted her head and narrowed her eyes. There was a particular thrill in being exposed to her keen gaze, the object of her scrutiny. He was aware of a detached professionalism absent from Louise's frustrated attempts.

"You may talk, if you wish," said Anna, "until I concentrate on the mouth." This was unusual in a man, she thought, well shaped and full. "You have exceptionally good bone structure, " she commented. "I would like to do a bust of you, but that takes a lot longer and I have no materials here."

"You sculpt as well?"

"Nothing big. I prefer carving with wood."

"I have picked some wonderful pieces of driftwood," said Peter. "I've polished them and some of them I've already built into larger pieces by adding bits of net and pebbles." They were scattered around his garden. He'd never thought of pointing them out to Charlie.

"That's interesting," said Anna. "Objets trouvés in themselves can be marvellous, but it's fun to make them into something else."

"Would you like to see them? Charlie could bring you to my place."

"Yes, I would. Now please keep your mouth closed for a bit. I've nearly finished. It's rough, but I think I've caught something."

She worked for about ten minutes more before putting down her pencil. "There. You're a good subject. Look. You can keep it if you like it. Or maybe I should give it to Charlie."

He did like it, he liked it very much. Now they were both more at ease she asked him about Louise, curious that he had a tempestuous French mistress. Encouraged by her interest, he opened up, presenting himself as passionate brokenhearted lover.

This man isn't right for Charlie, thought Anna.

Peter had a sense of losing his footing. He had felt Anna's power. She was beginning to remind him of Louise as she had been when they first met. Although Louise's beauty had been more unconventional, there was a similar flame inside, ignited in Anna again after being quenched for two years.

"You two look very cosy," observed Charlie, finding them absorbed in each other. She was out of sorts, cold and tetchy. Her prepared greeting – 'I'm sorry I've been so long' – seemed totally irrelevant. It was rather as if she might be an unwelcome interruption.

"I could do with a hot dinner. I'll ask Mrs. Branson to serve it immediately."

Even two helpings of jugged hare failed to revive Charlie's flagging spirits. Her dark mood affected the other two, destroying the peaceful atmosphere they had established. Peter said he had to go home as soon as they'd eaten.

"Charlie, you might bring Anna to tea with me tomorrow, if she's up to it," he suggested, giving his fiancée a peck on the cheek.

"If you want." Charlie almost scowled.

"A demain, alors," said Peter to Anna.

"A demain, peut-être," she replied, with a smile.

Charlie escorted him to his car.

"You seem to have quite taken to her," she said.

"Yes, I have," was all he replied. "Goodnight, I'll see you tomorrow afternoon."

"A demain alors," she shouted as he drove off. Her accent was much better than Anna's.

"So what do you think of the man I'm to marry?"

Anna was still sitting at the dining table, looking pensive.

"He's nicer than I thought." She wondered whether that was an adequate response.

"He's a good chap." Realising there was an apparent lack of enthusiasm in this, Charlie added "I've become awfully fond of him."

Anna wondered whether this was classic British understatement or whether there was no more than great fondness between them

"He was telling me about the woman he used to live with," she ventured.

"Oh, Louise? She led him a merry dance," said Charlie, with feigned casualness. She was startled that Peter should have broached private emotional matters so quickly.

"Yes," was all Anna said. She was studying Charlie, now seated opposite her. The lift of the chin, the hard set of the mouth, the slight narrowing of the eyes, were difficult to reconcile with a woman in love and loved.

She appeared to have withdrawn into her own thoughts for the moment, tensely flexing her fingers.

Charlie could not look at Anna, who had a particular radiance that evening. I shouldn't have invited her here, she thought, she'll only cause complications.

"I'm glad you're getting well," she said.

"So am I. I won't be a burden to you much longer, I hope,"

"You should know that you are welcome to stay as long as you like."

You don't mean that, thought Anna, you're just being chivalrous.

"Please don't feel obliged to take me to Peter's tomorrow, if you don't want to."

"Why shouldn't I want to?"

"I don't want to intrude on your times alone."

"He doesn't mind or he wouldn't have asked you."

"You mind, though, don't you?"

"Not at all."

Oh but she did, very much. Her face belied her words.

In that second of unguarded misery in her eyes, Anna glimpsed a profound loneliness. She wanted so much to reach out again, to cut through the barrier of pride.

"Charlie," she said softly, "I'm sorry you don't like me, because I like you very much."

Then Charlie did look at her, at the slender form in the soft blue dress, at the perfect features, the open lips, into the depths of the violet eyes.

"I like you," she said gruffly. "I'll go and make you infusion that Mrs. Branson insists you still need before you go to sleep. I shall turn in myself soon. I've had a tiresome day." She rose and strode into the kitchen.

Anna blinked back tears of disappointment.

The next day was bright and unseasonably warm, so Anna decided to get up and have a walk round the grounds. She put coloured pencils and a sketchbook in a bag and set off to the top of the slope behind the house, where she would be able to command a long view of the landscape. Arriving at the summit slightly breathless, she found a convenient stone seat. She gazed across the undulations of the downs towards Lewes, the county town of Sussex. The air was so clear that details of distant cottages were quite distinct. The shape of Finborough village with its church and inn held her attention. She was absorbed in the kind of drawing she hadn't done for some time when someone spoke, close by.

"Oh, I didn't think anyone would be here. There's never anybody here!"

There stood Violet. They had been hidden from each other by a clump of shrubs, as Violet had climbed up from the opposite side of the hill nearest to the Doderill farm. Neither of them knew quite what to say.

"Would you like to sit down?" asked Anna eventually, closing the sketchbook. "I was just leaving." This was certainly not true, but she stood and brushed down her skirt.

"Don't go because of me. I can see you were busy." Violet turned to retreat. She was more tentative than the previous time they had met. Anna sat down again.

"Please stay, Violet. I really will need to go down to lunch soon. We didn't have much opportunity to talk the other day."

Violet only hesitated for a moment. The seat was wide, four people could have sat there comfortably.

"I come up here most days when it's fine," said Violet. "Nobody minds. Toby and I used to sit here and talk about changes we would make to the park. She sounded wistful rather than tearful. "We had so many plans. I don't expect Charlie will do anything much. She'll be too busy writing plays. And Peter won't care, he'd just let things go to rack and ruin. He's very irresponsible, you know," she added, primly. "This marriage is very unfortunate in many ways." She sounded so much like a maiden aunt that Anna found it hard to keep a straight face.

"They appear to suit each other," she proffered, gently. Violet made a noise which could only be described as dismissive.

"I don't think so." She glanced sideways at Anna. "Charlie and I are very old friends. I think I know what suits her." There was a certain smugness in her expression. "You haven't known her for long, have you?"

"No, not very long. But I've heard a lot about her from mutual friends. In Paris," she added, tempted to assert some sort of superiority over this strange person who was part little girl, part old-fashioned spinster.

"Oh, Paris! I expect she's finished with all that." (What did she imagine by 'all that', wondered Anna.) "I suppose you're dying to get back there, though. Life here must be very dull for you."

"I'll leave as soon as I can."

"You won't be here for the engagement party?"

"No."

"I am going to help organise it. At least it will all still be in the family. When they get married Peter will still go off fishing, I imagine. I'll keep Charlie company. I'm looking forward to that." She gave a secret, sly smile.

She really is rather odious, thought Anna. "I'd better go down for lunch," she said. She started down the slope, then turned. "By the way, Peter has asked Charlie to take me to his house this afternoon, to look at this driftwood collection. You've seen it often, of course?" She suspected that Violet had never been to Peter's house.

"Er . . . yes, of course." Violet was not a good liar. She felt deflated as she watched Anna walk away.

The sky clouded over in the afternoon, bringing a damp chill to the air.

"Are you sure you want to come out?" Charlie asked Anna anxiously. Upon receiving a definitely affirmative answer, she sought out all the car rugs she could find.

"You should be warm enough now," she said as she tucked Anna into the passenger seat of the car.

Anna enjoyed being coddled.

"That's very snug," she laughed.

Please don't look at me like that, thought Charlie.

She was uncomfortably aware of Anna's body next to hers, as they started for the fishing village. All the more so since Anna would occasionally turn towards her with exclamations of delight at some particularly charming bit of the road. The discomfort gave way to a warm sense of well-being, however, so much so that Charlie began to wish the journey was much longer. Every so often she glanced at her companion's profile, happy to see her eyes sparkling and her lips parted with pleasure. She nearly swerved into a hedge when she found Anna looking back, for she too had been observing the fineness of the profile beside her. For a while after that they both stared at the road ahead.

Charlie parked the car in the usual place, a street away from Peter's cottage. She insisted that Anna keep the warmest blanket around her shoulders, like a great shawl, because now a strong wind had blown up. She held her firmly as they rounded the corner, afraid that in her delicate state she might be blown over. Shielded from the more violent blasts by Charlie's tall athletic form, Anna meekly allowed herself to be led. They arrived at Peter's huddled together like refugees.

He sat them down immediately by the fire. It was not a day for lingering in the garden, unfortunately, so the examination of the driftwood sculptures had to be postponed. Watching Anna unwrap herself from her layers of clothing, taking blankets and scarves from her, he experienced a similar shock to when she had entered the library in her blue dress. This time he felt the warmth of her body on the wraps and she was discovered to him like a jewel in layers of protective tissue. Sitting there as her simple self in a blouse and skirt she seemed to add a special light to the room. Outside the wind began a threatening moan.

"Oh dear, that sounds bad," said Charlie.

"Unexpected," said Peter. "Sometimes at this time of year a gale blows up from nowhere." He was thinking that they ought not to have set out on such an uncertain day, but he was very glad they had.

As her host busied himself preparing the hot drinks, Anna looked round the room approvingly. It was clean, ordered, bare compared with most rooms she had known, yet the size and shape, the black leaded range with a kettle on the hob made it feel very familiar. She was scrutinising one of three pictures on the wall opposite when Peter placed the teapot on the table.

"That is a view of the harbour from the upstairs window," he informed her. "Louise felt confident enough to have it framed. The other two are of villages in France, painted when we were on holiday the year before she left.

She had a delicate but sure touch, thought Anna. There was a freshness, a concern with overall impression rather than detail. "They're rather good," was her verdict.

They talked about the particularities of watercolour painting, about the challenge of changing light, about the problems and delights of working outdoors, for Peter too had tried his hand at capturing the moment in a holiday sketchbook. Anna persuaded him to show them, perceiving when he did a latent talent.

"You know, these have something," she said, lingering over two attempts at describing the sunrise in the bay. "Don't you agree, Charlie?"

Yes, Charlie agreed. She had seen Louise's painting on the wall without ever asking about them. To her they were just one part of the setting Peter had created for himself. She had never thought to ask who did them, nor had Peter thought to tell her. And she had no idea that Peter himself dabbled in these things.

The gale was beginning to acquire almost hurricane force. Peter took them up to the tiny attic room with its dormer window overlooking the channel. Way out as far as they could see, each dancing wave had a white crest. The breakers crashed against the harbour wall sending spray flying high into the air.

"I hope there aren't many boats out there," said Peter anxiously. "I'd better be prepared. I'm a member of the lifeboat team," he explained. "The ferry won't be able to get into the port if this goes on."

Charlie remembered a trip where she had spent nine hours tossing on a rough sea, to be turned back finally to France, even though they were tantalisingly close to the English coast. She was very worried, having envisaged driving home whilst it was still light. She was never happy driving in the dark and she was uncertain how her motorcar would behave in high winds. Most of the country road was protected by hedges and trees, but these brought a danger of falling branches. The exposed stretches were even more treacherous.

"You can't leave now," said Peter firmly as they descended the stairs into the kitchen.

"How long will it be before it blows over?" asked Charlie.

Peter shrugged. "Who knows? Maybe an hour or so, or it may go on all night."

Charlie gazed at him, horrified. All night!

"You really can't go out in this. If it gets any worse you would hardly be able to stand up in the street. I have a spare room where you could sleep, if necessary. It wouldn't take long to make up the bed."

The prospect of sharing a bed with anyone except a person to whom she had just made love was anathema to Charlie. Her expression communicated something of this to Peter.

"Or one of you could have my bed and I could sleep by the fire. It might be better if I'm to be on the alert."

If Charlie had been alone, she might have risked the journey. Her sense of responsibility for her fragile passenger made her accept the wisdom of his arguments. He had enough food to provide them with a delicious supper of a large plaice caught that morning. They were all excited by the crisis, stimulated by the extraordinary circumstances. All formality disappeared, as they shared the preparation of the food, the clearing away. Afterwards they exchanged tales of adventures from their childhood, most of Peter's being stories of his boarding school days. Charlie found consolation in recalling her wild escapades with Toby, reliving a happy period of their lives. A surprising number of her reminiscences involved Violet. Anna's childhood, surrounded by so many siblings, fascinated the other two. Encouraged, she no longer had inhibitions about describing the tension between her passion for the beauty of the woods and fields and her hatred for the ugly, smoky redbrick of the mining communities. It was midnight before, in the natural pause between their narratives, they realised that all was silent.

"The wind's dropped," said Charlie. "We can go now."

Peter opened the door. Every cloud had blown away, leaving an inky-black star-studded sky with a half grown moon reflected in the now gently swelling water.

"You could still stay." He envied them the drive through such a night. He would feel curiously bereft at their departure.

"I'd rather get going. Would that be all right with you, Anna?"

Please say no, wished Peter.

"Yes. It will be fun."

Peter gathered up all her blankets and scarves, handing them to her one by one.

"Thank you so much for you hospitality," she said, reintroducing a more distant politeness, as she tied a red muffler round her neck.

"It's been a great pleasure." The way he looked as he said this told her the remark was not pure politeness. "Come again whenever you like. You haven't seen the garden yet."

"I will." She smiled and put out her hand. He wanted to kiss it, but shook it instead.

"Thank you for looking after us so well." Charlie was standing outside.

"You know I will always look after you, my love."

There is a falseness there, thought Anna. Aren't they going to kiss each other goodbye?

Peter put his hands on Charlie's shoulders and kissed her lightly, on each cheek, in the French style.

"Drive carefully . . . darling."

Charlie grunted. "You know I always do," forgetting he'd helped pull her out of a ditch.

He watched their two figures in the flickering light of the streetlamp, Charlie shortening her usual stride to keep pace with the other woman.

He went inside, built up the fire and poured himself a glass of rum. His senses were aflame. There would be no sleeping.

Charlie drove very carefully indeed, partly because she wanted to take as long as possible. Neither she nor Anna spoke, for they were too enthralled by the quiet of the night to utter anything commonplace. It was enough that they could hear each other breathing, softly, evenly. They no longer needed to look at each other, they had seen each other in the soft lamplight, at some profound level they had recognised each other. Now in the darkness they listened and through the layers of clothing, their bodies touched.

When they came to a halt at Finborough Place and Charlie turned the engine off, they sat for a long time. Then Charlie said, "We'd better get you to bed. You must be exhausted." Never had Anna felt so alive. In spite of this she went straight to her room, whilst Charlie prepared her herbal drink.

"Won't you stay awhile?" she asked when her medicine was delivered. She was wearing a silk kimono in turquoise and gold, not yet in bed.

Charlie stood looking down at her, an unfathomable expression in her eyes.

"No, I think I'd better not," she said. "Good night."

"Goodnight," Anna sighed.

Chapter 14
Revelations

The next morning, Charlie received a letter from Gaby. She was expecting a baby. It was a long letter in which she described all her fear, joy, doubts and hopes for the future. For the moment she was content with life in the country, surrounded by all kinds of animals, some of them injured wild creatures she was nursing back to health. She did foresee a time, however, in the very near future when she would need to refresh herself with the bustle of Parisian life, see all her friends.

And you, Charlie, she wrote, *when are you going to tear yourself away from Anglo-Saxon society? Have you become addicted to tea? Or beer? I do miss you, you seem a very long way away. Tell me all your news. I hear nothing because I have not told many people my address. We lovers had to be alone and undisturbed. Now my darling husband has discovered he has work to do (administrators can be so boring) and I have begun my next novel. My darling Charlie, I think of you often and compare your grand house with this rather ramshackle castle I'm living in, where there is no clear border between the gardens and the farmyard, where the hens come in for breakfast and the ducks quack outside my turret bedroom every morning to tell me night is over. Will you come to Paris? Or, better still, visit me here? I miss you very much.*

Charlie missed her too. She sat down to write an immediate reply, but when she picked up her pen she wasn't sure what to say. She had several attempts, littering the floor with screwed-up pieces of paper, each one covered with a different version of her present circumstances, none of them honest. Exhausted with the mental effort, she settled for a short note.

Darling Gaby,
How wonderful to hear from you. And you are to be a mother! Congratulations! May I be a godparent or whatever? I'm afraid I won't be able to come to France before Christmas because I'm very busy here. I'll explain, but not now, it's too complicated. You probably didn't know my artist tenant is over in England and staying with me. I'll give her presents when she goes back, for the baby No, I'll wait until it's born, instead I'll send a gift for its mother. Do look after yourself,
All my love,
Charlie.

Reading this through the words 'reserved' and 'British' came to mind, especially setting it beside Gaby's outpourings. Too bad, she thought, as she sealed the envelope.

Anna's writing table was also covered with discarded sheets of paper, drafts of a letter to Betsy. She knew how much she had hurt her sister by running away at a time when Betsy would dearly have liked her to be beside her. It was absolutely clear to Anna that she was not needed, that there was no point in exposing herself to humiliation leading to frustration and anger, in trying to accommodate Betsy's dream of a happy reunited family, into which to bring a new generation. The anger was there each time she tried to explain, anger at having to account for herself and her actions. She strode up and down her room. Should she write at all? Shouldn't she make a total break again? By lunchtime she had given up and decided to get her pencils together for an afternoon sketching in the rose garden. Recently she had been waking to visions of the canvases left behind in Paris. She could work later on flower studies made at Finborough Place, especially as some of the rarer blooms had an exquisite sensuality. In spite of the lateness of the season there were still plenty of bushes in flower and the afternoon promised to be warm.

Just before twelve o'clock Violet and Peter arrived almost simultaneously. Peter had driven up as soon as he had dealt with his fish and had a shower, anxious to find out whether Anna and Charlie had arrived home safely. Violet was in a state of high excitement over a huge elm tree which had blown down across the roof of the stables during the night. Three of the horses had been badly injured and had to be shot. There had been a dreadful crash, they had all been awake most of the night. Her father was in an awful temper, her mother kept bursting into tears, so Violet escaped as soon as she could.

Mrs. Branson had no difficulty in producing a meal for two more. All attention was centred on Violet as she recounted the drama, relishing every detail, turning the narration into a performance with a captive audience. When she stopped and began to eat, she was able to observe that there was a subtle change in the relationship between the other three, a deeper intimacy expressed in the way they looked at each other.

"Of course you took Anna to see Peter yesterday afternoon, didn't you, Charlie? Fancy having to drive home in that wind! I'm surprised you weren't blown over." Her raised eyebrows indicated a question.

"We waited until the wind dropped," was Charlie's terse response.

"But that was quite late in the night." Again this was a question.

"Yes."

There was a finality in this which prevented Violet from continuing this line of enquiry, so she returned to her own story, adding bits she'd forgotten the first time round. It was so rare for her to be able to take centre stage in this way, she wanted to prolong the moment as long as possible. When she had dredged up every detail, she said,

"My father wanted to know if he might come over to see you some time soon."

"What for?" asked Charlie. Mr. Doderill couldn't possibly have anything good to say to her.

"I don't know. I daren't ask. He's terribly upset you know." She paused to help herself to some more treacle tart. "We all are. They were lovely horses. Two of them belonged to other members of the hunt who were stabled with us. The other was my father's favourite thoroughbred, Flashman."

Charlie knew the horse well. He was a fine big creature, brave and loyal. His master had been proud to own one of the best hunters in the county. For the first time in her life she felt sorry for Mr. Doderill.

"Tell him to come this evening before dinner at six-thirty. But Violet, make it clear that if there is one word of criticism about my behaviour, then I'll never, ever speak to him again. He will be banned from my house."

Violet wasn't sure that she could convey this message to her father, although she promised to do so.

They all parted company for the afternoon, Anna to the rose garden, Charlie to her room to do a few rewrites she had promised for the new actress taking over the leading role in her West End production. She had prevaricated until the last minute. She was to see the director and the actress concerned the next day. Peter went to tea with his parents and distant relatives who were visiting. He felt particularly unprepared to act out the part allocated to him, since he had no doubts about his growing attraction to Anna.

At six-thirty sharp Emily showed Mr. Doderill into the library where Charlie was waiting. His forced smile and firm handshake showed he had not come to attack.

"Please sit down," invited Charlie. "Would you like a glass of sherry?"

Yes he would, thank you very much. And the cigar she offered next. He seemed to be having some difficulty in opening the conversation.

"I'm so sorry to hear about your disaster last night," Charlie began. "It is a great loss."

"Yes, it is," agreed Mr. Doderill. "A very great loss." He sipped his sherry. "Flashman is irreplaceable. He and I understood each other."

Could there possibly be tears in his eyes?

He drew on his cigar.

"The other two were fine horses. Excellent stock." He sipped his sherry again, nervously. "It was a great loss in more ways than one."

Charlie tried to guess what was coming.

"Of course you can use my stables, if you like, whilst yours are being rebuilt."

The stables at Finborough Place would need a bit of cleaning, that was all.

"Thank you. That's very generous of you. I might well do that."

"We don't have stable boys any longer. I don't think Dan is so good with horses, so you'll have to send your own staff over."

"Yes, of course."

"Would you like another glass of sherry?" Charlie noted that after the initial sips he had drained his glass in one go.

"Thank you." He looked at her warily. "I should have had that tree cut down. It was diseased. I knew that, I just hadn't got round to it. There are several others in the same state, not far from the house. It's a costly business getting them felled. So, in a way, it could be said to be my fault this happened, I suppose."

This is something else, thought Charlie. "You mean the owners of the two other horses will hold you responsible?"

"Perhaps." He frowned. "They were very valuable animals."

Charlie was beginning to understand why he had come, but she wanted him to suffer at least some embarrassment, so she said nothing.

Mr. Doderill cleared his throat. "You must realise, Charlotte, that Violet's proposed marriage to your brother led us into various expenses. As our two estates would be one, your family fortune shared by Violet, we felt secure in making certain investments. We were encouraged by your brother, who would indeed have been happy for me to manage his affairs."

Oh would he, wondered Charlie.

"He more or less promised to back us up in whatever we decided to do."

Oh did he, thought Charlie.

"You see his tragic death put us in a somewhat precarious financial position. Very precarious in fact."

Go on, thought Charlie, ask me to lend you money. Or maybe you expect me to give it to you. There was a long silence. Mr. Doderill knocked back his second glass of sherry. Eventually, he cleared his throat and spoke.

"So given these circumstances, I imagine you might see your way to helping out."

"Helping out?" Charlie was determined he should be specific.

"With some money." The words stuck in his throat.

They looked at each other. Charlie could have said that she would never give, or lend, money to a man who despised her, called her unnatural, an abomination, to this red-faced blustering yeoman farmer who had been counting on extending the boundaries of his territory and increasing his bank balance well beyond his own earning capacity. To him Toby had been an economic windfall, not a person. He had been all greed, now he was desperation.

"How much?" she asked him.

He hesitated, a glint of hope in his shifty eyes.

"Ten thousand pounds."

Charlie's fortune was such that such an amount would scarcely be missed.

She spoke slowly, deliberately.

"I will have my lawyer make out a document giving that amount of money as an interest-free loan to Violet. As far as repayment is concerned, there will be no pressure, as long as we all live in harmony." She had no idea whether such a condition could be specified in a legal document, but no matter. She knew he would be infuriated and that was what she wanted. Let his pride suffer from permanent indebtedness not only to herself but to Violet.

"Is that acceptable?"

There was no reply.

"Is that acceptable?"

He looked as if he wanted to strike her.

"Yes," he growled.

"Then we'll shake on it. I'll make arrangements tomorrow morning."

His hand was hot and sticky. He squeezed her cool fingers as if he would break them.

"Now, if you'll excuse me, I have work to do." She rang the bell. Emily appeared so immediately that she must have been listening at the door.

"Please show Mr. Doderill out."

"Yes, ma'am."

"And Emily, come straight back, I want to speak to you."

Emily returned to the library almost bursting with suppressed excitement.

"Under no circumstances are you to tell anyone, and I mean anyone at all, about the conversation that has just taken place." Charlie was at her most severe.

"What conversation?" Emily was all innocence.

"Don't take me for a fool." This was said very sharply. "If I find out you have breathed a word of this, you will be instantly dismissed. Is that clear?"

Emily realised this was to be taken very seriously indeed, so not even Mrs. Branson was made party to the agreement made that afternoon.

It took Charlie until dinnertime to write out instructions to her lawyer. She thought about the wording very carefully, so as to give Violet some power of her own, some liberation from the domination of her father. As she sealed the envelope, she realised she didn't know what she was doing, and not for the first time compared the constraints of life here with her life in Paris where she was so much in control.

"Did you have a good afternoon?" she asked Anna, as they ate their meal.

"Rather frustrating," was Anna's reply. "I was very dissatisfied with what I achieved. Not in the right mood, I suppose. Instead of the roses I was drawing, I kept seeing images of those poor frightened horses. It was all very upsetting, wasn't it?"

"Yes it was."

They didn't say much else. They had just finished desert when Emily announced Peter's arrival.

"Show him into the library," said Charlie. "And bring a bottle of the old tawny port. A glass will do us all good."

It was unusual for him to call round at this time.

Emily hesitated.

"He said he wanted to talk to you alone, Miss Charlotte. He's a bit . . . flustered."

Charlie looked at Anna.

"I'll go to my room," said the latter. "I'm tired anyway. I'm already too much in the way. You two must have so much to discuss. Goodnight." There was a palpable absence when she'd left the room.

Flustered was not a word Charlie would have chosen to describe her visitor. Agitated would have been more precise.

"Charlie, I have to talk to you," his voice was urgent.

"Sit down and have some of this fine port." Emily was just setting down the glasses. "Emily, you can go now."

Peter sat down, put his head in his hands, ignoring the glass Charlie was holding out to him. She sat down opposite.

"What is it?"

"I can't go through with this charade. This afternoon, the way my parents were behaving, so pleased and proud. They can't wait for the party to spread the good news around to even the most distant relatives, people I've hardly heard of. It's unfair. They're getting older. They deserve a real engagement, a real wedding. They're even dreaming of grandchildren. I can't do this to them."

He stopped, looked up. Charlie saw in his eyes the unspoken accusation that it didn't matter to her; she had no parents to destroy. And behind that was something else. She waited.

"We have good times together, you and I. I've never felt as easy with anyone as with you. The first time I saw you, the only time I've seen you looking feminine," he gave a wry smile, "I admired you as woman. I could desire you."

There was no response. She was still waiting.

"There have been moments when I have thought about this marriage as a reality. Imagined what kind of a couple we'd be. I was lost, bereft. You brought me the warmth of friendship I needed, that I've never had. Your friendship is very, very valuable to me."

She waited.

"I believed I could never fall in love again."

Ah, she thought.

"But I can. I have."

At last! He was going to tell her what in her heart she already knew.

"I'm in love with Anna."

During the silence which followed the ticking of the clock seemed unnaturally loud. As Charlie said nothing he began again.

"I would like to get married. I would like to marry Anna." Then an almost desolate cry "I want her, Charlie."

In the depths of her pain, Charlie thought, so do I. The blood had drained from her face.

The clock was surely ticking hours, not minutes. Charlie raised her glass.

"Well, good luck, mon ami," she said, drank the port, and walked out.

Charlie caught an early train to London after delivering the letter to her lawyer. Her nerves were stretched to an almost unbearable tautness. She was sulky with her director and haughty with the new actress, whom she found very limited in her understanding of the role. Having managed to get through the day without anyone losing their temper, she took a cab to George's house. Fortunately he was in, preparing for a visit from Simon.

He greeted her with alarm. "Darling, you look wrecked. Whatever is the matter?"

Charlie condensed the matter into a few words.

"Peter doesn't want to play any more. He's in love with Anna."

"Well there you go!" He shrugged. "That's straight men for you! Can't rely on them."

Charlie was flabbergasted at this flippancy.

"Forget it. It doesn't matter now. Remember you only started it to keep off unwanted suitors. Simon, to be precise. I can assure you, dearest heart, that there is absolutely no danger from that quarter. He's rather a poppet, still wet behind the ears in spite of his travels. This weekend is going to be the big moment. Do you know, I'm quite excited. He isn't Toby, there'll never be another Toby, but he is very sweet."

Charlie had the feeling that she had been abandoned on a desert island. She spent the evening being 'cheered up' by George's account of his wooing. In a curious way it was restful and he could always end up making her laugh. He tucked her up in his four-poster bed with the gold embroidered silk curtains. He kissed her on the forehead, looked at her seriously for the first time since she'd arrived and whispered, "Don't cry, Charlie, you'll get over her sooner or later. We always do."

He's shrewder than he pretends to be, Charlie thought before falling into a troubled sleep.

She had another session with the new actress the following morning, trying to explain her character's inner motivations. She remembered Adrienne. At least she had understood what was going on. Perhaps it was necessary to seduce this one to make her understand. She rejected the idea. In fact she didn't care any more. They were playing to full houses all the time anyway. She should be getting on with the next script but she had no heart for it.

On the train back to Brighton she made herself imagine Peter and Anna together. An image flashed before her of them together in the library, that first time they were alone. If she were to be dispassionate, which was impossible, she would say that they looked good together. She couldn't blame Peter for falling in love nor for his honesty in refusing to continue the pretence. Nor could she be angry with him. She was jealous, deeply, distressingly jealous. It would need a superhuman effort of will to transcend that, to wish him good luck with a sincerity lacking two days ago.

She went to his cottage before going home. He wasn't there. As it was a brilliantly sunny day she went down to the harbour where she found him mending his nets.

"Good catch today?" she asked.

He was relieved by the friendly tone.

"Yes, very good. Did it go all right with your actress?" Charlie grimaced. "So-so."

The polite formalities over, she continued, "I'm sorry I was so abrupt, the other night. I meant what I said. Anna's a lovely woman. You and she seem to get on. There's no point in you and me going on."

"Our friendship must go on. I couldn't bear to lose that. I do love you, Charlie, I always will. It's just that . . ."

She cut him short. "I know. I shall tell her tonight our engagement is off. That we've broken it off by mutual agreement. Then your way will be clear. I'll make myself scarce."

"Thank you. You are an exceptional person."

Oh yes, thought Charlie, I'm that all right.

Anna listened thoughtfully and sympathetically to what Charlie had to say, which was that she and Peter had been coming to a gradual realisation that it wouldn't work, that they had talked at length when he came round two nights before and had agreed that it was better to break it off now. They were, and always would be, just good friends.

"Well, I can say this to you now," said Anna, "I didn't think you were right for each other."

"No, he needs someone more . . . artistic, more ... feminine."

"And you, what do you need?" She surprised Charlie with this question.

"I don't know. I've realised that what I *don't* need, is a husband." A wife, I need a wife, she thought.

She had agreed with Peter that if the next day was fine she would drive Anna, if she so wished, over to see his sculpture garden. She would leave on some errand in Brighton and Peter would drive Anna back. She outlined the plan to Anna, who was pleased, although she regretted that Charlie couldn't stay. They passed the

evening agreeably enough with Anna showing Charlie
her sketches and describing how she would develop
them. She also asked Charlie probing questions about her
past liaisons, especially the period with Adrienne, receiving only vague, discouraging answers. At nine o'clock
Charlie yawned pointedly, claimed extreme fatigue and
bid Anna abruptly goodnight. Anna sensed her acute distress beneath the veneer of nonchalance, so she felt sorry
about the upset the rupture had caused. She had to admit
to another sentiment though – lightness of heart.

The following day was as perfect as anyone could
wish. The sky and sea had that transparency particular
to early autumn days. Anna awoke with the dawn, lying
entranced by the rose light turning to gold. She was looking forward to her outing, especially as she now felt so
at home with Peter. The air was mild enough to be almost
warm, so she refused Charlie's offers of blankets as she
clambered into the passenger seat. In spite of the breathtaking countryside, the fields still bright with flowers, the
trees fading from bright green toward pale yellow, she
did not enjoy the ride as much as last time. Charlie
appeared to have a malicious intent towards the road,
she glared at is so fixedly. If she was aware of Anna's
eyes upon her, she didn't show it. She swore at a rabbit that ran in front of her and shouted that it should be
in bed, which would have made Anna laugh if it weren't
for the savage look in the driver's eyes. They swerved
violently at a bend to avoid a hay cart, almost over-
turning, so that Anna was thankful that they and the car
were still in one piece when they came to a halt at last.
Peter was at his gate, lean, handsome and bright-eyed.

"Have a good day," said Charlie through gritted teeth.

"I though I might take Anna to Lewes and some of the
villages around. There's a good inn where we could have
lunch. If the weather's still fine this evening, perhaps, she
might like to go out along the coast? I've spruced up
Lady Louise – there's not a fish scale in sight." He was
looking rather doubtfully at Anna's straw coloured skirt.

"What fun!" cried Anna. "Are you sure you can't join
us Charlie?"

"No, I'll be busy all day. Whatever time you come back, the door won't be locked, but I'll probably be in bed, if you're after 10 o'clock." Off she went.

Looking round the most expensive men's outfitters in Brighton in search of a new waistcoat, she met Simon, so changed that at first she didn't recognise him. His hair was longer, curlier, his clothes much more flamboyant. He was looking at cravats. He blushed when he saw Charlie.

"Why, Simon," she said, "you're looking very pretty." She could think of no other word for it. She looked at the yellow silk tie he was holding. "Hardly your style, I would have thought."

"No. I'm looking for a present for George. You see he's invited me for the weekend, and I want to take him a gift. You know his taste, would he like this?" Charlie was certain he wouldn't. She suggested a tiepin might be better, more discreet. Nothing expensive. She abandoned the search for a waistcoat to accompany the young explorer to a nearby jeweller, where they decided on a gold pin with a small agate in the centre.

I hope he knows what he's letting himself in for, thought Charlie watching him disappear into the Lanes with his precious little package.

She didn't want the waistcoat after all, it would be out of place here. Her wardrobe in France was full of clothes which would have been inappropriate for Sussex, even in her Brighton circles. Reminded of Brighton circles she decided to call on two acquaintances in Hove, Ethel and Margaret, whom she hadn't seen for some months. They had been together for thirty years, since they were more or less Charlie's age, and had become a legend for fidelity. They lived in a rambling flat in a mansion block, where one of them worked as a dressmaker and the other proof-read manuscripts. They had very little money to spare for luxuries, so Charlie called at the grocer's shop on the corner where she was able to make up a small basket of extravagant foodstuffs.

Their welcome was heart-warming. They had a very soft spot for the younger woman, who was more often in their thoughts and conversation than she would have ever imagined. They had been to visit her in Paris on two occasions, where she had entertained them most royally. She always sent them tickets for her plays in London. Today they fussed around her, scolded her for bringing the gifts, insisted on sharing their soup, in general helping to alleviate the loneliness she had been suffering since depositing Anna at Peter's door. She looked around with fresh eyes at the shabby furniture, the long table strewn with pieces of fabric at one end and manuscripts at the other, the threadbare carpet. There was a bedroom, she knew, and other rooms they only used in the height of summer because they couldn't afford to heat them, but this big high-ceilinged space was truly a living room, the centre of their lives.

"I do so envy you," she said, a slight tremor in her voice. She swallowed and blinked hard.

They stared at her, concerned. They had always seen her happy and confident. They had sent their condolences when Toby had died, but the Charlie they knew was a young woman with a busy existence quite apart from her twin, so they supposed her grief, though profound, would not affect her life in any major way. Now she was so suddenly deflated, her expression so miserable, that they were shocked.

"My dear, you poor thing, you look so unhappy." Ethel moved to sit beside her, patted her hand.

Then Charlie began to cry and they let her go on, producing handkerchiefs when necessary. At last she stopped, wiped her eyes, blew her nose and sat up straight.

"I'm so sorry. I don't know why I did that," she said.

"Just generally overwrought, I expect, dear. You've had a lot to do, what with one thing or another." She'll tell us in her own good time, thought Margaret

"You two are always so kind to me."

"It's not difficult," smiled Margaret. "You're the sort of person one wants to look after."

"Really?" Charlie saw herself as strong and independent.

"Haven't you found that?" asked Margaret.

"Perhaps. Yes, I suppose. I don't need looking after, though." Charlie remembered being abrupt with the lovers who had tried to organise her life, cook her meals.

"Everybody likes to be spoilt occasionally," ventured Ethel. She smiled affectionately at her partner. "We spoil each other."

"I don't know what I'm doing back at Finborough Place," said Charlie suddenly. "I can't deal with it."

"No well, it's not really you, is it?" Ethel herself came from a good Yorkshire family, from whom she had run away at the first opportunity, never to return.

"What is really me, do you think?" Charlie looked wistfully from one to the other.

"Ah, that is a very difficult question. You'll know when you find it," and Ethel squeezed her partner's shoulder.

Charlie didn't stay too long as she didn't want to interrupt their working day. Time for them was money. She had enjoyed seeing them and they made her feel better for a while, but walking along the seafront lawns she felt lonelier than ever.

"Looking for a good time, mister?" The husky voice was that of a coarse looking girl with fiercely rouged cheeks, leaning against the iron railings. The parted red lips, the insolent gaze and the way she leaned back provocatively, were very exciting; Charlie wondered what would happen if she took up the invitation and the girl discovered the 'mister' was a 'miss'. Perhaps she wouldn't care. Although the temptation was strong, Charlie shook her head and walked on. The arousal lingered, making her painfully aware of unsatisfied need.

She walked all afternoon and into the evening, until dusk. She wondered whether to stay at Vine Place, so great was her reluctance to drive back to Finborough. It was only her consideration for Emily and Mrs. Branson that made her start back. Passing through Newhaven she fought against a wish to call at Peter's cottage. Finding on her return that Anna was still out, she ordered Mrs. Branson to serve dinner for one immediately and then go home. Having little appetite she threw most of the food away before trying to settle down in the library with a novel.

She was startled by a ring at the door. Anna would have come straight in. It was nearly ten o'clock. What crisis could this be? She went through the hall in some trepidation. It was Violet. Charlie caught a drift of expensive perfume which she had never known Violet wear before.

"May I come in?" She was winsome rather than urgent.

"What do you want?" Charlie's tone was not inviting. She looked Violet up and down taking in every detail of her careful toilette.

"How did you manage to cross the fields in those shoes?" she asked, still blocking the doorway.

"Please let me in, Charlie, I want to talk to you."

"It's late."

"Not very."

For a farming family it was late enough. Mr. and Mrs. Doderill were likely to be in bed by now.

Violet slipped past whilst Charlie hesitated. The smell of the perfume trailed behind. It was one Charlie particularly liked. In fact Adrienne had always worn it. Violet was taking off her coat as she made for the library, which she guessed to be the warmest room.

Oh no, thought Charlie, as Violet's new softly fitting dress was revealed.

"I would really like a glass of brandy. Toby and I would occasionally drink it, you know."

"It's all gone," lied Charlie. Of course Violet wouldn't believe her, but that didn't matter. "Violet, what's this all about?"

Violet spotted Charlie's half-drunk glass of port and the equally half-empty bottle beside it.

"I'll have some of this then." Without waiting for some of her own, she took a long draught of Charlie's. She draped herself over the sofa and undid her top two buttons. "It's rather warm in here."

Charlie grabbed the glass angrily.

"Stop it! Whatever you have to say, say it and go home."

"What I want to say," Violet leant forward, dewy-eyed, her breasts falling gently as she did so, "is thank you.

You are wonderful, you are . . ." she grabbed the glass back and drank as she searched for words, "a miracle worker." She graciously handed the glass to Charlie. "My father told me you have made over some money to me, which he needs, and that I am to be nice to you. I am going to be nice to you, Charlie, really, really, nice."

That man is selling me his daughter, thought Charlie in disgust.

"I can stay all night. He won't say a word. I can stay every night until you're married, then we can come to some arrangement."

"Get out of here!" Charlie's voice was a whiplash.

"I'm frightened to go back. There was a bull loose." She fell to her knees imploringly. "Take me to bed, please take me to bed."

Pent-up desire made Charlie's heart beat wildly.

"I don't love you."

"I don't care. You want me and I want you. Make love to me, make love to me, please, please, please make love to me." She kissed Charlie's knees, her thighs and Charlie felt her hot mouth even through the rough wool.

"I'll never love you. I may despise you in the morning."

"I don't care. I need you to touch me."

She needs somebody, anybody, to touch her, thought Charlie. At the most basic level, they both needed relief from sexual tension. She put her hands under Violet's elbows and lifted her to her feet.

Emily had lit a small fire in Charlie's bedroom, as she had started to do when the nights were chilly. The coals were still glowing, a point of dim light which their eyes became accustomed to, so that their flesh was revealed with mysterious softness as they undressed. There was still the faintest glimmer when they lay back exhausted three hours later. Charlie's lovemaking that night was strong, rougher than usual, spurred on by Violet's ecstatic moans. They had just fallen apart when they heard footsteps ascending the stairs and a bedroom door opening and closing.

"Anna," said Charlie.

"Oh, I'd forgotten about her," said Violet. She moved closer. "Kiss me again Charlie, all over."

"Go to sleep now" replied Charlie, kissing her on the forehead. There was no more lovemaking that night, and Violet did go to sleep almost immediately, whilst Charlie stared into space, sinking into melancholy.

Chapter 15
Recognition

"Get up, Violet!" Charlie gave the sleeping form beside her a shove. She had to repeat the action several times before Violet opened her eyes and stared vacantly at her tormentor. Then she remembered.

"Oh, Charlie!"

"You have to go home."

"It's not morning yet."

"Yes it is."

"It doesn't matter. My parents won't care if I stay all day."

"I care. I don't want you here when Mrs. Branson arrives."

"Why? She'll have to get used to finding me here."

"Go, now!"

"You don't mean that." She rolled over towards Charlie opening her arms. She looked as if her body had blossomed in the night. Charlie slipped out of bed and put on a dressing gown, covering her own lithe form. Violet sighed.

"I'm hungry."

"We'll go down and make you some breakfast. But you can't stay long."

Violet spied another silk robe, similar to the one Charlie was wearing, hanging behind the door. She leapt up.

"I'll wear this, then we'll be matching." She made for the door before Charlie could order her to get dressed.

She had just stepped out of the bedroom when Anna emerged from her room down the corridor.

"Hello Anna," said Violet breezily as she brushed past. "I hope we didn't disturb you. We did make rather a lot of noise, but you know what it's like when you're carried away." She was perfectly aware that their lovemaking had ceased when Anna came home.

Anna was supporting herself on the doorframe. Her lips were white, her pupils dilated. She looked at Violet's loosely tied robe slipping off her shoulder, she saw Charlie's door was open, though Charlie herself was invisible, frozen inside by Violet's words. Silently she stepped back and closed her own door, turning the key in the lock.

Violet became quite the little housewife in the kitchen, laying the table with bread, butter, jam and honey, making tea.

"Would you like an egg, darling?" she asked when Charlie appeared, by now fully dressed.

Charlie sat down.

"What happened last night was a mistake."

Violet's chunk of bread and honey was suspended mid-air.

"You don't mean that."

"Stop telling me I don't mean what I say. You are an irresistibly attractive woman, you must go and test your wiles on a man. For goodness sake, Violet, you need a husband, a real man. It's no good fooling around with me. And if you say 'You don't mean that' once more, I'll hit you. Go and tell your odious father that I'll give you, actually *give* you, a generous dowry, and you'll see how he will invite all the bachelors in the county, of whatever age, to call."

Violet was no longer hungry. Tears were welling up.

"I thought last night you loved me."

"No. Did I say that? Did I once say 'I love you, Violet'?" Charlie made a point of never saying 'I love you' unless she meant it.

"You said I was luscious, that you could eat me, that . . ."

"That isn't the same. If you'd had any experience of lovemaking you'd know. How many times do I have to repeat I do not love you and I will never love you." She did not add that the pleasure she had in their love-making had been intense after a period of abstinence, but she continued more gently, "I promise you, you will find a man who will love you and satisfy you, and" she hesitated before finishing, "give you children." Then, seeing Violet's forlorn expression, she added, "I'll be a godparent to you first baby, and I'll give it lots of presents."

This was a new thought. In some ways Violet was her father's daughter, so the idea of a child of hers who would have a special meaning for Charlie, who might even inherit Finborough Place, who knows? had a certain appeal. But she was still flooded with a blissful warmth, hitherto inexperienced, which was at the moment supremely important. "You make me feel so good," she said. "We just melted into each other. Can't I come round again tonight?"

"No." It took some determination for Charlie to refuse, for she too was basking in a tingling glow. However, unlike Violet, she had lain awake regretting her weakness.

"Aren't you going to sleep with me ever again?" Violet's chin trembled.

"I'd better not." She wanted to drive an even more frustrated Violet into the arms of the first suitor, whoever that may be. Simon was obviously a lost cause. "You really do have to go home now." She leaned across the table to give Violet an affectionate kiss. "I'm going to be very busy for the next few days. Come round to lunch on Saturday, if you like." She buttered herself a slice of bread.

Understanding the finality of this, Violet started back upstairs.

"By the way," Charlie called after her "keep that robe if you like, as a souvenir. I have several."

Passing Anna's door again, Violet tapped on it lightly. "Goodbye Anna. I'll see you soon."

There was no response

Not trusting Violet to deliver the message, Charlie wrote a letter to Mr. and Mrs. Doderill, proposing a dowry for Violet, as well as the loan. She had failed to turn up a proper suitor, it was up to the parents to do better. She sent Dan to deliver her missive. She sat in the library, listening for Anna to come down for coffee, as she usually did at about ten o'clock. She was ashamed of having spent the night with Violet, and would rather have avoided the subject, but since Anna knew all about it, then something should be said. Also she hoped to have an account of Anna's day out, in spite of the pain she knew she would experience. When there was no sign of Anna at eleven o'clock, Charlie began to feel anxious. She went up to knock on Anna's door. There was no answer and the door was still locked. She called her name several times. There wasn't a sound. She knocked harder, rattled the knob. A faint voice said, "Please leave me alone."

Charlie got into her car and drove straight to Peter's house. The man who greeted her was a Peter she had never seen before. His face was dark, almost threatening. She was unnerved.

"What do you want?" His voice was harsh.

Charlie was too shocked to reply.

"Whatever you've got to say, I don't want to hear it. I don't care what you've heard from her."

"I haven't spoken to Anna," stammered Charlie. "I haven't seen her. She's locked in her room."

They confronted each other. He was bristling, like a dog about to bite.

"What are you trying to do to me?"

She didn't understand.

"If you wanted to destroy me, you've nearly succeeded."

What was he talking about?

"Peter, I'm your friend, not your enemy."

He was swaying slightly. He smelled of rum. He gave a bitter laugh.

"Some friend! Come in, you might as well. I'll tell you about my day yesterday. Would you enjoy that?" He stood aside to let her enter. "It's a bit untidy."

The usually neat little living room was in a state of chaos.

The pictures lay on the ground, the glass smashed. Chairs were overturned, one was broken, its staves scatted on the floor. Around the fire were scraps of burnt paper.

"Have a glass of rum," he pushed the bottle towards her.

"No thank you. I'll make myself some tea."

His glass was full, however he left it and took the tea she passed to him. He stared into his cup reflectively.

"Women are bitches, aren't they, Charlie?"

He was sober enough to see her anger. He covered his face with his hands, took a shuddering breath and broke into racking sobs. Charlie waited, her mind in a turmoil. At last, when he was quieter, she asked, "What happened, Peter?"

Red-eyed, haggard, he repeated the question, then added one of his own.

"What happened? Did you know how unbalanced she is?"

Charlie shook her head.

"All right. I've been thinking you knew, that you set this all up, to punish me for something, I don't know what. If that's what you wanted, you've done it."

Her dismay was evident.

"I don't know what you're talking about."

He searched her face keenly, decided she was telling the truth and leaned back with a deep sigh. He spoke haltingly with many pauses.

"We had a wonderful day. I hadn't been able to sleep thinking about her. She was everything Louise had been and more. I was in a state of grace, that's the only way I can describe it, with her beside me. I drove her round the prettiest roads, then we had lunch, came back here, spent a long time in the garden looking at my sculptures. I took her out to sea. You know what a lovely evening it was – she was enchanted by everything – the light on the water, the white cliffs, growing pink in the sunset – everything. Then we had dinner here. It was perfect." He stopped. Charlie said nothing for a while, before prompting gently, "and then?"

He raised his head.

"I was certain she felt as I did. She was so gracious, so attentive. I didn't want her to leave me. I had to tell her how I felt, that I had fallen madly in love with her. She looked at me with a kind of panic. When I said I'd never ever felt quite like this before, she stared at me and said 'I think I'd better leave now'." He paused, noticed the glass of rum, and drank from it.

"You know the French word *allumeuse*?"

Charlie did. A woman who set you alight, then left you to burn.

"It was as if she'd slapped my face. I thought, I know she wants me, she's just worried about you. So I said you wouldn't care, it didn't matter, she and I were so right for each other, I don't know what I said, anything that came into my head, and she said nothing, nothing, just stared at me. I was beside myself. I took hold of her and kissed her. I couldn't let her go. Then she did slap my face. She became hysterical. She fought like a demon. She bit me, I hit her. When she went completely dead on me I released her and drove her to Finborough."

Neither of them knew what else to say. After what seemed an eternity, Peter rubbed his brow wearily. "I must sleep," and he stumbled up the stairs.

"Anna, please answer me! Are you all right?" Charlie banged hard on the locked door. "Are you all right? I've been to see Peter. I know what happened. Are you all right?"

A scarcely audible voice answered "Leave me alone."

Charlie was in a stare of extreme anxiety. At first after Peter's account she had been suffused with guilt. It was true that she had set the situation up, thereby creating mayhem. Then she reacted against this assumption of responsibility. It was not her fault that Peter had fallen in love, not her fault that Anna had rejected him. At this moment the only thing she cared about was Anna's well-being.

"Let me bring you something to eat!" She realised that food was not what Anna needed, but it might be an excuse to open the door.

Silence

"You're not well yet. You'll make yourself ill again."

Silence

"You don't have to talk to me I'll just sit beside you."

This time the response was louder, sharper.

"I don't want you! Leave me alone!"

Charlie turned away. She had better come back later, try again She didn't know what to do with her restless energy. She couldn't turn it into writing, it was too powerful, it had to have a physical expression. She must walk, walk all afternoon until she was tired out. And think, sort out her disordered emotions, put herself back on an even keel. She set off along a path she knew out of the estate, through the forest, ending up back on the cliffs a few miles down the coast from Finborough. On another day she might have dawdled, stopped to look at the badger's set, examined the owl pellets on the path as she loved to do when she was a child. She would have taken a picnic, been out from morning until evening. On this day she walked fast, taking no notice of her surroundings until she came suddenly in sight of the sea, a flat gleaming expanse, with that peculiar late summer, early autumn shine which was as if it were lit from below. She caught her breath and stood still. It was a rare moment, like ones she treasured from her past when she and Toby had sat on the beach, holding hands, united in their silent contemplation of the infinite. She marched on, scaring rabbits back into the gorse bushes, up and down the chalk folds which marked the end of England, not slackening her pace, plunged back into the turmoil of her mind. It was dusk when she reached the track that turned inland to Finborough. On the top of the last rise she saw a figure standing on the edge of the cliff, a silhouette against the darkening sky. She recognised Anna and it was as if she was plunged into a deep pit.

"Anna," she screamed, flinging herself forward, racing to prevent another dreadful tragedy. She caught her foot in a rabbit hole and there was a searing pain in her leg. She fell to the ground and everything went black.

When she came to, Anna was kneeling beside here.

"I think you might have broken your ankle," she said. She touched the ankle gently and Charlie winced. "I'll have to get help, you won't be able to walk on it. Violet's parents are the nearest, aren't they? I'll fetch Mr. Doderill. I'll be as quick as I can."

"Anna," said Charlie, "I though you were going to . . ." she couldn't finish the sentence.

Anna's eyes widened.

"Oh no! I just wanted some peace, to lose myself in nature."

"I couldn't bear it. " Charlie was beyond pretence. "I would have died too."

"I understand. George told me about Toby."

"It's not about Toby. It's about you. I couldn't bear it if I lost you." She winced again as she tried to move her foot.

"I'd better go," said Anna. She sped away, skipping lightly but carefully over the grassy tussocks.

When she returned she was accompanied by Mr. Doderill, a couple of farmhands and Violet, who was all overwhelming concern.

"My poor, poor Charlie! I'll come back and look after you. It's all swollen!" She was on the point of saying "I'll kiss it better," but decided against such demonstrations in her father's presence.

So Charlie was carried home, the doctor was called and diagnosed a bad sprain not a break. Charlie sat by her bed, wrapped in bandages whilst Emily and Mrs. Branson fussed around. Violet was despatched home as more hindrance than help. Anna had melted away again into her own quarters.

"Shall I stay the night Miss Charlotte?" asked Emily.

"No thank you. I can manage." A good strong stick had been provided which enabled her to hop around. "Before you leave, would you ask Anna if she would come to see me."

"I don't know if she will. She's been very funny all day."

"Just ask her."

The request was conveyed. The house was silent and Charlie had almost fallen asleep when Anna finally came to her.

221

"I will leave tomorrow," said Anna. "You have no need of me, with Mrs. Branson and Emily and Violet to care for you. I will only be in the way." In the way in Derbyshire, in the way here. The words were chilling.

"I am perfectly well enough to go back to Paris now. I need to work." She was not as determined as she sounded. She had never seen Charlie look so vulnerable. Her heart went out to her. She continued, her voice a little unsteady, "You have been very kind, thank you for your hospitality."

Charlie was bruised. Her spirit was bruised. She remembered what the doctor had said about Anna's wounded soul. She was at the end of all subterfuge, all invention. She wanted no explanations. She stretched out her hands imploring:

"Kiss me," she said.

Anna was a rigid statue.

"Kiss me, please kiss me." There was anguish in her voice and eyes.

It was as if a hot sun began to thaw the iceberg inside Anna's skin. In Peter's embraces had been an ugly power which repelled her as Robin had repelled her. Drawing close to Charlie there was no resistance to an attraction she rejoiced in. When their lips finally joined there was a startled realisation of a mysterious fusion of body mind and spirit.

It was in the early morning that they began to talk. With instinctive trust they dared to say the hitherto unsayable, starting the long process of healing. Anna fetched them breakfast which they fed to each other, admiring in daylight the other's beauty. Charlie watched Anna dress and Anna helped Charlie on with her clothes. As she turned to return to her room, Charlie held her back.

"Don't go," she said, "Stay with me."

"But the Bransons . . ."

"It doesn't matter about them. Let's stay here all day. Emily can bring our meals up."

They were under a spell. If they left the charmed circle of the room it would be broken, thought Charlie.

"I love you." These were words she had made actors utter in a dozen plays, a cliché that could trip so lightly off the tongue, but practiced in so many different ways that it was almost impossible that it should express the overwhelming emotion which had taken possession of Charlie. Yet what other words were there?

"Je t'aime." She had not the slightest doubt that this was an absolute truth.

Anna had heard enough about Charlie's past conquests to make her question the sincerity of the statement, but she didn't. Nor did she ask what it meant. She knew with a knowledge beyond language.

They did as Charlie wished. Clouds blew over and it started to rain heavily. Charlie had kept the fire going, so they sat beside each other holding hands, sometimes talking, sometimes not. Visitors were to be turned away with the message that Charlie needed complete rest. Emily was overjoyed to be made part of a conspiracy, particularly when Violet called round.

"Miss Charlotte must have complete rest," she repeated, with malicious pleasure. "No visitors at all. Doctor's orders. She's sleeping."

"Don't be silly, Emily." Really, the girl was impossible! "She'll be happy to see me. I won't disturb her."

"No, Miss Violet, not even you. She said so."

Violet went away in a temper, and Emily bounced back into the kitchen, where she and her mother chewed over the events.

"Funny thing is," Emily mused, "Charlie didn't ask me not to tell anyone. Perhaps she actually wants me to spread it around. I don't think I will, though."

"No," agreed her mother. "I'm glad you're learning to keep your mouth shut."

"You know," Emily was preparing a tray to take upstairs, "they look quite sweet together. Do you think . . .?"

"I don't think anything," snapped her mother. "Get along with you."

For five days and nights they hardly moved and ordinary life was suspended. The only visitor allowed admittance was the doctor checking up on his patient. He declared that she was doing remarkably well and he was gratified to see Anna blossoming.

"Whatever it is you're doing, keep on doing it," he prescribed. "It's obviously good for you."

On the sixth day they came down for lunch, and were ready to receive in the afternoon. To their surprise there was no sign of Violet, who had come by every other day. Peter had not been near. At four o'clock, Emily announced George. He only needed to glance from Charlie to Anna to draw the right conclusions.

"Well, well, my dears!" he cried. "Here's a turn up for the books! Congratulations," and he gave each a resounding kiss. Charlie remembered how odd it had sounded when Anna congratulated her on her engagement to Peter. This time she beamed proudly.

"And I was imagining you lying racked with pain," he perched on the sofa. "When all the time – well, you sly little minxes!"

"But she has been in great pain, she's very brave," Anna was protective.

"Who told you about my accident?" Charlie was never sure how word got around.

"Dan. Last night. I met him in Brighton,"

Charlie raised her eyebrows. George pursed his lips.

"He's a handsome lad."

"What about Simon? He was looking forward to his visit to Chelsea."

George reflected for a moment.

"Simon could be a big thing in my life. He's very pure, perhaps it's living with all those savages."

Charlie didn't understand the logic of this, but made no comment.

"We had a beautiful weekend. Didn't rush it. I surprised myself by being so restrained."

Hence Dan, thought Charlie.

"I hear that Peter has been keeping bad company in the Newhaven bars these last few days."

This met with no response.

"I understand why, looking at you two. He was obviously besotted with Anna. Can't say I blame him. You're exquisite, my dear," he said to Anna, and to Charlie, "you're a lucky old so-and-so." He leapt up and embraced her in a spontaneous rush of affection. "Oh god, I was so afraid you might actually marry that man!"

He stayed for dinner. As they finished Charlie suddenly asked, "How did you get here? How are you getting back? Do you want to stay?"

George blushed. An unusual occurrence for him.

"Well, I have to confess that I asked Dan to fetch me and take me home in your car, as you wouldn't be using it. He's lurking about until I'm ready. You aren't cross?"

She wasn't. Dan was a good driver and she herself would be out of action for some days, if not weeks. She would need him for all kinds of errands, she would make it clear that he should not take the initiative again, and certainly should not use the motor as if it were his own.

"I'd like to have a word with Dan when he brings the car back," she said as George kissed them goodbye. "Don't delay him too long."

"Don't worry. He's not one to hang about," replied George, cryptically.

They sat for several hours in the library, contemplating the future. More than ever, Charlie felt the house to be a great weight round her neck. She longed to go to Paris with Anna, to escort her proudly to Mabel's soirées, to take her to see Gaby in her run-down chateau, to enjoy life. Anna was torn between the need to work and the wish to remain by Charlie's side. She would take care of her beloved until she could walk more easily then she would have to go. She was conscious that she had no home of her own nor had she ever wanted one, disliking the idea of permanency. She had thought she would always live alone, so if Charlie had wanted to return to Paris, she had expected to move out, inconvenient though that would have been.

"Would you live with me here?" asked Charlie. "You could have a dozen studios."

Anna tenderly stroked her lover's curls.

"I couldn't. Would you really want me to?"

225

No, she wouldn't. They would certainly be ostracised, which, though she didn't mind on her own account, she would not accept for Anna. They were both totally sure that, however it could be managed, they wanted to be together for the rest of their lives. They would find a way, they must find a way.

Charlie requested Dan to fetch her old friends in Hove over for dinner. She could hardly wait to introduce them to Anna. Like Mabel and Belle, they were models of a commitment and friendship which would survive all obstacles. They would be so glad that Charlie had found a soul mate, for that was what Anna was. Meanwhile as the day was fine, they walked in the gardens, Charlie with a stick, her arm through Anna's. They were surprised not to have heard yet from Violet who had been so persistent. Anna climbed to the top of the hill where Violet had claimed to sit every day, only to find the stone bench empty.

"She must have taken the hint at last," said Charlie, only slightly concerned.

Peter's continued absence was an immense relief. Neither of them was ready to meet him yet. Learning about Robin, about Anna's nightmares, Charlie had some insight into Anna's reactions. Trying to soothe her companion as she lay shuddering in her arms, recounting the horrors, she vowed that she would never force herself on this delicate being, that she would always proceed with infinite caution.

Margaret and Ethel had dressed up to come out. They were a handsome couple, looking younger than their years. Margaret clapped her hands with glee when Charlie presented Anna as 'my friend, my best beloved'. They were too tactful to voice the thought that just over a week ago Charlie had come to them in despair.

My darlings, I am so happy for you!" Ethel hugged them both at the same time.

It was while they were chatting over the evening meal, that it suddenly came to Charlie what she should do about her landowning responsibilities. She addressed Ethel:

"How would you like to take care of my estate?"

They all looked at her with incomprehension.

"You and Margaret, you could live here and I would pay you a salary to look after my affairs. You could give up that uncomfortable, expensive flat, have no rent, and be earning money. What about it?"

The suggestion did not arouse the enthusiasm she had hoped. Margaret gaped at her, Ethel spluttered over her pudding.

"Look after this place! Don't you know I ran away from that sort of thing?"

"It's not the same." Charlie would not be put off. "It's not yours. The headaches would still be mine. I would be so grateful.

Margaret began to be rather excited. Her own circumstances had been more modest than Ethel's.

"I would quite like to live in a manor house. And this is so lovely, with the park and gardens. We wouldn't have to do the gardening, would we?" she asked, fearfully.

"No. Dan does that. There'd be Mrs. Branson and Emily and anyone else you needed. I'll pay their wages. You'd just have to manage them."

"It's a long way from town. How do we get there?" Ethel was not convinced.

"Dan will drive you. Unless you want to drive yourself."

"I can't drive."

"Maybe Dan could teach you. Wouldn't you like that, darling?" Margaret was becoming keen on the idea.

Here at last was something which caught Ethel's imagination. She saw herself at the wheel of Charlie's car, bowling along the secluded roads.

"You can do your other work just as easily here. It will be better for Margaret, she could have a large room devoted to dressmaking, where she could spread out her cloth." Charlie pressed home her advantage.

"Oh Ethel, why don't we do it?" Margaret's face was pink. How could Ethel refuse what seemed to be a magnificent gift?

"I'll think it over," the latter conceded.

"You would be doing me the most enormous favour," urged Charlie. She knew this was probably the most persuasive argument and when she saw Ethel squeeze Margaret's hand she guessed she had won.

That evening Anna spent some time in her own room writing at last to Betsy. This time she had no hesitations, her pen raced over the page.

Dearest Bee,
I left because it was better to do so, I'm sure of that. My life is so different and separate. I love you and I know you love me, but we have grown far apart. Mother hates me, she will have told you she's glad I'm gone away again.
The most incredible and wonderful thing has happened to me. I've fallen in love. I was never really in love with Robin, I was drawn to him in spite of myself. I loved his beauty, his strength, but his masculine will was a steel wall between us. All that I needed from him I have found and there is no steel wall. When we make love we become as one. I never knew there could be such ecstasy. We have scarcely left each other's side for a week. At last I can give myself freely with no fear, no resentment. As you give yourself to Alan. All my senses are so alive, Bee, yet I am extraordinarily calm. Is that what heaven is like? A heightened awareness of the peace at the centre of the universe?
And my beloved is in the same heaven. She and I walk undivided. I am in love with a woman, who has become the light of my life. She is Charlie Price, who owns the studio I rent in Paris. I am staying with her at Finborough Place, near Brighton. We want to be together for the rest of our lives. I think we shall not leave here for some days, so you may write to this address. I wish for every blessing for you and the baby. Explain to the others as best you can.
Give my best regards to Alan too.
All my love, Anna

She was sealing the envelope when the doorbell rang. It was ten o'clock. She went to Charlie's room as the ringing persisted, to ask if she should see who it was.

At this hour there must be some emergency.

"I suppose you'd better see what it's about," said Charlie.

Anna had not quite reached the bottom of the stairs before the door was unlocked and opened. Dan and a friend stood either side of an almost unconscious Peter. "He's in a bit of a state," announced Dan, unnecessarily. "He got into a fight, fell down and hit his head. He hasn't got anybody at home to look after him, so we thought we'd better bring him here. I drove his car."

They half-carried him through the hall into the library where they dropped him on the sofa. He was dazed, confused, like a punch drunk boxer.

By now Charlie had limped downstairs with the aid of the stick."

"I didn't know what else to do Miss Charlie," Dan turned to her apologetically. "I couldn't leave him."

"No, it's all right, Dan. We'll take over."

The young man shuffled out leaving the women gazing at Charlie's erstwhile fiancé, who smiled idiotically, keeled over and fell deeply asleep.

Charlie threw a rug over him. "He'll be all right till morning," she said.

Chapter 16
Resolutions

Mrs. Branson arrived early, whilst Anna and Charlie were still asleep and Peter dead to the world. She was cross with Dan for what he'd done, but admitted that he had few options. The dishevelled, prone figure in the library reminded her of her dead husband, whom she had often received here, in a similar state, after a drunken brawl at the Finborough arms. He didn't move when she gently wiped blood off his lip, so she kissed him lightly on the brow, muttering "you poor soul," believing Charlie's infidelity to be the source of his trouble.

"Leave him to me, mother, I'll take care of him," pleaded Emily, who arrived an hour later. Playing nurse to this handsome, tragic youth would be much more interesting than dusting and cleaning. She adjusted the rug, was concerned about the bruises.

"You leave him alone." Mrs. Branson knew better than to leave a helpless man in her daughter's clutches. "Get on with your work."

He was just beginning to stir when Charlie came down for breakfast leaving Anna resting. He got up unsteadily, and staggered to the kitchen where Mrs. Branson and Charlie were discussing the situation in hushed tones.

"Could I have a cup of tea?" he asked, steadying himself on the table.

"Of course, dear. Glad you're alive and kicking."

Kicking he was certainly not. He took the cup with trembling hands.

"Mrs. Branson, would you take a tray up to Anna? She's rather tired. And then perhaps you would go and pick some vegetable for lunch. Emily can have the day off, it's time she had a holiday. Neither of you will need to come back into the kitchen for a while, will you?"

"No, Miss Charlie." Mrs. Branson quickly grasped the tray, she did not point out that they had all the vegetables they needed for two or three days. They watched her activities in silence, until the door had closed behind her and they could hear the footsteps going towards the stairs. It was Peter who spoke first.

"What am I doing here?"

"Dan brought you."

He made an effort to collect his muddled thoughts.

"I was in a fight."

"Apparently."

"I don't know what it's about. Nothing." He drank the tea in one gulp and pushed the cup to be refilled. Then he said "I haven't been on the planet since I last saw you. I've been out of my head. I haven't been near the boat."

Thank goodness for that, thought Charlie.

"I remember going to the harbour one night. There were a lot of us. I fell in. They pulled me out. I think I went mad." His mind was clearing. "Does Anna hate me?" he asked suddenly. Since Charlie didn't reply, he added "Do you hate me?"

"No."

"I hated both of you. I could have murdered you. That's over now. It's all over. I don't care."

"Anna and I are in love with each other." For better or worse she'd said it. "But we were afraid to admit it. I honestly believed she could love you, would love you. Now we have realised the truth, and we're not going to hide it."

"So she's like that, she's one of you after all. I should have known when she pushed me away."

Charlie flushed with anger.

"She is not 'like that' whatever that may mean. One of 'us', who do you think 'we' are? Anna is a woman who has lived, suffered and finally found her other half." Charlie regretted the expression, but she was too roused to choose her words carefully.

"Other half, is it? Well, keep her under lock and key, away from any men, or she'll cause trouble."

If women are bitches, men are wolves, thought Charlie, remembering Peter's words when they last met.

Charlie pushed her chair back. "Dan will drive you back in you car whenever you're ready."

"I can drive myself"

"As you wish."

"That's the end of our friendship, isn't it? What did it all mean, anyway?"

"I don't know." Charlie had thought she loved another Peter, not the one sitting before her.

"Don't try to play with little boys, Charlie, stick to your own kind."

This cut more deeply that he could ever guess. She lifted her chin defiantly.

"Some little boys are rougher than they seem. I'll try to be more discriminating." She hurried away, fighting back the tears.

Fifteen minutes later, her head on Anna's shoulder, she heard his car starting down the drive. She wondered whether they would ever see each other again, except by accident. Their paths may never cross.

Since Charlie's ankle was so much better and the day was bright, she decided to have Dan take them into Brighton, to show Anna Vine Place. Anna clapped her hands with joy at the sight of the overgrown garden, somewhat neglected during the past weeks. A tranquil haven in the middle of the busy town. She was completely entranced when she stepped inside the cottage.

"This is our own special place," said Charlie proudly. "When my foot's better, I'll carry you over the threshold. I chose it, the Langham Price ancestors have nothing to do with it. Toby used to escape here too. Do you want to spend the night here? It's always ready for guests. Dan can take the car back tonight, let his mother know and fetch us in the morning, what do you think?"

Anna was delighted by the idea of such a total change of scene. It was almost like a honeymoon. Like any lovers they walked arm-in-arm or hand in hand on the Pier.

That night they went to the music hall, where they met women friends of Charlie's, who took them back for a candlelit supper, toasting their union with a dusty bottle of champagne, saved for just such an occasion. They talked and laughed, exchanged hugs and kissed, then walked round the corner home, where they fell asleep as soon as their heads touched the pillow.

Next morning they called on Ethel and Margaret, to find out if they had come to a conclusion overnight about Charlie's offer. Anna had taken an instant liking to them so when she saw how poor and sparse their flat was, she was just as anxious as Charlie that they should accept. They had, in fact, reached their decision as they were being escorted back to Hove. Turning round to take a long look at the building from the drive, they responded to its dignified simplicity. As they approached Finborough village, Ethel asked Dan to stop, so that she could climb into the front seat beside him to have her first driving lesson. There were lots of arrangements to be made before they could move in, however, so they were trying to keep calm. It was yet another cause for celebration, this time with a drop of ginger wine, which they kept for cold winter nights. The weather was mild, but it was all they had to give. They would have shared their soup too, but the visitors declined politely.

Charlie sent Dan away again when he came for them. "Come back the day after tomorrow," she ordered. If this was a honeymoon, it was going to last longer than one night. "And tell you mother to lock up the house tonight and take the day off tomorrow. All of you have the day off. Why don't you take them on an outing? Somewhere pretty where you can all have lunch. Here." She went into a back room and emerged with a handful of banknotes, "you can have anything you want." On second thoughts she found an envelope, into which she put the money before she sealed it with a wax seal and wrote 'Mrs. Branson' on the front.

"Give this to your mother. I'll ask her how much was in it." Her generosity did not extend as far as subsidising Dan's drinking with his chums.

Dan went away whistling cheerfully, reflecting that Miss Charlie wasn't at all a bad sort.

During the next few days Charlie was a most attentive and tender lover, seeking to please her partner in every way. Anna, who had half expected to wake up one day from this dream of completeness, of oneness with another, allowed herself to be possessed, transported. They opened up to each other with a trust which left them raw and exposed. Whether they were dining out, sitting on the beach or in bed, in company or alone, they were bound by invisible cords, and they were glad. They made their love plain for all to see, without fear of derision. For who could deride these beautiful creatures, who carried their magic circle with them?

"By the way, Emily asked me to tell you Miss Violet called this morning." Dan announced this from the back seat of the car, where he was luxuriating in the unusual experience of being driven, as Charlie had wanted to take the wheel. "She's going to come back this afternoon, she said."

Come back she did. Charlie was sitting in the rose garden, Anna was in her room. Violet was bursting with news she was relishing. She would take her time to reveal the source of her suppressed glee.

"How are you, Charlie?" she began solicitously.

"Much better thank you. How are you?" Charlie could see for herself how Violet was. Her whole demeanour expressed a newfound sexual confidence. What had attracted Charlie before, she now found slightly repellent.

"I'm very well. I'm sorry I haven't been to see you recently, I've been very busy."

"As a matter of fact, so have I."

Charlie's business was of no concern to Violet.

"A lot has happened since I last saw you."

Charlie waited.

"Really such a lot. You'd never guess."

Heaven be praised, she's found a husband, thought Charlie. Well done, Mr. Doderill, he was quick off the mark there.

Violet could contain herself no longer. "I've fallen in love. I'm sorry."

Charlie smiled. "Is it something to be sorry about?"

"Well, after our night together I though you'd mind."

Yet again, Charlie was amazed by Violet's stupidity. "My dear, I was just whetting your appetite."

"Don't you want to know who it is?"

"Who is it?" Charlie didn't care who it was, really.

"It's Roderick. There! Aren't you surprised?"

Who on earth is Roderick, thought Charlie. Her blank expression betrayed her ignorance.

"You know, Roderick Harding!" Then, as she perceived no enlightenment, "The lawyer from Alfriston, who has the large farm."

"Oh, the bloodhound!" She remembered Emily had said, never mind about his face, he was reported to be pretty good where it counted.

Violet flushed scarlet. "Don't call him that."

"All right, tell me all about it." Charlie gave a resigned sigh.

Roderick Harding did not have a fortune like the Langham Prices but he was just about the most eligible bachelor in the county. Mr. Doderill had wasted no time in inviting him over, after receiving Charlie's letter. Violet was still glowing from her night with Charlie, as the latter predicted, she was irresistible to any red-blooded male. She was not impressed with Roderick's looks, his soft, slightly puffy face bore no comparison with Charlie's finely sculpted features, and it was true that it would readily sink into mournful wrinkles. However there was a glint in his eye which excited her, so she was not averse to her father's suggestion that she might show him round the stable yard, explaining that the rebuilding work would soon commence.

How romantic, though Charlie ironically.

It was when they were looking at Violet's new young stallion, Firefly, that it happened. Roderick kissed her on the neck from behind. It was like an electric shock, it was incredible. He spun her round to face him and bit her lips.

"I was helpless" Violet almost gasped at the memory. "He pressed himself against me and .."

"Spare me the details" Charlie could imagine the rest only too will.

"We did it in the hay!" Violet was positively triumphant. "I think Firefly must have been jealous because he kicked Roderick as we were leaving.

Well done, Firefly, approved Charlie. Ah, country life!

"We're going to get engaged."

"I'm very pleased for you." This was one plan which had succeeded. She was sure that Violet and Roderick would make a wonderful couple and have lots of children and horses. It was irrelevant to mention her own happiness, so all she said was "I'm going to be leaving Finborough soon. There will be two women in charge of the estate."

"Two women!" Violet frowned. "That's unusual."

"Isn't it? I'm sure you'll get on with them. One of them can make you a wedding dress."

"You'll come to the wedding?"

"I wouldn't miss it for the world," Charlie lied.

"You won't forget what you said about being a godmother to our first child? It could be soon."

It most probably would, thought Charlie. They'd better fix the wedding date for the very near future. "I won't forget," she promised, "as long as you call it Charlie, or Charlotte (seeing Violet's dubious face), amongst other names, if you like".

Meanwhile, Anna was looking again at the letter from Betsy which she found on their return from Brighton. She was trying to read between the lines.

Dear Anna,
I must tell you how shocked I was to hear your news. First of all you are so wrong to think you are no use here. Of course you could be an immense help, to me and to us all. I am very, very disappointed in you. Don't you care any more about any of us, especially me? How can you be so selfish?

I suppose the infatuation with this person has blinded

*you to the values of normal people, ordinary, good peo-
ple who care for their families. You must know such
women are doomed – she will wreck your life as well as
hers. How could you possibly compare my love for Alan
with your feelings for that creature. I only hope this is a
time of madness which will pass and you will come to
your senses. Quite frankly, you disgust me,*
   Betsy

She must have sat down to reply as soon as she received
Anna's missive. There was no measured reflection here.
Why was she so harsh? Couldn't she understand that love
was not just about men and women? Anna had hoped
her sister would recognise that at last she had found
what she had been searching for, that Charlie would allow
her to fulfil herself and that she would therefore be a
better not a worse person. Instead there was this dreadful hostility. She pressed her hands to her forehead,
shaken, trembling. If her own, closest sister couldn't
accept her new life, who could? Was it her husband who
had made her write these damaging words?

In fact, Alan had advised Betsy not to post the letter,
when she showed it to him, but she would not listen.
She must express her outrage. He argued that she would
open up the gulf between her and Anna to an unbridge-
able width. She accused him of intellectualising, she
wanted nothing to do with reason, she must express what
was in her guts. Surely she was speaking for them both,
surely the idea of Anna with another woman turned his
stomach? It was shameful, she must keep it secret, she
begged him to tell no one.

Alan's own reaction had been quite different, though
he dared not say so to Betsy. The news came as a revelation, which to some extent helped him to absolve
Anna from her part in Robin's death. In a curious way,
he was happy that after Robin, Anna would sleep with
no man again, that she had joined the women of the
shadows, a clan apart, doomed to sterility. He pitied her,
yet he understood her, in a way. Also in Betsy's absolute
rejection he perceived a jealousy she would not have
experienced had Anna fallen in love with a man. So he

had resolved that he would write his own letter of response, but not yet.

When Charlie bounced in to describe her conversation with Violet, her good spirits evaporated at the sight of Anna's stricken countenance.

"Whatever has happened?" she cried

Anna pushed the letter towards her. When Charlie raised her eyes from the page, there was in them a mixture of sadness and fear.

"I thought she would be glad for me," Anna whispered.

Glad, thought Charlie. No, never glad. Pitying, tolerant at best, not glad. Anna had to learn about the knocks from the 'real' world from which Charlie had so far protected her, but this was too sudden a blow.

"She is telling you what most people believe."

In her whole life Anna had taken no account of what 'most people' believed.

"If they believe in God, they think we'll go to Hell. They'll call us names, insult us, even our so-called friends will snigger when our backs are turned, make jokes about us. Are you ready for that?"

She took a deep breath before her next statement.

"If not, then we cannot have a life together."

Anna came towards her, took both her hands.

"Charlie Price, I want to take you for my partner in sickness and in health until death us do part."

They both burst into tears.

Later, when they lay chastely side by side, Charlie said, "You missed out for richer for poorer."

"That seemed rather silly," said Anna, caressing Charlie's silk pyjamas.

"We will leave for Paris as soon as possible." Charlie flexed her ankle. "Get away from these shores. I'll make arrangements. The Bransons can hold the fort until Margaret and Ethel move in. Don't you agree?"

Anna agreed wholeheartedly. She was beginning to feel claustrophobic. There was no way forward here, in an odd way they were more confined and trapped in these endless, echoing rooms than in many a more humble dwelling.

"We must take off again, fly over the Channel, to a place where we can be free to live and work." She was struck by a sudden thought. "By the way, I owe you a lot of rent."

Chapter 17
Celebrations

Mabel and Belle organised a special dinner in their honour. Belle produced a veritable feast, trying out extravagant new recipes involving esoteric spices. Twelve of them sat down on Saturday in Mabel's studio where Anna saw lots of new paintings hanging, including her own.

"You haven't an inch of wall space left," she remarked.

"We do have some room in our country house," said Belle as she laid a plate of quails stuffed with pâté de foie gras down in front of Picasso. "These are for everyone, Pablo," she warned as she saw his hands move towards the plump birds.

What a relief to be at this table, with these friends, thought Anna. She grinned back at Elisabeth, who hadn't been able to stop smiling all evening, since she congratulated herself on having brought about the happy event.

"Aren't you grateful I brought you out of Germany?" she kept asking Anna. "You are my biggest success. Not only is there a long list of customers waiting to buy one of your paintings, impatiently, I might add, but through me you've met the love of your life!" And Anna had to admit it was all true.

Charlie had always been less comfortable than Anna in this milieu, suspecting that she was considered old fashioned by this fast avant-garde set. She had never taken to Picasso, who was too much of a king pin, and she disliked the way he and most men of his group treated women. Mabel and Belle's extravagance shocked her slightly – in the way they used emotional endearments and baby talk to each other, the way they ate (the quails were to be followed by jugged hare in champagne and cognac, duck stuffed with beef fat and chestnuts, amongst other things and the crowning glory, banana flambéed in kirsch with a bitter chocolate and cointreau whip) and the way they spent money on ugly pictures. Nor could she understand any of Mabel's writing. Nevertheless, she was prepared to suspend judgment this evening, praying that her liver would stand the strain of the rich fare. She had been disappointed that Gaby was absent, being stuck in the country, but she was comforted by the latter's promise of a visit very soon, a long visit until the baby's birth, so that it would be a proper Parisian.

Between the duck course and the Roquefort salad with walnuts, coriander and fresh ginger, Mabel stood up to make a speech.

"We must all be very happy," she declared. "Happiness is happiness is happiness. Charlie and Anna are Charlie and Anna is Charlie is Anna, so my dearie dear and I and all of us are happy. Anna is Charlie's dear and Anna's dear is Charlie isn't Anna."

What nonsense and she's completely sober! thought Charlie, although the rest of the company were listening intently.

"So let us drink to the two dears who are who they are, to wish that they will forever be Anna and Charlie." She raised her glass and everyone did likewise. Before the dessert Marie proposed another toast to the happy couple. By then she had forgotten that Mabel had already done so. Then she sang a suggestive music hall song, forgot the words and was pulled back into her seat by Guillaume. When the petits fours came with the champagne, Picasso, who hardly drank, stood up in his turn.

"I scarcely know these two young women, but they look so good together it must be right. May their beauty never fade!" He was looking at Anna as he said this, and he added, "Charlie, you're a lucky fellow, damn you."

There was general cheering. The table was cleared to make way for dancing, which went on late into the night. Charlie and Anna took the floor together, as graceful a couple as one could ever expect to see. Then Charlie propelled Marie round the room whilst Pablo danced with Anna, who remained unimpressed by his firm grip and hypnotic black gaze. Belle and Mabel were content to watch, holding hands.

"Why don't we go to Les Halles for some onion soup," suggested someone just before dawn.

Charlie and Anna declined, deciding to walk back to Passy as the sky began to lighten. They were about to cross the Seine when Charlie noticed a familiar looking figure sitting under one of the arches.

"I think I know that person," she said to Anna. They went down the steps.

"Duchess!" Charlie wasn't sure that the shape huddled in a man's overcoat was the woman she knew. The figure turned, revealing the face, the hollow cheeks, the blank brown eyes.

Charlie sat beside her whilst Anna hovered nearby.

"What are you doing here?" Had she not recognised her she would have thought this was a tramp, a beggar.

"Oh, Charlie," this was said with no surprise, nor pleasure.

"What are you doing here?" Charlie tried to sound normal, whereas she was horrified.

"Nothing. Looking at the river, as I do every night. One night I'll have the courage to jump in."

"Will you come home with us?"

"Us?" The Duchess glanced towards Anna.

"With Anna and me." Charlie was almost ashamed of her happiness beside such wretchedness.

The Duchess took a longer, harder look at the woman still keeping a discreet distance, before turning back to Charlie.

"You're lucky. Do what ever you can to keep her. I tried, God knows, I tried with Gaby. In the end, it was no good. I could never be enough." The river water was lapping gently against the banks. "You know she's expecting a baby?"

"Yes," replied Charlie simply.

"I knew her husband, Giles. They won't last, her and

him. The city is littered with his discarded mistresses. He's a rake." There was a flash of anger. "You know I would never have deceived her, don't you, Charlie? I would have given my life for her."

"Please come home with us." Charlie was afraid Anna would be feeling cold.

"No. You take your lady to bed. I'm no fit company. Go on!" she insisted as Charlie didn't move.

"Promise me . . ." The Seine looked dark and deep.

"I'm promising nothing. Leave me!"

"You know where I live. Come round any time."

But the Duchess was already closed again in her own grim thoughts.

Charlie and Anna held each other very close as they walked the quiet streets. The sky was that particular blue which heralds sunrise as Charlie unlocked her front door. She swung Anna up and over the threshold, kissing the tips of her ears. When she set her down, she said,

"Do you think you might ever want a child?"

Anna understood the importance of the answer.

"No." She cupped Charlie's chin in her long white hands. "No. But it's possible . . ." she rubbed her nose against Charlie's, "it's possible, I might want a dog!" And she ran into the bedroom. Charlie followed. It was not the time to brood, it was a time to rejoice.

Autumn was fair. Shiny horse chestnuts gleamed on the pathways in the Champs Elysées and the leaves had turned gold. Chimneys smoked all over the city, there were mornings when the grass was stiff with frost and the few remaining flowers lay down defeated. The summerhouse at the end of the garden in Passy was just right for a studio during the long warm days when the doors were open and inside and outside became one. Now it was different. One morning Charlie found Anna painting in an overcoat, a shawl and muffler, and mittens on her hands.

"You can't work in here," she declared, "you'll get a chill. When real winter comes it will be quite impossible." She had come from a warm study, where a coal fire burned all day every day, and she was attempting, in vain, to write a new play. Anna had to agree. The ends of her fingers were numb, making it difficult to hold a brush and, moreover, the paint wasn't drying. She was trying to recapture the vision of the riotous mass of natural colours she had seen in August and the spectacle of the wilted browning vegetation. She was persuaded to come into the main house where Charlie prepared a bowl of hot chocolate. She loved to watch Anna sipping the rich, spicy drink delicately like a little cat.

"We'll have to make a space for you in here, a winter studio," said Charlie thoughtfully. "The spare bedroom, or you might even share the study, it is plenty big enough." She enjoyed the thought of them working side-by-side, breaking off every so often to make love – it might help her to find the motivation she was lacking.

"My sweetest, I must work alone, unless I am painting a portrait. Then the other person is an object of scrutiny, not a distraction. I could not share a space, especially with you. That was delicious!" She drained the bowl, then as she placed it carefully on the saucer, "I was talking to Gaby about this when she came to see my work the other day. The temperature in the studio was very low."

Gaby had been back in Paris for a couple of weeks. She paid them frequent visits and she and Anna had become firm friends. Charlie wasn't sure whether she was pleased or not. Gaby could be a disturbing influence. Beside she was still at the stage of not wanting to share Anna's attention with anyone else. However, she realised that to be over-possessive would be a great mistake.

"What did she have to say about the matter?" Charlie lit a cigar.

Anna appeared to change the subject.

"The little gate beside the studio, leading to the garden the other side of the wall has always been locked, has it?"

"Ever since I took out the lease. I don't have a key."

"Do you know you neighbour who owns the garden?"

"No not really. Isn't he Russian or something?"

"Of Russian origin. It doesn't matter. He was a sculptor. He has just died. Gaby knew him."

Charlie drew on the cigar.

"The lease on his studio is for sale. His daughter has inherited it. She is a friend of Gaby's and if Gaby knows someone interested in taking it she will be pleased. He lived and worked there in all seasons."

Charlie's cigar went out. She did not relight it.

"Do you want me to buy it?"

"No. *I* want to buy it. I have never owned any place and I would like to now."

Charlie went cold.

"You want to leave me?"

"I'll never want to leave you," Anna kissed Charlie's hands, then looked at her earnestly. "This is why I must take this chance. I have to have a space to sculpt and paint in, a big space. I want to get back to sculptures, to create large figures such as I've never made before. We will open up the dividing gate, Charlie, we shall sometimes be apart but undivided."

Charlie wanted to object. She was still afraid of letting Anna out of her sight for too long, which is why she interrupted any thought processes to look out of the study window towards the studio where she could make out the busy painter. The garden wall would be too high, there were trees growing the other side, blocking the sculptor's house from view. She would feel a wrench as Anna disappeared though the gate. Yet it must be done one day if she was ever to write again.

"Are you getting tired of me?" This was so wistful that Anna took her in her arms and rocked her like a baby, murmuring such loving things that Charlie was reassured.

The next day they arranged to meet Tatiana, the sculptor's daughter. She was clearly relieved and pleased that another sculptor might be taking over. The house was dilapidated, the living arrangements rudimentary but the studio was vast and warmed by a great iron stove. It was the place Anna had dreamed would some day be hers. Tatiana gave them the key of the gate and they walked through.

"You.see," cried Anna triumphantly. "I promise you when this is mine I'll throw away the key."

So began their next phase, learning to be with and without each other. Charlie pined for days whilst Anna moved and installed herself as she wished, but then an idea for a plot came into her head, and she set about inventing the characters. Their domestic staff was shared, although Anna wanted no interference with her work in progress, so housework by a stranger was banned. Occasionally, when inspiration was at a low ebb, Charlie would slip through the open gate and sit quietly while Anna chipped away at a block of marble, a new and exciting material for her. The sight of a form gradually emerging from stone was a revelation to the writer, who even found in it a kind of dramatic inspiration. Her approach to theatre was slowly being affected by the Bohemian set, in spite of the fact that the short plays by Mabel, which had occasional Saturday night readings were totally beyond her comprehension.

Violet wrote to Charlie.

Dear Charlie,
I am so sorry you missed the wedding. It was a very grand affair. I insisted that father should send his only daughter off in style, and you know I have certain means of persuasion!!! The weather was fine enough for us to be outside, which was just as well since there were so many guests. The whole county came. We didn't include your caretakers because they would have been uncomfortable, we don't know them, they're not part of our set, after all. Thank you for your present which arrived just before the big day. Such beautiful crystal, it must have cost you a fortune, but then you have a fortune to spend. Roderick is keen to buy some of your land, by the way, but I don't suppose you're interested. He has some modern ideas about farming. He's so clever. He'll take care of all our finances. He says I needn't bother my head about such things, which is just as well because I'm not good with money. He's already invested my dowry in something or other.

Now, the great news – I'm going to have a baby! We are so blissfully happy about it; we've brought lots of baby things and had lots of presents already. If you're thinking of sending something, perhaps a christening robe would be a good idea. And don't forget you promised to be godmother! Oh, Charlie, I never believed I could be so happy.

Other news, Simon has gone off again to South America and, guess what, my cousin Peter had joined the expedition. He sold his boat and his cottage. My aunt and uncle are distraught. After you two broke off the engagement they were broken hearted, now they feel like disinheriting him. He was always a wastrel, he'll probably get himself killed and eaten by savages. If they do disinherit him, they'll probably leave the farm to me, don't you think?

I hope you are well. When might you come back to Sussex? Your estate could do with some proper management you know. Two old ladies are not good enough.

Love, Violet

Charlie was in regular communication with Ethel and Margaret. Ethel was an excellent accountant, keeping Charlie informed about her financial affairs. It might be a good idea to sell off some of the land, if the bloodhound could make good use of it. She had once dreamed of buying her own small theatre, perhaps she would use the money to do that, find some derelict building – it could be a project for herself and all their friends.

As for Peter she was glad he'd moved on. The day after receiving the letter from Violet she received one from George.

My Poppet,
Sorry I haven't been in touch, but you know how life takes you over sometimes. I'm desolate! Simon has gone back to the jungle! We swore undying love for each other before he went, but I've seen pictures of those natives with it all hanging out and I'm very much afraid he'll find them hard to resist. Never mind, I think his heart is mine and it will only be for a few months(!!) Meanwhile, your man

*Dan and I are getting to know each other quite well. Your
erstwhile fiancé is also off to the jungle. I expect he will
go native and stay there with a harem of nubile charm-
ers, who will feed him dainty morsels and hang garlands
round his neck. Or am I mixing up my primitive tribes?
Geography was never my strong point. Kiss your lovely
lady for me,*
   Warm embraces, George.

   The winter passed and in late spring Gaby's daughter,
Nathalie, was born with difficulty. It was a long hard
labour which left the mother wrung out. She was debil-
itated for weeks on end, unable to do anything except
adore the perfect little being she insisted on feeding herself. Giles had hoped for a son and heir. He had fathered
several daughters already by different women. His wife's
consoling piece of folk wisdom "Never mind, chéri, it
takes a man to make a girl" only irritated him, as did
the wrapt exclusive attention she gave to the baby. He
began to work late in the evening and Gaby didn't care.
Both Charlie and Anna were devoted aunts. Cradling the
tiny helpless girl in her arms, Anna said to her lover,
"Don't worry, I don't want one of my own, borrowing
one when I want to is just right!" She thought often about
Betsy, who must have given birth by now. There would
have been rejoicing. Clara, who had always adored
babies, would have come to life again. When she was
sad gazing at Nathalie it was not because she was child-
less, but because of the pain of Betsy's rejection. This
was one of the few subjects she never discussed with
Charlie, who she knew would hold herself responsible.
   She was working a maquette for a fertility goddess, to
be cast in bronze, one of the largest pieces she had
attempted, when Charlie came over for a break, bringing her a letter from England. Anna worked on for another
hour then she put her tools down, wiped her hands and
picked up the envelope. She didn't recognise the writing. She tore it open, unfolded the paper and looked at
the signature. Alan. She read it with rapidly beating heart.

Dear Anna,

I have sad news which I thought you should hear. Our son, Thomas, has died. We don't know why or how. He was healthy, happy, then one morning he was dead in his cradle. What a short life! I have taken time off work to be with Betsy who is too distressed to be left alone. The doctor says it sometimes happens and we should not be afraid of starting again, but we cannot think of it yet.

Betsy doesn't know I'm writing to you. She is hurt, confused and bruised all over. I do not share her feelings about you. I think what you have done is right. Robin was wrong, he should have realised it, you should have realised it, but you didn't and there was an end to it. I used to enjoy Charlie Price's plays in my youth, by the way, I think she has some talent as a writer.

Anna, we are all very raw, unapproachable. Given time Betsy will welcome a visit from you. Little by little I will prepare the way. She does need you now, she will recognise this. Do not answer this letter, I will write to you again,

Yours, Alan

The light was fading when an anxious Charlie returned to a cold studio, where Anna was sitting beside the grey cinders of the stove. "Betsy's baby's dead." Anna's voice was a hoarse whisper. Charlie took off her jacket, placed it around Anna's shoulders and led her across the gardens to the warmth of the neighbouring kitchen.

Alan did write again in July. They had talked much about what they should do next. He had resigned from a job he hated and wanted them to break free, travel the world, change their perspective. In the end Anna was right to leave the country, perhaps Betsy would come to understand this, though she found it hard to cut her ties with Derbyshire.

He was taking Betsy away for a holiday in London. They would stay in a flat belonging to old friends of his in Hampstead. The air of the Heath would do her good and they would be in easy reach of museums and theatres. She had mentioned Anna often recently, so he felt the time was right for them to meet. If Anna could come to London in August, it would be an excellent moment to effect some kind of reconciliation. He let her know the exact date and the address in London to which she should send her reply, so as to keep the whole business secret until the last minute.

Anna wanted to go and didn't want to go. Her indecision lasted for days, preventing her from doing anything except walk round the Bois de Boulogne, churning over her past, present and future. Charlie made no attempt to influence her, although privately she had no doubt that the meeting must happen, since Alan had made the circumstances so easy. One morning Anna came home and announced that she had bought her return tickets, allowing herself only three nights in London.

"I'm sure that's right," said Charlie.

They travelled to Dieppe together, clinging fast to each other before Anna boarded the ferry. Charlie stood on the harbour until the boat was well out to sea and she knew it was impossible for Anna to see her waving any more. There was a fresh breeze blowing towards England, in a few hours the passengers would be disembarking in Newhaven.

'She'll soon be back,' thought Charlie.

Sitting on the top deck, watching the receding French coastline, Anna thought, 'Whatever happens now, I'm glad I'll soon be back.'

ONLYWOMEN PRESS publishes political, literary and cultural criticism as well as fiction and poetry. Our books are available from bookshops and libraries throughout England, Europe, Australia, Canada and USA.

See our website, www.onlywomenpress.com for more information.

A selection of Onlywomen books:

What Night Brings
by Carla Trujillo

Altogether Elsewhere
by Anna Wilson

Hatching Stones
by Anna Wilson

Bulldozer Rising
by Anna Livia

The Vinland Sheep
by Helen Shacklady

The Patterned Flute
by Helen Shacklady

Stoppage Time
by Helen Shacklady

Something Wicked
by Jay Taverner

All In The Game
by Eleanor Hill

For a free mail-order catalogue, please write to:
Mail Order Department
Onlywomen Press
40 St. Lawrence Terrace
London W10 5ST, England.